FORGET
ME NOT

FORGET ME NOT

JULIE SOTO

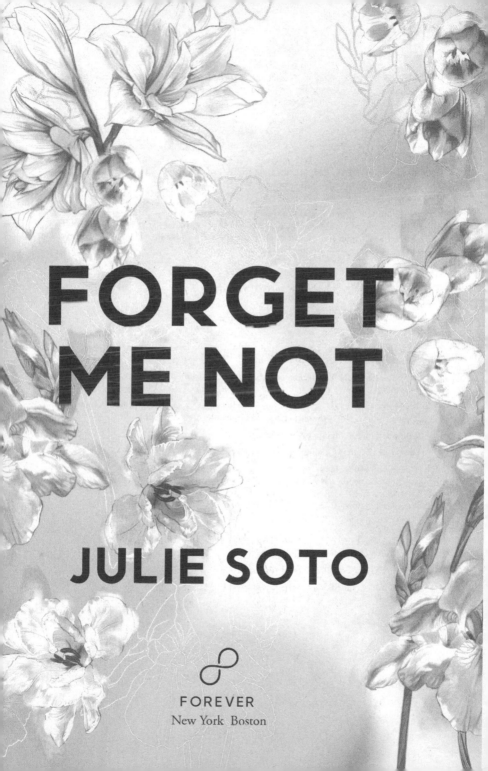

FOREVER

New York Boston

Copyright © 2023 by Julie Soto
Reading group guide copyright © 2023 by Julie Soto and Hachette Book Group, Inc.
Cover illustration and design by Nikita Jobson. Cover copyright © 2023 by Hachette Book Group, Inc.

Hachette Book Group supports the right to free expression and the value of copyright. The purpose of copyright is to encourage writers and artists to produce the creative works that enrich our culture.

The scanning, uploading, and distribution of this book without permission is a theft of the author's intellectual property. If you would like permission to use material from the book (other than for review purposes), please contact permissions@hbgusa.com. Thank you for your support of the author's rights.

Forever
Hachette Book Group
1290 Avenue of the Americas, New York, NY 10104
read-forever.com
twitter.com/readforeverpub

First Edition: July 2023

Forever is an imprint of Grand Central Publishing. The Forever name and logo are trademarks of Hachette Book Group, Inc.

The publisher is not responsible for websites (or their content) that are not owned by the publisher.

The Hachette Speakers Bureau provides a wide range of authors for speaking events. To find out more, go to www.hachettespeakersbureau.com or call (866) 376-6591.

Print book interior design by Jeff Stiefel

Library of Congress Cataloging-in-Publication Data

Names: Soto, Julie, 1988– author.
Title: Forget me not / Julie Soto.
Description: First edition. | New York : Forever, 2023.
Identifiers: LCCN 2022057942 | ISBN 9781538740880 (trade paperback) | ISBN 9781538740903 (ebook)
Subjects: LCGFT: Novels.
Classification: LCC PS3619.O865 F66 2023 | DDC 813/.6--dc23/eng/20230127
LC record available at https://lccn.loc.gov/2022057942

ISBNs: 978-1-5387-4088-0 (trade paperback), 978-1-5387-4090-3 (ebook)

Printed in the United States of America

LSC-C

Printing 2, 2023

For Mar and Cat.
Thanks for holding my hand
under the table all these years.

FORGET ME NOT

1

Ama

MARCH

I have five rules for planning a successful wedding.

(Lies. I'm sure there are more, but if I said, "I have seventy-six rules—sit back," I think I would have lost you.)

Rule #1—No live animals. They eat rings, bite flower girls, and poo everywhere.

Rule #2—DIY doesn't mean the wedding party will Do It Themselves. It means the couple went on Pinterest and now it's the wedding planner's problem.

Rule #3—A nightclub DJ and a wedding DJ are not interchangeable.

Rule #4—Don't ever find yourself alone with a groomsman.

And finally, Rule #5—Always talk them out of the gazebo. Always.

I march down the aisle, thighs burning to keep my heels from sinking into the grass. The carpet arrives in twenty, and I'm glad I insisted on it, because the bride would have been tugging her legs out of this like a marsh.

My photographer and favorite ex-stepsibling—a tall Indian woman who gets mistaken for Priyanka Chopra at least twice a day—is lying on her stomach in the middle of the park, camera pointed upward at the gazebo, where my assistants have been kidnapped to stand in for the bride and groom.

"Mar, dear," I say through a fake smile. "Jake already *has* a job." With a snap of my fingers, Jake—another stepsibling—bolts down the gazebo steps and back to the loading zone, where he's supposed to be directing the vendors. "And I gave you Sarah for ten minutes."

As her long limbs bring herself to standing, Mar's beautiful face scowls down at me from six inches above my head. "Gazebos, Ama?"

"The couple insisted. I know you hate it—"

Grabbing my arm, she jerks me to her side and turns the camera preview window toward me. "Latticework. *Latticework.*"

I look at the frames as she clicks through them. The ceiling of the gazebo is crisscrossed, and as luck would have it, today is a radiantly sunny day. There are shadows on Jake and Sarah's faces.

Mar leans down to me. "They look like—"

"Apple pies. They look like apple pies." I huff, glaring up at the sun. There are clouds in the west, but will they be here on time? "What do you have in your car?"

"A bunch of stuff that would look terrible during the actual ceremony."

I nod my head, staring at the gazebo. Mar knows to let me think. I shove a hand through my dark hair, still getting used to the shorter length even though it's been maybe two years since it ran down between my shoulder blades. (In fact, I know *exactly* how long it's been since I crawled into the salon and begged my hair gal to make me "different.")

I turn to Sarah, who's plopped herself on the gazebo steps.

"Sarah, as soon as the ceremony starts, you will take Mar's keys and drive her car to the loading zone. You will *discreetly* bring everything she tells you to bring to that big-ass tree, and as soon as they say 'I do,' you and Mar will set up. We'll pull the minister and the couple and get a few shots that don't resemble baked goods."

Sarah, another ex-stepsister, who has absolutely no interest in wedding planning—and *it shows*—blinks at me sleepily. "Who's gonna cue the DJ?"

"I guess I will." I check my watch and lift my brows to Mar. She nods, agreeing. "Okay, Mar. During the real ceremony, get the kiss, the big moments, but focus on the crying family members."

"Crying family members are my bread and butter."

I leave them at the gazebo and wave down the floral delivery. As the florist's assistant weaves garlands of roses through the chairs, my eyes search for petals that are browning, and I pluck them right out of the buds. The assistant's lips tighten every time I do it, but she knows better than to say something.

I step back and look over the venue. We're almost there. I have signage to put up and a sound check to do, but it's coming together. When the carpet is delivered, the gruff man in the truck is unfamiliar. He sweeps a gaze over me and asks if I'm Ama Torres's assistant. When I correct him, he doesn't seem to trust that I'm the kind of person who could place chairs in a straight line, much less coordinate a wedding, but he shrugs and rolls the carpet down the aisle.

As I'm observing the DJ play with the sound levels, the Bluetooth in my ear beeps—yes, I'm *that* person—and I answer, "This is Ama."

"Um, hi." I don't recognize the voice. "You're the wedding planner, right?"

"I am," I say as cheerfully as possible. "Who's this?"

"This is Erica. I'm the groom's cousin."

The bridesmaid who decided to dye her hair green last week. "Hi, Erica. Something sounds wrong."

"Yeah…Eloise has locked herself in the women's lounge." I stop dead. "The other girls didn't want me to call you, but it's been like forty-five minutes, and the makeup girl hasn't even started on her—"

"Got it. Thank you, Erica. I'm on my way."

I tap my earpiece like a Bond villain and pivot like a dancer, making my way to the hotel across the street. The bridal party is stationed in a small downstairs conference hall that the hotel was smart enough to transform into a suite after a trend of downtown weddings took off. I walk straight to the front desk where Bernie, my favorite concierge, is already reaching into the drawer.

"Emergency?" he says.

"Nothing I can't handle." I beam at him and take the skeleton keys from his outstretched hand.

My short legs stride across the lobby and directly into the suite without knocking. Six perfectly coiffed heads snap to me, and Erica pretends to be just as surprised by my arrival. Carmen, the maid of honor, snaps her head up from where she's leaned against the wall outside the bathroom, talking through the door. She looks half relieved to see me, half put out that she couldn't be the savior.

But that's my job.

I head straight for the locked door. "Carmen, everything is going to be fine. Will you make sure the makeup girl is ready for Eloise in five minutes?" Carmen blinks at me, but I unlock the door, enter the bathroom, and lock it behind me before she can speak.

The bathroom is a 1940s design with Tiffany shades over the sconces and deco tile. A clawfoot tub sits against the far wall, and inside it is Eloise soon-to-be-Reynolds, white chiffon overflowing the porcelain enameled sides. She doesn't look at me, just stares into space.

My heels click on the black and white tiles as I approach, and with a quick look, I confirm she didn't turn on the water— no repeats of the Winchell Wedding Disaster of '22, thankfully. I take out my Bluetooth, toe off my shoes, and step into the tub, sitting across from her.

Her lashes flutter as I register in her mind. Then her lip quivers, and a squeak escapes her throat. A hand comes up to cover her face as the tears fall. I don't say anything until she's done. She's pressing her palms into her eyes, tipping her head back to keep the new tears at bay.

I say softly, "What's one thing that you would change that would make this day perfect? One."

She bites her lip, staring at the wall. "The groom."

Ah. Well, that I can't help. Not in an immediate fashion anyway. I nod, as if I understand, as if I'm considering.

Patrick Reynolds wasn't my favorite groom. He proposed at a baseball game, Jumbotron and all. I can always get a good sense about a couple when I ask about their engagement story. I'm not saying it's a proven method to know if they're going to make it, but . . . the brides with the loveliest engagement stories are the ones I haven't done twice.

"Do you wanna go?" I ask her. "Sneak out the back?"

She chokes out a wet laugh. "Are you serious?"

"Yeah. We can bounce. Just you and me. Or just you and Carmen." When the confusion doesn't leave her face, I say, "I mean, I've already been paid, so what do I care if the wedding happens or not."

She snorts and runs her hand down her face. "What would happen to the vendors? The caterer, the DJ?"

"Nonrefundable the day of, I'm afraid. You'll be eating chicken or fish for the next fifty-seven days."

Her lip wobbles. "Is it weird that I hate the idea of canceling the reception more than canceling the ceremony?"

"Nope. It's pretty standard to be more excited about the party with all your friends than the altar bit."

"Can I just have the party without the wedding?" she mutters, fluffing her dress aimlessly. I smile and let her think. "I really hate the idea of going through with this, when I know it will be for nothing. I didn't want to end up like my parents—just making it work until the kids are in college." She sniffs. "Is it worse to have a wedding for the *fun* of it, when you know it's not going to be your *last* wedding?"

I swallow tightly. I promised myself I'd stop doing this— stop getting close. It always—*always*—leads to disaster. Eloise had invited me to her bridal shower because I was already too close. But my job is getting her down the aisle. So I take a breath and stop holding back.

"My mom has been married sixteen times."

Eloise stares at me like I just threw her wedding cake onto the ground.

"*How* many?"

"Sixteen. My father was number five. I'm her only biological daughter, but Mar—the photographer? She's number nine's daughter. I have upwards of twenty current and ex-stepsiblings running around the greater Sacramento area, including my two assistants working today."

I can see her mind working, counting, doing math. "That's... horrible. I'm sorry, I don't mean to be rude about it—"

"It's okay. It was really challenging when I was young—to bounce from stepfamily to stepfamily like that. But I eventually met some really cool people." I clear my throat and refocus. "I'm only telling you this to say, as much as you want it to be your only wedding, it doesn't have to be. My mom has full ceremonies and receptions every time. Only *one* of those sixteen weddings was at city hall. So, if you plan a different wedding in three years, all these people will still be there for you. No one gets tired of weddings. *Trust* me."

She nods slowly. "Is that why you became a wedding planner?"

I smile. "Pretty much. By eighteen, I knew everything there was to know about weddings. I'd done everything from flower girl to maid of honor to DJ."

Eloise laughs. "Have you ever been married?"

"No," I say. "Ever since I was young, I wasn't interested in it." And before I tell her that I don't even believe in long-term commitments on the day I'm trying to get her to make one, I take a deep breath and shift. "So you have a choice, Eloise. You have the power. You can go out there and have cake, dance, and make a solid attempt at keeping these vows. Or we can sneak out the back door. I'll send my assistant around to call it off." I reach for her hand and squeeze it. "A wedding is not a marriage. Marriages will never be perfect. They're always a work in progress. But weddings? Weddings are just a moment in time, striving to be perfect. Let me make you a perfect moment, Eloise."

Eloise worries her bottom lip between her teeth, staring down at the engagement ring. When she looks back up at me, I know I've pulled it off.

We climb out of the bathtub, and when I open the bathroom door, Carmen is still standing there, bouncing from foot to foot.

"We're good. Ladies!" I say to the room. "We have some work to do to get this going on time, but what will not save time is asking Eloise what that last hour was about, okay?"

I wink at her, and Eloise nods her head in thanks.

As I hand Bernie back the keys, I try to tell myself that I did the right thing by opening up. We're already at the wedding day. Giving a little of yourself isn't a bad thing, despite what I've been told to believe.

By the time I get back to the park, Jake is speed-walking toward me with a fevered look on his face.

"The caterer just called from the venue," he blurts out in a panic. "He says the linen delivery didn't show up."

Damn it. That's a brand-new linen company I was trying. I fold my hands in front of my stomach and let my fingers calmly play with the long chain necklace that lands between my breasts. "Jake. How much am I paying you again?"

He stammers out, "Uh, one hundred dollars?"

Jake's a bit of a Muppet. He's a sophomore at CSU Sacramento, studying theater. I hoped I was getting a stage management major, but apparently I got a drama major. He's my only current stepbrother, as his father is currently married to my mother. I say currently, because...well...it's only a matter of time.

I scroll my phone for the linen company in my contacts. The call in my ear gets sent to the Linens and Love front desk, and I say, "My name is Ama Torres. Your company is now an hour late with a linen delivery. What can you tell me about that?"

The guy on the other end stammers and says, "The truck is en route. It's just—there was some car trouble—"

I take my car keys out of my bag and say, "Can I send someone to meet the truck, seeing as you're delaying my catering staff?"

He tells me where the truck is stopped, and I put him on hold, taking Jake's arm and dragging him toward the parking lot.

"Jake, I am now paying you two hundred dollars because you're going to the gas station on Howe. You are going to load everything into my car—I mean everything; you will strap boxes to the top if you have to—and then go straight to the venue and help catering get back on schedule. Got it?"

Jake starts to sputter again, and I say, "Or you're not getting paid at all. Because currently you're getting in my way."

He swallows, nods, and then zooms to my car. Once he's pulled away, I walk back to Mar in the gazebo, turning my Bluetooth back on. "My assistant is coming to meet the truck. Please let your delivery driver know that if you are an hour late, *you call*, and please let your manager know that Ama Torres is very displeased. I will not be adding Linens and Love to my list of approved vendors."

I hang up on him as he starts to apologize. I take a deep breath, roll my shoulders back, and find Mar on a ladder, practically hanging from the ceiling of the gazebo to set up a small light. "Alright here?" I say.

"What was the drama?" she asks. "I saw you heading to the hotel."

"The bride almost ran. I talked her out of it."

Mar lifts a dark brow at me. "How'd you do that?"

I press my lips together. "I told her about my mom. And how I believe marriages don't matter, but weddings do."

Mar laughs. "That was bold of you."

I shrug. "She had one foot out the door. I thought it was time for some honesty."

She steps down from the ladder and says, "If anyone can convince someone that first marriages don't matter, it's the daughter of Cynthia Jones Rutherford Reed Dyer Lee Torres—"

"I can't believe you still have it memorized."

"Smith Smith Nelson Jaswal Matthews Andrews Evans Benjamin . . . plus three." She takes a breath like she's run a race. "I only have it memorized up until Cindy started marrying a bunch of first-name-as-last-names."

"All downhill after your dad," I say, and she lifts her camera to take my picture. "The girls will be ready for you in ten minutes. The bride and MOH weren't in makeup yet when I left."

Mar scrunches her nose and checks her phone. "Are we going to be la—"

"Don't say it!" I point a finger at her and move swiftly to the minister's car as it pulls up to the curb.

We get through the rest of the setup without another hitch, and before you can say "I do," the guests are arriving. Once the valet is there, I'm able to check in at the hotel again. When I come into the suite, Mar has Eloise looking out the window with sunlight dappling through the lacy curtains. Eloise looks over her shoulder at me and nods, smiling.

Looks like we're off.

The bride walks down the aisle to "A Thousand Years," like they always do, and I stand in the back next to a relative with a fussing baby, waiting for the next music cue. When Eloise and

Patrick walk back together past their guests, newly married, I see her smiling up at him with wet eyes.

It might just work out.

I take them to the right, away from the guest exit, and hold them as the bridal party joins us, letting Mar and Sarah set up everything for our fake wedding photos. Someone's aunt tries to follow the bridal party and sneak in their private pictures, and I go off Eloise's expression when I firmly tell her that this is a private area and no one but the bridal party is allowed. She sniffs at me and stomps away. I sense a strongly worded email coming.

I love postceremony onward. The hard parts are done, for me and for the happy couple, and the vendors are doing their thing at the next location. It's basically corralling toddlers at this point, getting the bridal party from point A to point B. And when Mar is contracted as photographer, she doesn't put up with wandering groomsmen or random family members hanging around. She has a magic touch with wedding parties, because she's bubbly and engaged enough for the bridesmaids to feel endeared to her, but smoking hot enough for the groomsmen to listen to every word that comes out of her pouty mouth.

And like me, she doesn't forget Rule #4—Don't ever find yourself alone with a groomsman.

It's cake once we're at the reception hall. Jake is hopped up like a junkie by the time I walk in, talking a mile a minute. He's folding napkins into shapes that *almost* look right, telling me that the delivery guy was very apologetic.

Not good enough. Linens and Love is not going into my Rolodex. (Yes, I have a literal Rolodex. It's from the fifties and it's adorable.)

I finish the napkins with him, redoing the ones he's fumbled, and then the guests are arriving.

What I miss most about working with a huge wedding planning company is that I used to be able to peace out as soon as the cake was cut. When I was with Whitney Harrison Weddings, they were always able to hire three Jakes to be there for setup and breakdown. Now that I'm doing my own thing, it's me at dawn and me at dusk. One day I'll get there. One day I'll be doing three weddings per Saturday and two per Sunday, like Whitney. But as is, I can only do one per day, and I have to book smaller packages on Sundays because I will be completely unavailable the day before their ceremony.

What I really need is a feature article from Martha Stewart or TheKnot.com, like Whitney had in her twenties. She was thrust into the spotlight with the wedding of the mayor's daughter and single-handedly put Sacramento on the map for the wedding industry. By the time I was working for her, she was twenty-five years into her career and had San Francisco connections to boot. She hardly ever showed up on the day of, unless it was a widely publicized wedding.

I actually really like the day of. I like the hectic hustle of the ceremony, I like the bumps and dips, I like the first dance. But, yes, one day I'd love to be charging enough to get two more assistants in here so I can just point. That would require sacrificing a bit of my brand, which up till now has been Millennial Modern Affordable with a personal twist.

"Why are you frowning at the DJ? Did you find him snorting coke in the bathroom again?" Mar snaps a picture next to me.

"You think I still work with that guy?" I say. "I got him blacklisted. He works solely on cocaine weddings now."

"Excellent." She switches lenses. "Are you thinking about tomorrow?"

Well, I hadn't been. But now that she'd brought it up..."I'm not nervous," I rush out.

She laughs. "Good. There's nothing to be nervous about. They'll either want you or not. There's nothing else you can do."

I nod, taking a deep breath.

Speaking of big breaks, tomorrow could be it. Hazel Renee, an influencer with 4.2 million followers on Instagram and 8 million subscribers on her YouTube channel, has fallen in love with a girl from Sacramento. I saw their engagement announcement last month on Instagram, and I thought, *What lucky LA planner will get to do* that *wedding?*

Well, it seems *I* may be the lucky planner to do that wedding. Her fiancée, Jacqueline Nguyen, wants to get married in her hometown. She emailed me two weeks ago to set up an interview. I'm trying not to get my hopes up. I'm fully prepared to let them know what I offer and what I don't. Even if they plan to keep the list under thirty, there are agencies who have much more experience in the style they may want (read: fancy as fuck).

But if I click with Hazel and Jacqueline...If I do a wedding seen by millions...

That's all I need. That's the golden ticket to upscale (read: fancy as fuck) and high exposure.

I just need to make sure I'm ready for it.

Eloise stumbles to me at the end of the night, barefoot and love-drunk, kisses my cheek, and tells me I was the best choice of her life. I send her off in her town car, smiling to myself for a moment.

Whitney Harrison's cool blue eyes flash in my mind, the motherly voice she reserved only for me saying, *Be careful, Ama. At the end of the day, you're the wedding planner, not their maid of honor. Don't expend so much of yourself on people you will never see again—people who probably won't even say goodbye to you at the end of the night.*

Well, take that, Whitney.

I sigh, rubbing my brow. I've been trying to set clearer boundaries. The line of professionalism with the clients and the vendors has always been my weakness. I love getting to know people and finding out what makes them happy. But blurring the lines always gets me into trouble.

Always.

2

Ama

MARCH

Deciding what to wear to meet someone who has their own makeup line, three upcoming projects listed on IMDb, and their face in Times Square on the reg is a nightmare.

I was in high school when Hazel Renee booked her first *Marie Claire* cover. We're roughly the same age, so she's had my friends and me whipped for a long time. I've been following her Instagram for ten years at this point, so I know exactly what to expect when she walks into the coffee shop in an hour.

Usually in a first interview with the couple, I dress for the client. Through some light social media stalking, I'm able to determine whether my Stella McCartney skirt suit or my bohemian witch vibe is more likely to do the trick. Hazel and Jacqueline are young and trendy. They don't need Stella. I toss a fitted black shirt and a black blazer over jeans and slide my feet into black heels. I spend an extra-long time on my makeup, because it's *Hazel Renee*, and it's her makeup line I use. It was Hazel who taught me how to contour in her YouTube videos when I was a teenager, and I still do it her way, because with my round face, I get mistaken for a kid all the time.

With a spritz of perfume and a hiss from my cat, I set out into the warm March morning.

I bought a two-bedroom house a few years ago in the sweet part of the City of Trees. What I mean is, I moved into a two-bedroom house. I will officially buy it in approximately eighty-four years. In a place like Sacramento, it's hard not to get caught up in the roommate thing in the middle of Midtown. There's a five-block radius that feels a little like New York City—a bar below your apartment, a mini-mart on the corner, and no need for a car. It's addictive. Mar is still in Midtown, but she comes to me fifteen blocks east when she needs "a vacation." I decided to break from the millennial stereotype when I stopped renting. Don't worry— I still spend $6,000 a year on avocado toast. They let me keep my membership card.

And actually, if there's anything I spend six grand on every year, it's donuts.

I push open the door to J Street Donuts, and Mr. Kwon waves to me over the head of the woman he's helping. When I get to the counter, he's already loading up my half dozen.

"Let me guess," he says. "New clients."

"How'd you know?"

"You are dressed to impress." He seals the top of the box and takes my ten-dollar bill. "The peanut butter one is on the left, wrapped in paper."

"Thank you, Mr. Kwon." I waltz out before the woman ahead of me has even pulled out her card at the register.

Mr. Kwon knows to keep the change, just like he knows that although his Peanut Butter Dream donut is his best seller, I'm allergic. He used to give me a few for clients in a separate box, but I finally convinced him after a few years that just separating them is fine.

Donuts are my love language. I bring a box to every potluck, party, cocktail hour—you name it. There is nothing in the world that cannot be solved by the first bite of a perfect donut. I am, of course, excluding serious world problems—but even then, I think that if we could all just sit down and have a donut, things might get better.

Donuts are also a tactic for me to get to know the clients. I can figure out which brides have started dieting for their wedding dresses, which grooms prefer their fiancées don't eat sweets, and which couples are already stress eating. And while I get to know the clients, I get to have a donut. Or six, if they *are*, in fact, dieting. My mom went on crazy intense diets for about a third of her weddings, and that told me a lot about where she was emotionally with that person, with his friends, with that point in her life, etc.

I park outside of Weatherstone, a trendy café in a brick building that used to be a horse barn back in the day. I don't know what day that was, but it was back. The baristas here know me too because I peddle their coffee for receptions. I even did a thirty-guest wedding in the coffeehouse two years ago—which is why the barista with the goatee doesn't say anything about the donuts I bring in.

I grab the open corner of the rustic dining table smack in the middle of the café and set up facing the door. I order just a drip coffee—they bring it to you in a little personal carafe, so you can feel extra bougie—instead of my usual: espresso shot with a cold brew chaser. My legs are bouncing enough as it is.

I've never been this nervous for the initial meet. Except maybe my first. That was over three years ago now. Whitney had sent them my way when they balked at her prices, and while it sounds like a pity fuck, it was at the time in my career when I needed as many pity fucks as I could get. Deciding to leave Whitney Harrison Weddings could have been the most colossal mistake of my life, but thankfully I had Whitney in my corner.

At two minutes past nine, the door swings open, and it takes me a second to truly trust that I'm seeing the person who used to live solely in my phone. I was expecting runway, but I got girl-next-door. Hazel is in jeans and a cardigan, with her dark blond hair tossed up; the only thing making her stand out as a celebrity is the aviators that she keeps on even as she walks indoors. Her fingers are laced with an Asian girl's who has round cheeks and bright brown eyes—Jacqueline. She catches sight of me waving first and points.

"Hi, Ama?" Jacqueline drops her bag on the table next to me and offers me a handshake.

"You must be Jacqueline."

"Jackie is fine," she says. "This is Hazel."

I shake Hazel's hand. "Good to meet you." She's got a strong grip and a beautiful face, and the whole thing is making me a bit dizzy.

"Jesus, your skin is perfect," she says, and then I'm practically laid out.

My fingertips reach for my cheeks and I say, "Oh, thank you. It's actually your line."

"Amazing! I love that for us." She flashes me a brilliant smile and turns to Jackie. "Hazelnut latte?"

Jackie nods and takes the seat across from me as Hazel moves to the register. Jackie's about to say something when her eyes catch on the pink box between us. "If those are donuts, I'm going to lose my fucking mind."

I grin at her and open the box. She squeals like *I'm* the one who dropped to one knee with a diamond, and searches the half dozen for her favorite.

"If peanut butter is your thing, that's their specialty. It's this one." I point to the one wrapped in wax paper.

She doesn't hesitate to stuff it into her mouth, and I think I'm obsessed with her already.

"Ohmygod," she mumbles around the pastry.

Hazel arrives back at the table just in time to get the donut shoved toward her face with a "Babeyougottatrythis."

"Mm!" Her eyes pop wide. "I love that."

Good. Good, I can officially like them.

I always like to keep the conversation from jumping straight to business. I think it helps ease everyone into talking about this horribly awkward thing—a wedding. Whitney disagreed. She liked to get the ball rolling. But when you're Whitney Harrison, people stop talking when you start.

"So, Jackie, you grew up here in Sac?"

Jackie nods as she sips her latte, her lips smacking with pleasure. "I went to Rio Americano. Class of '15."

"Oh, same year as me!"

"Really? Where'd you go?"

"St. Joseph's," I say, a little sheepish.

Some kind of lightbulb switches behind Jackie's eyes as she says, "Oh. Yeah."

My mother grew up with a lot of money. She spent that money on two things: my private schooling and her weddings. When I tell people I went to St. Joseph's, one of the four private Catholic schools in Sacramento, they look at me with new eyes. I hate it. I personally have none of my mother's money, because she's still spending it on yearly table arrangements and string quartets, but also because I don't want to ask for it if I don't need it. Since working with Whitney practically out of high school, I haven't needed it. And the fact that I *didn't* go to college is actually a blight on St. Joseph's otherwise untarnished reputation. One of the only good things about coming out of that school was that my friends and acquaintances are all getting married. Some of them can afford to go to Whitney, but a lot of them have used me in the past three years.

"And what do you do?" I ask Jackie.

"I'm a legislative director down at the capitol."

"Cool! I mean, it sounds cool. I have no idea what it means." Jackie laughs. I flash her a smile and turn to Hazel. "And I obviously know what you do. But what's drawing you to Sacramento?"

"Jackie," she says simply. The two of them glance at each other, color popping on their cheekbones. "She's always wanted to get married here."

"It's a great city," I agree. "And there are some insane venues here too." Bringing it back around...

"We actually know the venue." Jackie beams, turning her body toward me.

"Excellent! Did you lock in a date yet?"

"Not yet," Hazel says. "Jackie wanted to make sure it cleared your calendar."

My fingers freeze inside my tote bag as I reach for my catalog binder. "Oh, that's..." I slip the binder onto the table. "You know, I'm really, really flattered that you wanted to meet with me. *Flattered* is not the right word, but super excited. Makes my day for sure." I look between their expectant faces. "I just want to make sure you're doing the best thing for *your* wedding. I don't know any of your details yet—how big, how luxe—but there are a lot of companies that have expertise in planning weddings of all sizes. Whitney Harrison Weddings is an amazing company, and I used to work there myself—"

"I've heard some not-so-good things about Whitney Harrison, actually," Jackie says, wincing.

"Oh, okay." I try for a warm smile, but I'm racking my brain to think of who could have reviewed Whitney poorly and lived to tell the tale.

"And on the flip side," Hazel jumps in, "you come highly recommended."

My mouth opens to accept the compliment, but I've never been good at that, so it just comes out as "Yeah, great!" I clear my throat. "Let's absolutely talk through what I can offer, and we'll make sure it's exactly what you need for your day."

They both nod, like little bobbleheads. I flip my binder around to face them and open to the first page. My hands are shaking a little. I had only a smidgen of hope that this was going to work out. I didn't even know if I could pull this off if they did like me, but I knew I wanted to try. This binder is essentially my pitch for myself, so I dive in.

"In this highly competitive wedding area, what I specialize in is *you*. Your vision. Your wedding. My company offers six levels of packages to fit your budget"—I almost make a quip about how money probably isn't an object, but I walk myself back from that stupid idea—"and your style." I turn the page to my pièce de résistance, my lookbook—ten back-to-back pages of the weddings

I'm most proud of. "What I offer that other smaller agencies cannot is experienced design, suited to your exact personality and dreams. Other boutique agencies hire a designer at an additional fee, or charge more for design. I don't. I'm an all-in-one."

"You should, though. Charge more."

My lips are parted, ready to talk about rates, but Hazel's murmur stops me. She looks up from my design pages.

"Sorry for interrupting. I just ... You should consider charging for it. This is ... " She points at my favorite wedding I've ever done, the Willow Ballroom, an explosion of spring inside a repurposed warehouse. "This is outstanding. Better than my entire Pinterest board combined. You clearly have the talent to charge."

Heat rushes to my cheeks as I stammer a thanks. "You're right. I could add a fee. But it's something that I love to do. And it sets me apart from the competitors."

Hazels hums. She sips her flat white. "I used to do my own makeup for print ads. My YouTube channel back then was just makeup tutorials, so I'd come to set with my makeup done, and the photographer would just allow it. It didn't occur to me until later that the makeup artist they hired was still getting paid. And in certain circumstances, still getting credited." She scratches a spot behind her ear. "Obviously you know what you're doing. I'm not trying to tell you how to run your business. But as one person who makes a living in the visual world to another? Beauty always has a price tag. You can ask for what you're worth."

My chest constricts, and my skin buzzes. I'm almost embarrassed, but also preening from the compliment.

"Sorry." Hazel laughs. "It means I care, I promise."

"She does this," Jackie says, rolling her eyes playfully. "She gets all entrepreneurial on you."

"No, I love it," I say. "I'm just stunned, that's all. It's something worth thinking about." I try to find my footing in my pitch—which just went sideways when Hazel Renee told me I was worth more than I ask for.

She seems to see me flounder for a moment and says, "Tell us about your packages?"

"Sure!" I flip the page. "I don't think in number of guests. Yes, that comes into play down the line for a bunch of different price tags, but when I talk about services, I'm thinking of what you need from me. What kind of commitment you are looking for."

"Full," Jackie interrupts. "Skip the baby steps. I want design, I want vendor selection, I want you walking me down the aisle."

I snort.

Hazel says, "I'm going to be pretty busy this year. It hasn't been announced yet, but I've been cast in the next Greta Gerwig project. It films next month."

My eyes go wide. "Amazing! She's from here, you know."

Jackie nods. "I'm really happy for Hay"—she squeezes Hazel's arm—"but I know that means I'm going to be doing a lot of this alone—"

"Not alone," Hazel argues, and I love the concern that creases her brow. "You know I'm available for this."

"No, I know. But we both decided we didn't want to push it a year. And that means I need to take point on the early decisions." Jackie addresses me, "Which is why I need you. Do you offer twenty-four-hour anxiety texting?"

She jokes. And I laugh. But it's something I used to offer. And it's a habit that needed to be broken.

It occurs to me as we all sip our coffees that this is going to be hard. I like them. A lot. My heart is fluttering like we're on an excellent first date, and I can see how this will all play out so clearly in my mind.

"I think we can work with that," I say. "Why don't you tell me what details are settled, where your priorities are." I slip my iPad out of my bag and tap open my notes. I scribble *Hazel & Jackie* and it appears typed in the center of the screen.

"The McKinley Park Rose Garden. It's been my dream since I was little." Jackie blushes, and Hazel wraps her arm around her waist.

"It's beautiful," I say, writing it down and attaching the words to *Hazel & Jackie* with a little bubble. "I've done several weddings there, so I know the location well. I actually live walking distance. They do fill up, though."

"Right," Hazel says, "I've called already, and they're holding a couple of dates for us. We were going to wait to hear your schedule."

I blink at her. It sounds like *I'm* a top priority for them, which boggles my mind. My cheeks are warm when I open my calendar app and ask, "What are the options?"

"October seventh is our first choice, but we also have April sixth."

"October of *this* year?" I squawk, my eyes bugging at my calendar.

That's seven months away. April of next year is clearly the better date. But before I can convince them of that, Hazel leans her elbows on the table with a dreamy smile and says, "I've always wanted a fall wedding."

And maybe it's because she's Hazel Renee, or because I'm already visualizing the *feature* article, or because Jackie gets as excited about donuts as I do (which is all I really need to know about a person), but I don't immediately tell them it won't work.

I can do a wedding in seven months. I've done plenty of weddings in less than a year and still made them incredible. And October 7 is open on my calendar.

I've been quiet for too long, staring down at my planner and flipping through the big weddings I already have on the books for this year. Aside from two weddings in September, they would have my full, undivided attention after my hectic wedding season.

Looking up at them, I find Jackie chewing on her lip and Hazel trying to read my calendar upside down with a tense expression.

"So...I can do it, but it would be very tight."

Jackie squeals, and Hazel kisses her.

"We like it tight!" Jackie gasps. "And that's not a sex thing! That's just something that came out of my mouth!"

Hazel bursts out laughing, and Jackie tries to apologize while catching her breath.

I'm laughing with them, watching Jackie flush scarlet and Hazel giggle into Jackie's shoulder. They're infectious. Seductive. I can see these next seven months. I can see the wedding. I see myself tagged in every photo. I see Hazel's wedding covered in *People*. Maybe *Entertainment Weekly*. I see reporters calling to highlight me. I see *The Sacramento Bee* running coverage in the wedding section. And just before their laughter subsides and their attention flickers back to me, I see Whitney calling to congratulate me. It feels like I've been swept up in a current, a wave rising higher and higher.

"I'll write you in on October seventh," I say. "I can call the Rose Garden today and secure everything. There are a few things to know about the Rose Garden. They don't have a reception area that I would recommend. Do you know what you want for the reception?"

"Not yet," they both say at the same time.

"We'll cross that bridge later, then, but I don't see this reception in the park." My language has shifted. I'm taking charge of this wedding, talking fast and letting adrenaline guide me. "If you like the general vibe of this Willow Ballroom wedding," I say, pointing to the page still open in my lookbook, "then I'll start brainstorming in that direction."

They nod in unison.

"Second, since it's a historic rose garden, there are only a handful of florists they allow to work in the garden."

"Yeah! Ours is covered. He works there all the time," Jackie says.

My next words catch in my throat, and all language leaves me for a moment. The current I was riding only seconds ago breaks. A wave drags me under.

Out of the five florists in Sacramento cleared by the Rose Garden, only one shop is run by a man.

My chest contracts, and I feel like I can't breathe. I force a smile and say, "You already have your florist?"

"Yes! Sorry. Florist and venue are the only things that are really important to—"

"Have you signed anything, or can we shop around a bit?" My words are sharp and pitched high.

Jackie blinks. Hazel's coffee pauses on the way to her lips.

I recover. "To find the best, I mean."

"I think we already have the best." Jackie laughs. "It's Blooming. Elliot—"

"Wonderful!" I smile so wide I feel my teeth will fall out of my mouth. "And he's locked in? You've discussed the October date with him?" Immediately, my pulse skyrockets. They can't have met with him yet. And if they did, he should have steered them to a different wedding planner or declined—just like I've been doing for two years.

"No, not yet. But he's a family friend," Jackie says. "I work with his mother at the capitol."

The literal sensation of a bubble bursting slams into my brain.

"Oh, lovely." And before Jackie says it I already know—

"Laura is why you come so highly recommended. You did her second marriage two years ago."

Champagne bubbles float through my mind. A slow dance and a warm hand on my lower back. And as quickly as it comes, it's gone. And the inside of my chest is cold and damp again.

"Of course." It feels rougher than my normal voice. "Senator Gilbert is a wonderful woman. And was a model client, if I may say." My skin is tight on my bones as fear swells. "You were at the senator's wedding?" My fingers clutch the coffee cup.

"I couldn't make it," Jackie says. "I was actually out of town in Chicago—where I met Hazel for the first time!"

"Oh my god, yes. Please tell me everything about you two," I say, happy to know she wasn't there and thankful beyond words for a change in subject. "We'll talk vendors later."

My ears are ringing, and I've lost feeling in my feet. I close my iPad and try to listen. Hazel and Jackie talk over each other, laughing about which of them had feelings first, and I should be taking notes. I should be holding every scrap of their personalities in my mind like marbles in a bag. I should be writing *October 7, 2023* on my iPad and attaching it to the bubble of their names.

But instead I listen like an old acquaintance, letting images of rustic barns and ivory tablecloths trickle out of my head like sand through a sieve. *Entertainment Weekly* and *People* flutter away on the wind.

Because I'm not doing this wedding.

3

Elliot

I fucking hate flowers.

Every other rosebud is wilting and hanging off the stem, petals browning. I'm sifting through them one by one at the head table in the outdoor tent, making sure that the bride's point of view and major camera angles are at least solid.

Dad says I'll get the hang of it, but I don't really want to. Flowers are his thing, not mine. He *loves* flowers. He's a magician with them. All while I was growing up, he used to say, "Flowers are better than people."

It was a weird thing to say.

But he would tell me that flowers need only three things: light, water, and attention. When I was fifteen and angry because I was too tall and too angular and too rude, I would say, "It could be argued that people need the same."

He'd laugh at me. "You'd think." He'd trail off, "You'd think…"

And now, as I mangle roses in front of the catering staff, stalling until Dad comes back with the rest of the centerpieces, I'm pretty positive that both flowers and people suck.

I fluff up the garland as best as I can, trying not to think about what Dad meant when he said, "You'll get the hang of it." As if one day I'll need to have all these random facts and anecdotes and genuses memorized. I should be studying for my final in Architectural Design Theory and Criticism, but the sound of Dad's hacking cough this morning makes me think it won't matter. Mom called last month and said my father looked like he needed an extra pair of hands when she visited the shop. But she didn't say for how long. They're divorced, but she still checks in on him—which is good, because I don't know how else we would have found out about the mass in his lungs. Certainly not from him.

I run a hand through my dark hair and glance over the head table again, not actually knowing if I'm making things better or worse.

A laugh bounces through the canopy tent, ricocheting off the tables and mocking me. I look toward it and find a brown-haired girl with a groomsman in only his tuxedo pants and shirt, standing off to the side of the ceremony chairs. Practically snarling, I almost tear a bud out in frustration.

I've only been doing weddings with Dad for five weeks, but I hate it when the bridal party gets involved. Opinions sprouting like spores. I watch under lowered eyelids as the bridesmaid turns to point at the bridal arch and the groomsman steps closer to her shoulder to "see it from her perspective." I'm waiting for the inevitable moment where he says, *You're right. One of the sides is leaning to the left.*

That's when I see the iPad in her hands. And realize she's not in hair and makeup yet. Not wedding party hair and makeup anyway. It was hard to tell before, because she's polished. Sleek.

I'm staring too hard at how she's referencing between the iPad and the arch, waiting for her to spin around and "find the person responsible for the imbalance," so that's why I see the moment when he leans into her neck, whispers something in her ear, and slides his hand over her ass.

She jerks away. I can see her eyes, wide and blinking, as the color drains from her cheeks. She steps back.

He steps forward again. And I drop the flower I'm trimming as he grabs her waist with two hands, leaning forward toward her lips.

Quicker than a crack of thunder, her fist connects solidly with his nose.

"*Fuck!*" The groomsman stumbles back, gripping his face between fingers covered in ruby-red blood.

I'm frozen in shock as the girl's hands come up to her surprised mouth. I see her apologizing, creeping forward with an outstretched hand to help—

"Fucking *bitch*!"

My fingers curl.

She's whispering frantically, her spine curved in like a cornered cat in an alley even as she takes tissues out of her fanny pack and tries to get him to tilt his head back.

They've got the attention of all the staff. The on-site venue coordinators are rushing over, but Whitney Harrison beats them all. She's a force to be reckoned with in her heels and clipboard. She's snapping her fingers to get ice and towels for the bloody nose. The girl is standing just at her shoulder, cowering.

The groomsman spits accusations, waving his hand around. Once he's ushered inside, Whitney snaps around, grips the girl's elbow in a vise, and pulls her very close, hissing in her face.

I catch three words: "Be a *professional*."

I'm still rooted to the spot, watching from a distance. I hear the people around me continuing to set up the linens, teeth clicking with gossip. I focus once again on the roses, hiding brown petals. I take the cart out of the tent and back to the van, trying not to watch as the girl nods, wipes her cheeks, and with downcast eyes, moves to help with the linen.

Whitney adjusts her dress, sweeping her hair back into place, and pastes on a smile. She catches my eye as I head to the truck, and I feel her move into step with me.

"I'm so sorry about that, Elliot." Her voice is silky with a sharp edge. "Completely inappropriate—and I'm going to deal with her."

"He made a pass at her," I say. "Aggressively."

Whitney's smile tightens. "That's a shame. Unfortunately, this is the third time I've told her she needs to create space between herself and the clients. She's far too involved." Tossing a look over her shoulder to where the girl is folding a napkin with shaking fingers, she says, "She got invited to the bachelorette party, for god's sake. Anyway, please don't think I support my staff flirting with the bridal party. She will be dealt with."

Something claws at my throat. "Most people don't punch someone they're flirting with."

She gives me a sweet, condescending smile. "Most people would have learned their lesson by now." She gives my arm a squeeze and says, "Say hello to your mom for me."

Whitney's one of those people who thinks she has clout because she has a connection to my mom, a state senator. As if she could "make one call" in special circumstances.

Whitney moves quickly around the edge of the tent, eyeing her rogue assistant. I pack up the cart with the next vases, letting my mind clear. Maybe Whitney is right. Maybe this was a lesson this girl needed to learn the hard way.

From the corner of my eye, I see the girl drop a napkin on the ground because she only has one hand to fold them with. Her right is curled into her stomach, bruised and battered from colliding with bone.

Weddings are fun, Elliot, I hear my father's voice say. *Don't let it be difficult.*

That's what is echoing in my head when I abandon the dolly, moving to the bar to grab a handful of ice. The cubes are burning my bare hand as I take them over to her. The others are giving her a wide berth, so I'm the only one who can hear her sniff as she restarts the napkin. She looks up at me and slaps away a tear.

"Hi, Elliot. Does your dad need help?"

Her voice is small and tight. I had no idea she knew my name. I don't know hers.

She turns her back on me to save face, continuing to fold napkins with one hand. I don't know how to respond, so I tug one of my dad's handkerchiefs out of my pocket.

"Elliot!"

I spin to find my dad parking the other van to the side of the tent, waving at me to come help him. I glance back at the girl, who's moved toward another table. She can't be much older than twenty.

I don't know what I'd even say to her. Just hand her a hankie full of ice? Tell her she should have kneed him in the balls too? Ask her if she'd like me to go beat the shit out of him? Out of Whitney?

So, when she moves farther away from me, I walk back to my dad, ice numbing my own hand by now.

"All good?" Dad says, heaving himself out of the driver's seat with a wheeze I don't like. "Any trouble with the roses?"

"Yeah. You'll need to check them," I mumble.

"What's the ice for?"

I look down at my hand, turning red from the cold. "It's ... That girl? Whitney's assistant? She hurt her hand so I was ..." I hold the handkerchief and ice out to him. "I'll get the centerpieces. Do you want to check on her?"

He takes the handkerchief and then looks at me. "Don't you want to?"

I shrug. "I'm no good at people, you know that."

He sends me a smirk as he walks toward her. "You're no good at flowers either!" He laughs at his joke as I glare at him.

I load up the dolly, watching out of the corner of my eye as my dad approaches her. Within seconds she's laughing, grinning at something he says. He wraps the hankie around her knuckles, and she laughs again, a sound like blossoms opening in spring.

I set up the rest of the centerpieces alone, letting Dad work the magic only he knows.

4

Ama

MARCH

I leave the coffee shop with a promise to call tomorrow to set up another meeting. I have their email addresses. I'm supposed to send my favorite vendors over tonight.

I won't be.

I need a little space to figure out how to decline. I need to figure out what kind of lie sounds best. Is "I don't work with that vendor" enough? Or does the whole truth need to come out? Will it come out anyway when Jackie asks her old family friend what happened? Will Whitney Harrison be doing their wedding by then?

I can't get my thoughts straight, and I almost drive directly home before remembering *I have the Ferguson wedding today.* I turn around and head downtown to check on prep.

I fall into my routine, allowing my brain to worry about schedules and late caterers instead.

I think I'm doing a good job too. That is, until Mar pulls me aside at the reception and says, "Where the hell is your brain today, girl?"

All of it rushes back to me, making my head spin, and I sprint to the bathroom. I'm splashing water on my cheeks when Mar finds me after finishing the cake cutting.

"You didn't get Hazel Renee?"

"I did get Hazel Renee. They're set on Blooming for flowers." My throat threatens to close up. Saying it makes me nauseous.

Mar curses. I look up and see her head thrown back, eyes on the ceiling. I check up there to see if the answers are written on the fluorescents.

Leaning next to me on the wall, Mar kicks her shoes off to make herself shorter. The hotel has carpeting in here, thankfully. "You could do it."

"Could I? Really?" I turn to her, and her hesitation tells me she doesn't believe it either.

She's silent for a bit before she says, "What if you correspond by email only? You explain there's a situation, but you'd be happy to work around it."

I consider it. It's far less professional. It may make me look weak. "You really think I could do a wedding without seeing him once?"

Her lips press together. "Maybe they don't want a lot of floral design?"

"If you're using Elliot Bloom, you want a lot of floral design."

Even saying his name makes my stomach tighten. Behind my eyes, I see white dahlias and spider mums.

I turn to her. "Go out and get more shots of the reception. I'll be fine."

"We can discuss this tonight. Drinks on me."

She disappears through the bathroom door, and I check the time on my phone.

I have four thousand new notifications.

Four thousand, two hundred and twelve, to be exact.

I open Instagram to see what's up, and I find a picture of Hazel and Jackie outside the coffee shop from this morning at the top of my feed.

Met our wonderful wedding planner for coffee today—@WeddingsbyAma. Check her out.

I have two thousand new followers. I have thirty DMs from strangers. I have notifications that my Pinterest pins have been saved. I have two emails from bloggers asking what we can expect to see out of Hazel Renee's wedding.

The notifications keep coming. I stagger back out to the Ferguson wedding and try to keep everyone on schedule. By the end of the night, my follower count has doubled. I have six more emails from journalists.

If I wasn't already regretting this, I would be now. This is far more exposure than I've ever handled, even under Whitney. And exposure means just as many opportunities for mistakes as there are for successes. Every wedding has its pressures, but not many have the possibility of advancing or ruining your career with one small swing of the pendulum.

When Mar and I eventually settle at the hotel bar at eleven, she's thumbing through my Instagram with weary eyes. She rubs her face.

"You can still say no," she says, almost a question with the way her vowels tilt upward at the end.

I nod, staring down into a martini. "I can."

"Or you could carry on. Be a professional."

My eyes close, I suck air through my nose.

Be a professional is a phrase that haunts me. Mar doesn't know she's hit a land mine, so I just breathe deeply to clear my head.

Be a professional. Is that what Whitney would say to me? I want to call her and ask, but then I'd have to tell her what happened at Senator Gilbert's wedding. And what had been happening for six months prior to it. And with whom. And she'd say "Ama," in that tone that told me I'd disappointed her. She'd know I'd never learned my lesson, and I crossed another line.

"Talk me through the worst-case scenario," I say.

Mar sits up tall. "You walk into his shop. You immediately burst into tears. Hazel Renee films it. It's live on Instagram titled, 'Woman Regrets Choice Made in Haste—'"

"You know I'd never be called 'woman.'"

"You're right. 'Sacramento Minor Could Have Had It All. News at eleven.' I think *E!* would get enough of the facts straight."

We drink some more, and when I get home, I email Hazel and Jackie the vendor list like I said I would. As if I'm actually doing this.

When I wake up on Monday morning, hungovery, Jackie's returned my email with:

Can we get in to see Elliot sooner rather than later? I want Hazel's input on flowers before she leaves for filming.

I laugh until I dry heave. And then I wet heave. When I'm done and refilling on electrolytes, I look at my calendar.

The odd thing is that Hazel and Jackie's wedding fits perfectly into my life. A few months back, when I looked at what this wedding season would be like for me, I wanted a large-scale wedding to work on this year. It was, in fact, my immediate goal. I wanted something that would get me noticed and satisfy my bank account while I continue to work on a smaller scale. I wanted to be able to rent my own office space by the end of the year, hire a permanent assistant, and pay someone else to run social media. Those were my long-term goals. But nothing came my way, and I told myself I'd catch my break next season. Hazel and Jackie would put me right on schedule.

Be a professional, Whitney's voice rings in my ear. Whenever I overstepped, she'd remind me that she got to where she is with professionalism, without crossing any boundaries.

Whitney never would have gotten herself in a situation where she had to work with an ex, but if she had, she would power through it. She'd be a professional.

I write back to Jackie and ask for their schedules this week. Then I text Mar that I need her to sober up and come over.

She knocks on my door at noon with sunglasses on and a box of donuts in hand. I'm halfway through my third when we speak for the first time.

"I'm gonna do it."

She nods, sipping her Gatorade. "Good."

"I need you to call him today to set up an appointment."

Cool Blue Raspberry dribbles out of her mouth as she coughs. I hand her the napkin I had prepared for this moment. When she recovers, she says, "Do you intend to speak to him at all? Or am I on contract?"

"I just need to get through this one thing. Then I think it will become easier. Businesslike."

Mar sighs. "Gimme some Advil, and then let's do this."

We're sitting on my living room floor an hour later, the box of donuts empty. Mar is clutching her prewritten script in one hand as her thumb pokes the number I'm giving her into her phone. She takes a deep breath before hitting dial, and I feel my own catch.

It rings four times. Long enough for me to hope that we'll get the machine. Midway through the fifth, I hear a click and wait for his father's old message from ten years ago, inviting us to leave our name and number.

I breathe out. It's over. It was easy. I can just wait for an email back.

"'Lo?"

The single syllable sets my skin on fire. I hate him for never enunciating. I hate him for not having a standard "Blooming, how can I help you?" I hate him for picking up at all.

But more than anything, I hate that I can't move. I'm staring at Mar as she crinkles the notes in her hand.

"Hi, I'm calling on behalf of WeddingsbyAma." She rushes the words together like we practiced. "I wanted to set up a meeting sometime this week for her newest clients. Can I talk scheduling with you?"

The line is quiet. I can feel my heartbeat in my lips as I press my fingertips to them. Mar checks the screen to make sure he didn't hang up.

And then—

"Mar." He says it like a greeting. Like a fact.

My mouth opens. My throat is dry. He's said one and a half words and I feel like I'm in a trance. The static of the phone mutes the timbre his voice has in real life. The resonance in his chest.

Mar tilts her head back and closes her eyes. She pulls her full lips into a tight line and then says, "No, this is Kelsey!" in a high voice. "I'm calling to set up a client meeting—"

"Mar, put Ama on the phone."

He says my name like "Emma," like he used to. Back when it was our joke. Back before I realized it was just the way he slipped the vowel through his lips.

Mar's eyes are wide and staring at me, but I can't move. "Okay!" the Kelsey voice says. "I'll see if she's free!"

Dropping the phone onto the coffee table—*his* coffee table—she gesticulates in a panic, mouthing, *What do I do?!*

I don't respond. I can't respond. I stare at the phone. Then Mar takes off her shoes and walks them across the hardwood, like a Foley artist from the 1920s. She leans away from the phone and says, "Ama, call for you."

She's reaching for my slippers, ready to create the sound effects of two people walking, when I reach for the phone and say, "Hello."

He's quiet for a moment. I think I can hear him breathing.

"What time."

I swallow involuntarily. I can't even figure out what he's asking for a moment.

"They're free Thursday after four, or Friday all day—"

"Thursday at four."

The line clicks dead.

I hold the phone to my ear a little longer, wishing for more of his consonants. Hoping for more than a three-word sentence, just like I used to.

I pull the phone away and stare at it. Mar's phone screen is the two of us at thirteen, Halloween costumes on.

"Are you okay?"

I look up, and Mar has her hands on her cheeks like Munch's *The Scream*. Her doe eyes are searching mine.

"Thursday at four," I say. I stand and take the donut box to the trash. I wash the sugar off my fingers. "I'm gonna shower. Wanna get dinner later?"

I disappear into my bathroom before she can answer. The faucet covers the sound of my sobbing.

5

Elliot

Flowers are better than people.

"Yes, Dad, they are," I say to the empty shop.

I'm in the back room, working on a hoop that I can suspend from the ceiling above the register. It will have dahlias and peonies twined around it, a section on the bottom right, a smaller section on the top left. It's a miniature version of what some people want behind them at the altar.

Dad would have told me to focus on the register, don't dally in the back. But he was 5'7" and frail, kind to everyone. I'm the opposite. Nobody's coming into Blooming to fuck with me. And besides, I've always been more interested in behind the scenes.

There's still a lot of him at the shop—his voice on the voicemail, his name on the sign. But there are exactly four of his flowers that are still kicking, ones that I brought to his funeral when I thought he'd maybe like more flowers than people there. Mom has one, and the other three are still in the shop. And he was right. They only needed light, water, and attention. But it's not as simple as that. Because you need to know *how much* light, *how much* water, *how much* attention. But if you can get it right—if you can crack the code—flowers are infinitely better than people. Because you can find a person's ratio of light, water, and attention, and it still won't be enough.

For flowers, it's enough.

It took me a couple years to really understand. I was mad for a long time that I had to drop out of college for *flowers*, of all things, but this was my grandad's shop before it was my father's, so it was always going to be mine, lung cancer or not, architecture degree or not. But light, water, and attention—that I could do. It's almost instinctual now. I don't think I have the magic touch my father had, but after a while, I started adding my own magic. Like this hoop. A little bit of design and construction to brighten up the place. I can get lost for hours making things like this.

So when my father's bell on the front door chimes just as I'm starting to tie off the peonies, I huff a sigh.

My lips tighten. I'm so close to finishing this.

"Yeah, one sec."

Once the section is secured, I grab a rag for my hands and step out of the back room. A girl is running her fingers over the new imported flowers that sit in the front window. I hate when people touch shit.

"What." I place my hands on the counter and lean forward onto them.

She spins. She's familiar, but she looks too young to be one of my mother's blind dates. Her eyes slide over the tattoos on my arms, and I'm still trying to place her when her expression narrows and her arms cross.

" 'What?' Is that really how you greet someone?" she says.

The sound of her voice does it. She's Whitney's girl. I remember her now. Her eyes are dark oak-brown to match her hair. She's got it tossed up in one of those ridiculous high buns so you don't know how much hair she actually has, but mine's currently long enough to be tied back, so I can't complain. My gaze dips to the swell of her hips before I can stop it.

"Welcome to my store," I say drily. "You need a prom corsage?"

She blinks rapidly. "A—a *prom* corsage? I'm twenty-two!"

I shrug. "You look sixteen." She doesn't. But I bet it's gonna make her mad.

She steps toward the register with an arched brow, a swagger in her walk.

"Is that how you look at sixteen-year-olds?"

I push away from the counter with a sigh. She won that one. "How can I help you, ma'am?"

I see the *ma'am* hit her just as hard as the *sixteen*, but she straightens her scarf and moves closer. "My name is Ama Torres. You might remember, I used to work with Whitney Harrison Weddings. Now I've started my own business—"

"Congratulations." I turn my back on her, fingers already plucking up the petals left over from this morning. I busy my hands and listen to her sputter.

"Yes, thank you. Um, I wanted to come in and make a connection. I've always been a fan of Blooming, and if I can convince clients to hire you, I'd like to—"

"Whitney's had a discount for years." I move from behind the register and onto the floor, heading for the Stem Bar I set up so customers can make their own bouquets, priced by the stem. I grab some yellow buttercups. "My father set it up with her. It's much higher than anyone else gets, especially new wedding planners."

"I didn't come here for a *discount*, Mr. Bloom," she all but hisses. "I came to introduce myself."

"Great. And now you have." I find the petunias and return to the counter, grabbing some waxy lemon leaves.

My father used to do this. He was kind about it, of course, but he used to give a boutonniere or small corsage to people coming in to place an order, like it was a bit of luck to take with them. I expanded on it. I create it while we talk. Sometimes they're so charmed to have a free arrangement inspired by them that it erases the five minutes of rudeness they experienced.

"Okay," she says, and I hear the exasperation being pushed down. "I'd like to start again. I'm Ama."

My eyes leave the twine and petals. She's extending one hand toward me with a bright smile on her face. I relish the fact that mine are sticky with stem sap with dirt under my nails as I reach for her manicured fingers. Her hands are small. And I realize she can't be much over five feet, but she wears heels to cover it. I'm thinking too much about her body, so I say, "Emma?"

Her lips tighten. I've hit another nerve. "Ama. A-M-A."

I'm still holding her hand in mine when I say, "What the fuck kind of name is Ama?"

She takes her hand back, and her eyes flick to the floor before she gains her confidence again. "It's short for something, obviously."

And the fact that she won't tell me is delicious. I try to keep the grin from twitching my lips, but I think I fail. "Amateur."

She stares at me, then realizes it's a guess, not an accusation. Then realizes it's both. Then frowns.

It's a fun journey to watch.

"No." She pushes her bag up her shoulder. "My mother didn't name me *Amateur*."

"Amabella," I guess.

She tilts her head. "You read a lot of Liane Moriarty?"

"I have HBO."

She snorts. And it's not crass or unflattering. I start twisting the twine around the stems again. "Why did Whitney let you go?" I ask.

She takes a sharp inhale. "She didn't let me go. We're on good terms, I swear."

I look up at her. I remember her at venues, her hands in every pot. She'd be on ladders with the sound tech, refolding napkins, shifting chuppahs two inches over. She'd spot a wilted flower from a mile away, and while I was still setting up, she'd come over and tear out the offenders. She was excellent with design, and probably the true brains behind Whitney's success. But I also remember her laughing with bridesmaids, getting closer than Ice Queen Whitney ever dared.

And I remember the crack of her fist. The way she trembled when Whitney dug her nails into her arm.

"It's all the same, isn't it?" I say. "Whitney decides who stays and who goes. Whitney *let* you go." I slip the pin through the boutonniere, finishing with a thin ribbon. I watch her mind work, trying to figure it out.

"I told Whitney it was my dream to own my own business. So she supported me."

I place the purple and yellow boutonniere on the counter next to her hand. She picks it up and her fingers feather over the petals. I feel that bit of magic that Dad used to talk about—when you can change someone's day with a gift of flowers.

So I say something to ruin it. "The only reason Whitney Harrison would allow you to compete with her in the market is because she knows you'll fail. So she let you go."

Her eyes snap up at me. I see her fingers curl around the tied flowers. And before she can chuck them at my head, I say, "I won't do a vendor discount for the first six months." I pluck up our old business card that still has Dad's name, and I slide it across to her before grabbing the rag and heading into the back again.

I wonder if she'll look up *The Language of Flowers* and figure out I just told her, *You are immature and I resent you. Go away.*

6

Ama

MARCH

With Hazel's schedule being what it is, we're squeezing a lot into one week. We go to Blooming tomorrow afternoon, but my stomach is already a mess today, so I'm sticking to iced tea at our second meeting—this time, lunch at Cafe Bernardo, a casual farm-to-fork restaurant in Midtown.

I take out my iPad and say, "So, tell me what you know so far. List size, colors, dresses—"

"Ah." Hazel finishes her bite of salad. "I'm in a white pantsuit. Jac's in the dress."

"I love that." I lean forward on my elbows, smiling. "Both walking down the aisle? Just Jackie?"

"Well, it's been my dream to walk down the aisle at the Rose Garden," Jackie says with a smile, "but I want Hazel to have an entrance too."

"That doesn't matter to me though, babe—"

"I know, babe, but I still think your brother should walk you down the aisle…"

I sip my iced tea, letting them bicker. It's great to get a sense of people early on. Hazel is laid-back and open to anything, and Jackie, while she wants her hands in everything, only has one real demand—the Rose Garden. Hazel is happy when Jackie is happy. A different type of planner would have catered to Hazel, the celebrity. But now that I've spotted this, it's going to set me ahead.

"Can I ask about the proposal? I love hearing the story."

Jackie's eyes brighten, and she brushes hair out of her face. "It was at my parents' house. I brought Hazel home for Christmas, but she had already talked to my dad." Jackie smiles at her, and I see her eyes water.

"What I didn't know," Hazel says, "was that *Jackie* had a fucking ring in her suitcase too."

I gasp as Jackie elbows Hazel.

"So I had to wait there like an idiot in front of her parents when she shot out of her chair and ran upstairs without saying yes or no. I thought she'd gotten sick at the thought."

They laugh and lean together for a soft kiss.

Proposal stories are the best, and this is a good one. There's nothing wrong with a football stadium proposal if I feel the bride is as much a sports fan as the groom. And the simplest "Wanna get married?" stories that happen without a ring can tell me a lot too. Sometimes it's that they haven't thought it out, but also they might be more spontaneous than other couples.

Some people can tell if a marriage will last when they watch the groom's face as the bride comes down the aisle; some people can tell at the first meeting with the couple; I can tell when I hear the proposal story.

And Jackie and Hazel? They're the real thing.

I don't believe long-term commitments like marriage work out, but I do believe in love. It can be fleeting and undependable, rarely long-lasting, but I do believe it exists. I know my mom has been in love with many of her husbands, but marriage was the quickest way to kill it. I've been in love once, and it, too, ended.

I sip my iced tea to help swallow the lump in my throat that rises with that thought. Across from me, Jackie threads her fingers through Hazel's on top of the table.

It's not my place to hope that Jackie and Hazel will be together forever, but I can be happy they are together for now. I believe they are in love, and that that love will last a long time. End of story. Whenever I find these kinds of couples, I put more of myself into the design, and those weddings end up being my best work.

I get more of their details over lunch, writing myself notes:

- Jackie walking down aisle; Hazel TBD
- Jackie in dress; Hazel in pantsuit
- Both commissioned by Elle Stone—friend of Hazel
- Colors—TBD (H wants muted fall colors with drama; J wants pink)
- Live band at reception
- Cellist at ceremony—Xander Thorne—friend of Hazel
- AMA ACTION ITEMS
  - Reception venue
  - Make initial contact with Elle Stone
  - Contact Xander Thorne—don't go through agent—afitzmusic@aol.com

When I finish my bubbles and tie them to *Hazel and Jackie*, I say, "So we haven't talked guest list. Give me a ballpark as I look at reception venues."

Jackie looks at Hazel. "Well, *I* think it can be done under one hundred. But Hazel is worried about her publicist's list."

"I have a feeling that 'Hazel Renee's Wedding' isn't really going to be my wedding," Hazel says with a grimace. I nod, feeling like Hazel's publicist may be the equivalent of the mother-in-law in this case. "I think two hundred."

I try not to widen my eyes. An extra hundred for the mother-in-law is a lot. I write down *100–200* and bubble it. "Well, then. I guess it's time for money. What's the budget?"

Hazel sits forward. "I'd like to think of it as a Do Not Exceed number."

"That's wonderful for me. It's usually something I clarify anyway!" I make a note. "And you'd like me to come up with a general budget, knowing the Do Not Exceed?" When Hazel nods, I ask for the number.

"Two hundred and fifty thousand."

To my credit, my stylus doesn't slip out of my hand, roll onto the floor, trip a waiter, and bring a tray of drinks crashing down. But in my mind all of that is happening. And it is my career swirling on the floor with the mimosas.

That's more than I've ever worked with, except under Whitney. I'm filled with half excitement and half dread. Numbers like that usually come with vendors who are out of my league, venues I have no relationship with, and high expectations. I should have gotten this information before I agreed to this, but Jackie's only wish of the Rose Garden didn't indicate that budget.

"Is that not enough?" Jackie asks quietly, misreading my silence.

"No, it's great," I say. "It is ... a lot. I haven't seen that kind of budget since I was with Whitney, so I'm just trying to wrap my head around it."

I think of the promise I made Whitney when I resigned—that I would never intrude on her market. The way she waved her hand like it wasn't even something she was worried about. The hug she gave me. Firm, caring, vanilla-scented.

But what do I do now? Back out? Send them to Whitney, who can handle this size, who knows these vendors?

No. Absolutely not. This wedding is a window of opportunity that won't come my way again.

I know I can do this. I'm the right choice for Hazel and Jackie. And I can't wait to prove it.

I have a free morning before Thursday's appointment at Bloom ing, so instead of staring at the wall and sweating, I decide to check in at the WHW office. It's been a few months since I've visited, and I'd like to pick Whitney's brain about Hazel and Jackie's wish list.

With my signature box of donuts in one hand, I tug open the door to the brick building, neatly situated in East Sacramento— the hub of rich people. The front desk is occupied by a new girl I don't know, but soon enough, people are stepping out of their offices to give me a hug and grab a donut.

It was hard to leave. It wasn't that I wanted to stop working with Whitney, but I knew that if I continued there, I'd stay forever. And the clients that Whitney takes on are not *my* people. The budget weddings I've done in the past two years have been more satisfying than the six-figure ones I was doing here. I get to see the bride's face light up when I tell her what we can achieve, even with funds being tight. That's the heart of it.

Whitney has a corner office—not that it matters when you're not downtown—in the back, and as my old friends munch on the donut holes Mr. Kwon tossed in, I rap on the door and wait for her "Yes?"

I slip inside with a grin, and I'm transported back to my first interview in this office, fresh out of high school. My mother had a Whitney Harrison wedding the weekend of my graduation, and after tossing my cap, I ran to her reception and saw Whitney for the first time. She was an intimidating presence—tall and blond and disappointed with everyone. I watched her grab the wrist of a server as he brought the first entrées out ten minutes early, and with a bone-crunching squeeze and a honey-sweet smile, she guided him back into the kitchen. It was fantastic. I learned later that her assistant had canceled on her that day, which was why she was running the wedding. I didn't even wait for the job opening announcement to hit their website; I showed up on Monday with a lookbook from my mother's past four weddings, all of which I designed for her. With a calculating gaze, she offered me minimum wage to answer phones. Two weeks later, I was promoted to assistant; three more months and I was the design and production coordinator. While my classmates were starting college, I was already making a living, doing exactly what I wanted.

Whitney's the exact same as she was. Her hair is swept back into a thick blond ponytail. She's starting to get lines around her eyes, but I know she's just overdue for an injection. Her thin lips are downturned as she looks up to see who has disturbed her, and the moment she realizes it's me, her teeth shine pearly white at me.

"Ama, how nice!" She jumps up and smooths out her boatneck dress, sweeping me into her arms. "What's the occasion?"

Her soft perfume envelops me, and I breathe deep before saying, "Thought it was overdue."

I settle in the chair in front of her desk, and we catch up. She has four weddings this weekend. I have one, but she still wants to hear all about it.

"How's Mom?" she asks, crossing her legs and smiling at me.

"She's good. She just got married last month."

"What number is that?" She laughs, and I feel like I have to do the same. "Has someone checked the world record yet?"

My cheeks heat. It's not the first time I've heard that joke, and it won't be the last. My mother has never been ashamed of her marriages, but after the tenth, I started to realize that other people found it wildly entertaining. As a kid, I didn't understand there was anything wrong with it. I didn't know people talked behind her back or that she was the butt of jokes made by the people closest to her. I laugh along with them now so they don't see my discomfort.

I change the subject quickly. "So I need some professional advice."

"Of course!" She flicks her wrist, and her bracelet jangles. "What's up?"

"I scored the Hazel Renee wedding." Getting it out of me as quickly as possible is all I can do to not vomit. Though vomit may still come. It's early.

Her brows jump. "Oh really?" She smiles, but a small laugh pops through her chest. "How on earth did you land that?"

"They found me." I shrug, wincing. "I tried to talk them out of it—"

"Ama, no." She shakes her head. "You're perfectly qualified. You told them your services, your style, your scale, and they still wanted you."

I chew on the inside of my cheek. "Right. I'm starting to feel their scale is . . . more than they let on. Or maybe I didn't clarify. I don't know. And I wanted to be up front with you, because I said I wouldn't be encroaching on your list or your clients."

She waves her hand. "Well, that's not something entirely in your control. I know that." She levels a stare at me, a smile curling her lips without reaching her eyes. "I'm proud of you. It's a wonderful opportunity. When is the date?"

I wince. "October seventh."

She blinks at me. "Of *this* year? That's very soon."

I nod, chewing on my lip. "It's fast, but I can do it. I'm positive. I was just hoping you could point me in the right direction of vendors that may still be free."

The corner of her mouth tightens. "Of course. But . . . let me just advise you to be careful, Ama."

I take a deep breath, knowing exactly where this is going.

"Hazel is your age, I think?" When I nod, she continues. "The celebrity aspect may be difficult. It can be seductive. So just remember to keep your distance. Any misstep could be broadcast to her followers."

She says *misstep* like it's a missing wedding ring or forgetting to hire a DJ, but I know what she actually means. I was one week into my position as design and production coordinator when I texted a bride out of the blue to ask why she never brought in her Pinterest board. I'd been snooping around and had found her social media pages. The pins she saved were nothing like what we had settled on. Veronica, the bride, messaged me back to say she didn't think any of it was possible in their budget. The next day, I'd devised an entire plan of attack for the new wedding design and presented it to Whitney in front of the couple. Veronica was ecstatic. Whitney smiled and nodded and held her tongue until the couple left, and then released me from Veronica's wedding.

"Do you have any idea what it's like to call your rental company, your caterer, *and* your florist at the four-month mark and tell them you're redesigning? Oh, right, of course you don't, because *I'm* the one that has to do that!" she'd hissed at me.

In the moment, I thought it was the timeline and the relationship with the vendors that she was most upset about. But three months later, I attended a bridal shower for one of our clients, and when Whitney found out, she took me off that wedding too.

I tried to be better. I tried to decline invitations to bridal showers and bachelorette parties, but to Whitney, it was a Band-Aid over the real problem—they *liked* me. They liked me enough to want to be around me and talk about their wedding design privately. I began to focus not on how to keep them from inviting me, but on how not to get caught. I was the best designer Whitney had, and to keep it that way, I *had to* get to know the couple and their style. When she felt I'd improved my boundaries, Whitney promoted me to director of design, a huge position for a twenty-year-old. And a month after that, something worse happened. I punched a groomsman for putting his hand on my ass and suggesting that I suck him off. While I was crying and apologizing, my fist swollen and my clothes too tight on skin that didn't feel like mine anymore, Whitney tugged me to the side and said, "I'm surprised this is the first time, actually."

Whitney handled it. She smoothed everything over with the couple and got the groomsman cleaned up and to the altar. She convinced him not to press charges, which was something I hadn't even thought about. Once the reception had started, she hugged me to her side, pressed an ice pack on my knuckles, and whispered softly, "You'll learn, sweetheart. I took care of everything. I made it all go away."

I look into her eyes now, and force myself to smile. On days like today, I still wish I had her taking care of everything.

"Absolutely," I say. "I'm getting better at my boundaries."

She nods, and I'm not sure she believes me, but she pats the desk and reaches for her mouse. "October seventh? I'll let you know which vendors of mine are already busy that day."

I take a deep breath, steeling my nerves, and bring my chair around to look at her calendar—like old times.

7

Ama

MARCH

I haven't been to Blooming in two years. Two years, two months, one week, and four days, to be more exact. I tried to calculate the hours and minutes while curling my hair, but that was overkill. And I burned my wrist.

I've cut my hair since he's last seen me, and it's stupid to wonder if he'd notice when I'm actively hoping he *doesn't* notice me—that maybe I can hide behind an especially tall orchid for the entire meeting and let Jackie take lead. But it's still on my mind.

I'm not bringing donuts, because with him, it's never been the "endearing" thing to do.

I park down the street instead of in the three-car lot attached to the shop. My Apple Watch wanted me to call 9-1-1 six minutes ago based on my heart rate, so I'm actively meditating, imagining creeks trickling slowly over rocks. I wait for Jackie and Hazel to pull up, with the intense focus of a hunting hound, jerking quickly whenever a car with two women in it slows down. My check engine light is flashing at me, but I ignore it as usual.

This is the first time we'll be in the same room, breathing the same air, in over two years. I've driven out of my way to avoid Blooming every day of those two years, and I can assume he hasn't had a glimpse of me either. I started working with other florists, obviously, even though it was a huge hit to my style and creativity. There were even some weddings that I needed to cut him from after—well, *after*. Largely, I am able to put him out of my mind most days. It got easier as time went on, but it's just now hitting me how difficult this is going to be.

A cute little Prius puts on its blinker for the parking lot, and as soon as I confirm it's Jackie behind the wheel, I grab my bag and jump out. They're shutting their doors by the time I walk up to them. I think we all hug. I'm blacking out, so details are getting fuzzy. We're chatting up to the main door. I'm reaching for the handle.

"Hey!"

The bark freezes me like a statue. The three of us whip to the right, and there he is, a rag between his hands, black Henley, black jeans. He's stepping out from around the building where we just came from, out the side door that leads to the back room. His hair is long again. He has half of it tied back, out of his face. I called it a man bun once, and he gave me the silent treatment for the rest of the day.

I can feel my knees wobble. My heartbeat is kicking into "Is there an intruder in your house?" status again.

I wait for him to point at me and say "*She* can't come in," or "Meeting's canceled."

But he doesn't glance at me at all. He just jerks his head for us to enter that way, and disappears.

Jackie rolls her eyes and says to Hazel, "He's always like that. Rude is his brand."

It would have been funny to me if I didn't feel a sudden pain in my chest. Jackie *knows* Elliot. More than just "the boss's son." Forget anything about sexual orientation, but there's a person in his life who *knows* him well enough to make that joke, and I didn't know she existed until this week.

Jackie and Hazel link hands and walk toward the side door, and I follow them like a dog who's being led to a bathtub, cowering and shaking. I take the weight of the door from Hazel, and when I hear her say, "Oh, wow!" I look up and stop on the threshold.

The back room—it's transformed. Where there were boxes and broken things to be fixed, there are now two worktables, eight feet long with marble tops. Where there was peeling olive-green paint and rusty nails, there are now white walls with wedding arches hanging from the high ceiling, wreaths mounted, a ten-foot wall covered in roses—silks, maybe—spelling *Blooming*. Where there was one bare bulb ceiling light, there are now neons and LEDs popping clear violet light from above.

My eyes flutter with all there is to take in, and I remember—

"If you want to do custom installations, you'll need a studio, Elliot."

He rolled his eyes at me. "I made a couple things. I'm not converting the shop just to play ball with Whitney's high-end clients. My dad would never have wanted that."

I shrugged. "Why not both? What about the back room?"

I have to place my hand on the door frame before I fall down. I've never in my life felt unsteady on heels, but my legs don't want to cooperate.

"Shut the door," his gruff voice calls from across the room. He's standing at a smaller table in the corner that's more of a workbench. It's the only messy spot in the entire room. It's the only *Elliot* spot in the entire room.

"Elliot," Jackie says, "this is my fiancée, Hazel."

I let the door close behind me, and I watch from a distance of thirty feet as Hazel shakes his hand. He mutters something that must be "Nice to meet you."

Hazel gestures to the rose wall. "This is incredible. Your whole workshop is, really."

He nods, never one to say thank you. "This was my father's shop for forty years. He operated in bouquets and small-scale wedding pieces, but when I took over, I started experimenting with constructions and installations. Blooming now offers both."

They're the longest sentences I've heard him speak—ever. And I realize it's a script he's trying to pretend isn't memorized. The familiarity I feel around him sends an electric shock through my system, and I have to turn away. I face the wall and examine the way he's arranged the wreaths for spring.

I hear them give him the wedding date. I hear Hazel start to describe a couple of her wish-list items. I hear the low hum of his approval.

I should be over there in the thick of it. I'm designing this wedding, and that includes collaborating on the floral arrangements.

Under the guise of staring at the potted flowers on his tabletops, I wander closer just as he asks, "Where's the reception?"

"I'm working on that this week," I say. My voice is scratchy. When I slip my gaze to him, he's adjusting his sleeve, looking at Jackie. "Once I know, I can email you about a visit time."

"Rehearsal dinner?" he says.

"No details yet, but I'd *love* some centerpieces for that," Jackie says hopefully, clapping her hands together. He only nods.

His fingers reach for the stem of a fuchsia calla lily, tugging it out of an arrangement as he says, "McKinley Park Rose Garden.

Are we sticking to roses for the ceremony? Or are you interested in seeing variety?"

Jackie and Hazel look at each other, then at me. "I think variety sounds nice," I say, trusting his intuition.

He doesn't respond. Doesn't nod. No indication that I've spoken or even exist. I swallow tightly and watch him reach for the muted orange chrysanthemums at the other table. My heart skips, already knowing what he's doing. I'm buzzing, remembering my first boutonniere. Buttercups and petunias—immaturity and resentment. I shake my head free of the memory as Jackie says, "This is cool."

I turn my head over my shoulder and see what she's looking at. Leaning against the wall is a large clear box, split into four quadrants packed full of blossoms. It's about a foot deep and as high as my waist, and it's covered with a slab of clear Plexiglas. It looks like it could be hung on the wall as a faux window.

Elliot hums, and he leaves the flowers on the table. I step back to give him a wide berth as he comes over to the window box. He grabs a wall plug I didn't see before, connects it to an outlet, and before I can marvel at how sweet the fairy lights look inside that window box, he flips it flat onto the floor and steps on top.

It isn't until he extends his hand to Jackie to have her join him that we realize—

"Is this . . ." Hazel's eyes are wide. "Is this a dance floor?"

Jackie's jaw drops as she joins him on the Plexiglas.

"It's one-tenth of a dance floor," he clarifies.

He steps down and gestures to Hazel to take his place on the floor. When Hazel eyes it warily, Jackie whispers, "It's okay. He's an architect."

Elliot doesn't correct her. She steps up, and he turns the lights off in the workshop to let them get the feeling of an evening reception with the lights from below.

I'm honestly speechless. Which is fine, because he wouldn't want to hear from me anyway. I've seen LED dance floors before, but this is a floor made out of flowers and light. It's nothing short of magical, and it's only a three-by-three slab. Hazel and Jackie look at me with their I-want-a-fairytale eyes, and I say, "Include it in the quote."

The lights turn on, and as they chatter with him, he continues with the calla lilies and chrysanthemums, grabbing a feathery grass and some boxwood. He nods while they talk, winding the twine and grabbing a fraying rope to tie it off. When he places the bouquet in front of Hazel and Jackie on the table, they stop midsentence and stare down at it.

"Free of charge." He moves toward the door leading to the main shop. "Email me," he says to no one. Me.

Jackie picks up the bouquet and runs her fingers over the petals. "Wow. This..."

"Pinks like you want, fall colors like I want," Hazel says. She turns to me. "Did you tell him how we were arguing about colors?"

I shake my head. "No. He just...knows." I shift my bag on my shoulder and gesture toward the exit. "Shall we?"

Hazel snaps a picture of his studio before we leave and says, "Can you ask him if I can post it?"

I'd rather eat glass. "Of course."

When the door shuts, and we're walking to our cars, I realize I survived. He didn't look at me once. He didn't speak to me. But I survived.

"My god, if I wasn't into girls..." Hazel says suggestively.

"Or engaged?" Jackie pinches her side.

"He's aggressively hot."

I stare straight ahead.

"His mother says he doesn't date. Isn't that sad?" Jackie looks over her shoulder at the shop and lowers her voice like he could be listening in. "She said his last girlfriend broke his heart real good."

I trip over nothing, looking back like a large rock will appear, and Hazel says, "When was that?"

My stomach is in knots, but Senator Gilbert didn't know about us, I thought. How could she possibly—

"Last fall, I think? She was a girl from the office—Kate," Jackie says.

The twisting in my stomach turns violent. I look back at the shop. There was *another* girl that broke his heart? Since me? It's been two years, so I suppose it makes sense that he's dated. I've seen a couple people, but not anyone who could mean anything. He was the first person I'd let get that close anyway—the first I broke all my rules for—and I wasn't interested in doing it again.

I don't know what feels worse. The idea that he moved on, or the hope that he hadn't.

"Ama?"

I jerk toward Hazel and smile. "Yes? Sorry?"

"Anything else we need today? I'll be gone for two weeks."

"No! We're great. That dance floor is *amazing*. I think it will be a perfect centerpiece."

We say goodbye, and I walk the half block to my car, looking over my shoulder like an idiot. Hoping someone's watching me.

8

Elliot

I don't do social media. I could try to explain how it's rotting my generation, or that basing your self worth on your ability to photograph your eggs is useless. But the truth is, I never learned how to use it.

And I refuse to do it wrong. If I'm going to commit anywhere from one to eight hours of my day to a new hobby, I'm not going to make an ass of myself.

My dad wanted the shop to have an Instagram account. He had my cousin set it up several years ago, but Dad was terrible at adding to it. There'd be all caps in the descriptions, and he'd have fertilizer bags in the corner of a shot of some dahlias. It has about a hundred followers and gets maybe six likes per post.

My same cousin, Ben, works at the shop on days I'm setting up weddings, and I asked him for some advice. I built a chandelier by suspending a rectangular tray from the ceiling in the back room with a lightweight chain. I filled it with pink baby's breath and feathery blush flowers from an astilbe. I'm not even embarrassed—

it's a fluffy pink cloud, and I think it looks awesome. Ben thought so too, and helped me upload it with the right hashtags.

Two hundred likes, seventy new followers.

I hate social media. I'm in bed, staring at other posts from floral designers across the world. I don't care that they have one thousand times the followers or likes; it's that they *deserve* them. My skin is buzzing with inspiration and jealousy.

One of them has a wall of roses spelling a bride and groom's names. A wall. Of roses. How much are these couples shelling out for this shit? But even as I shake my head, I'm itching to sketch the construction. What kind of structure is the flower foam mounted on? Does it have to be a day-of installation, or is this actually sustainable?

Some other punk kid is doing Alice in Wonderland–themed bouquets, naked underneath his gardening apron. He's got twenty million followers. His Mad Hatter bouquet is driving me nuts because he clearly colored the peonies for it. I'm about to become one of those internet trolls I've heard about, ready to post "black spray on your peonies bro?" when a new like and a new follower comes in.

> *@AmazingAma liked your photo*
> *@AmazingAma started following you*

My eyes flick back to where I'm typing, trying to decide whether I want a comma after *peonies*, when I realize who it might be.

I leave the naked dude's page and click on my notifications just in time to see:

> *@WeddingsbyAma started following you*

I click the first profile and see her huge eyes staring wide at the camera under a hat brim. Account is private. My thumb hovers over the Follow button, but I decide against it.

Private accounts. Instagram's version of online dating, one rejected follow request at a time.

The banner at the top of the app drops down. WeddingsbyAma has sent me a message.

I sit up in bed, feeling oddly like I need to be not in my underwear for this. But I look at the time and *she's* the one DM'ing me at eleven thirty at night.

I click the message, and it's a link to my own post of the chandelier and a message from her:

This is fucking beautiful

I swallow. I know it is. But that's not what you're supposed to say. I'm still thinking of the annoying way she talked and the scent of her perfume that cut through the flowers even after she was gone.

I decide to say nothing instead of being rude again. Or instead of being forced to type *thank you*. I go to her WeddingsbyAma page and look at her posts. She's been using Relles Florist in Midtown. They're good. My father used to get dinner with Mr. Relles, and their entire family came to his funeral.

A new message pops up.

Can you make it for a 12-foot head table?

I stare at the screen, thinking of the trays I have. One tray is three feet. I wouldn't do four trays because it would outshine the table itself. I can connect three trays, maybe even link them together so there's more stability—

For next weekend?

I frown at the incoming message. It's Thursday. Nine days for a special order isn't unheard of. But not over Instagram. At 11:38 p.m.

In my head, I draft a response—my cousin said they can see you type—and after about ten minutes I disregard it. I just write back:

Call the shop tomorrow and we'll talk.

It's nine a.m., and I'm still trying to turn on the computer when the door swings open. That same brimmed black hat from her profile pic is on her head, and there's a broad smile on her lips. With her hair down, now I can see that it's long—to her mid-back. She looks like a witch.

"Good morning!"

I catch myself just staring while she approaches the counter and I grunt a response, turning to the register. She drops a pink box between us. I glare at it.

"Donuts! From J Street Donuts."

"Very inventive name."

Her eyes twinkle. "Well, Elliot Bloom of Blooming, we can't all be as blessed." She flips open the lid, and I spare a glance at the half dozen.

"I don't eat sugar."

She looks like I just burned down her house. "God, seriously? That's not possible."

"It is. I don't."

"Ever?" She leans forward on the counter. "What about soda?" When I shake my head, she blinks like she's having a stroke. "I have a donut almost every single day."

I glance her over, searching for signs that she's telling the truth. The curve of her hips catches my attention, just like last time, but I refocus quickly. "I told you to call."

"Why waste time?" she says, plucking a donut hole out of the box, popping it between her blush-stained lips, and reaching for her iPad in one movement.

I watch her chew, her tongue swiping out to catch the sugar. I think of Madison Bailey in middle school, telling any idiot who would listen that you should always eat in front of a boy. *It will make him think about your mouth.*

Fucking Madison. I didn't believe her back then.

"Okay," she says, swallowing, and I watch that movement too. Her fingers are quick over her iPad. "Wedding is next Saturday. The head table is twelve feet long, and the ceiling is about twenty high. I'm thinking the chandelier lands at seven to eight feet. Can you come to the venue today or tomorrow to measure and confirm?"

Her eyes flick up to me. The computer screen goes dark, task completely forgotten. I shake the mouse and pretend to look at my calendar.

"Noon either day. That's when my cousin can cover the shop."

"Awesome. Today, please," she says. She tells me the location, then says, "Can I see the piece? Is it still here?"

I head to the back, turning to hold the door open for her. She grabs a chocolate donut from her box and follows.

The single bulb flickers to life in the back room. I used a work light for the initial picture. It almost looked well staged, with the rustic green paint on the wall behind the chandelier.

She moves right to it, reaching up to touch the baby's breath, stepping underneath and staring at the trays. She's tiny, really. She just wears tall shoes.

"In the pinks, right?" I say, sliding my apron on over my head.

"Yeah, perfect."

"Is the client coming to confirm?"

"I am the client," she says absently, stepping back to observe where it connects to the ceiling.

Something in my chest drops. Like a bird shot dead.

"Congratulations," I mutter, watching her take a bite of the donut. Watching her mouth.

"Mm." She spins to me. "Sorry." She eventually swallows. "Not me. My mom. She's getting married; I'm designing it."

I drag my gaze to the mess of the back room, ignoring the adrenaline pumping through me, as well as the relief. I clear my throat and continue. "The trays are three feet. I think I'll do three of them to not overshadow. And then the flowers will overflow the ends and give more volume."

She nods and stares at me with a grin. "You can speak more than three-word sentences. Cool."

I roll my eyes and step up to show her where I'll connect the trays. I see her glance at the tattoo on the back of my left forearm.

"Which flower is that?"

I bend my elbow back. "It's a Vietnamese orchid. It's endangered."

She stares at the tattoo, the white petals and reddish-pink center. "Is it your favorite?"

I drop my arm, fingers reaching for my other sleeve to roll it down. "No, I don't have a favorite."

Her gaze flicks to my right arm as I cover it to the wrist, but she drops the subject. "Do you have more to do a centerpiece too? Just aesthetically, to match above and below."

"You don't have your centerpieces yet?"

"I do. I'd rather have this."

I move into the main shop, heading toward the Stem Bar for the feathery astilbe and baby's breath. "What are the other flowers?" I call to her. "I can match and fill the center."

"White dahlias." She surprises me by being right next to me.

She follows me into the back room again, and I take a low basin from a shelf, starting to arrange the sprigs to fan out of the sides. I can feel her watching my hands move. The center is bare, and I pull some thick white candles as an option. "I can fill the center with the dahlias or weave them in."

"What do you think is best?"

She's looking at me expectantly, and I feel like this is some sort of test.

I start weaving them into the baby's breath. Hopefully integrating the dahlias will help these centerpieces match the other floral design.

"Do you like the guy?" I ask.

She doesn't answer, and I glance up. "The guy?" she asks.

"Your mom's new husband."

"Oh." She snorts, waving her hand flippantly. "It doesn't matter."

Zero points there. "Okay."

"Sorry, I just mean—she doesn't stay married for long. So whether I like him or not is inconsequential. I'll spend the summer with him and his kids, maybe Labor Day, and then I probably won't see him ever again." There's a downward tilt to her mouth.

"That sounds hard," I try.

Her eyes flip up to mine. "Sometimes."

"Is your dad still around?" She doesn't answer right away, and I feel my skin heat. "Sorry, you don't have to—"

"It's okay." She flashes a smile and says, "He's in Connecticut. With a new family. More stepsiblings for me!" She laughs, like there's a joke there, but I don't get it. "I used to fly out every other Christmas, but it's been a few years. He gave me his car for my sixteenth birthday, and we started just calling each other on holidays."

I look up at her. Her eyes are glued on the centerpiece I'm making, but there's nothing sad or embarrassed about her expression. It's fact. I can't quite apologize for facts.

She pivots topic quickly, gesturing to the flowers as I finish up. "This looks great. If you weren't such an asshole, I would have ordered ten of these already."

"Oh, you didn't like your boutonniere?" I ask innocently, my lips twitching. I wipe my hand with a rag and lead her back to the counter.

She follows. "You mean the buttercups for immaturity, the petunias for resentment, and—what was that other plant you used?"

"Poison ivy." I grab an order sheet from the drawer and sneak a glance up at her. She's gaping at me like a fish. When she realizes I'm joking, I see her biting the inside of her cheek to keep from smiling.

I scribble the order down in my chicken scratch. "We charge an added ten percent for rush orders." She nods in agreement. "And there's a PITA fee."

She blinks, and then she hums her acceptance. She looks down at her phone, but I watch her eyes focus, trying to figure out what a PITA is.

It's the one thing my father ever did that convinced me we were related. He'd charge a PITA fee sometimes. Pain in the ass. It was only ever ten dollars, so he used to donate it to the library or the high school.

I write the order name at the top. *Ama Torres.* As I scribble the date, I say, "Amalgamation."

She pauses typing—probably looking up PITA—and stares at me. "You think my mother named me Amalgamation?"

I shrug. "There are so few A-M-A words in the world. Amaranth?"

"You are conveniently forgetting *amazing*. What is Amaranth?"

"I didn't forget; I disregarded. Amaranth is a plant. Drooping pink flowers that I use in bouquets sometimes."

The corners of her mouth tighten, and she hums. "Nope." Her eyes look away quickly.

I lean forward on the counter so I can see the small details in her expression that say I'm too close to the truth.

My eyes flick to the front window—the flower I caught her pawing the first time she came into my shop. The "Red Pearl" I'd gotten in from South America. The second bud just opened today, crimson red.

I move around the counter and take my mini shears from my back pocket. I run my fingertips over the dark petals, the stamen reaching outward to me, saying goodbye.

"Amaryllis," I say, my voice soft in the quiet shop. I lift my eyes to her, and she's pressing her lips together, a blush on her cheeks, a stain on her neck as vibrant as the Red Pearl amaryllis. "Is your mother a fan of musicals, or...?"

Her eyes sparkle again. "How does someone like you know a minor character from *The Music Man*?"

"How many times do I have to tell you? I have HBO." I slide my clippers over the stem of the older bud and snip. Moving slowly back to the counter, I grab a bundle of the pink baby's breath from my apron and say, "Amaryllis was a mean little girl who was very rude to a little boy with a lisp. And as a little boy who had a lisp..." Her eyes widen, like I've given her a year's supply of donuts. "I vowed to take my revenge on Amaryllises... by charging a twenty-dollar delivery fee."

She fights a smile. I grab a pink ribbon, tie off the amaryllis and baby's breath with a quick twist, and set it next to her copy of the order.

"See you at noon," I say, before disappearing into the back to clean up.

When I get to the country club later, she's pinned it to her blouse, above the swell of her breasts. I do a terrible job of keeping my gaze from dropping.

9

Ama

It's hard to focus on other weddings when I have Hazel and Jackie's looming over me. On Saturday morning at the Gutiérrez-Montoya ceremony, I sketched reception hall designs while the bridal party taught the waitstaff their choreography to "Be Our Guest," which the couple demanded to be performed as the entrées came out. I had two of my ex-stepsiblings there as plants, dressed like the waitstaff and learning the dance for fifty bucks.

My favorites of my mother's husbands are the ones with kids who need job experience.

But nothing I sketch feels right. It doesn't feel *Elliot*.

Surprisingly, the thing I hate about working with Elliot Bloom again is the creative *possibility* he always made me feel. He could send me a picture of a half-finished piece, and it would change my entire design for a wedding. Because I had to have it. Elliot has a way of creating something from nothing that's really addictive. You can say, "I want an eight-foot Eiffel Tower made of flowers," and he'll send the design and the quote the next day.

It's Monday, and I'm already on my sixth sketch of a reception hall that doesn't exist, based solely on his floral dance floor. I have three indoor and three outdoor designs. I'm actively ignoring the other weddings coming up over the next seven months, because I can't stop thinking about the *possibility*.

I stand from my desk in the bedroom I've converted into an office, pop my back, and go feed the cat. Lady Cat-ryn de Purrgh flicks her tail at me and ignores her chow. She wants the leftover sushi she smelled in my to-go box a few days ago. Mar took me out to dinner on Friday to talk through the meeting with Elliot. I lied and told her it went better than expected. She asked why I was lying, and I ordered another round of drinks in response.

Despite the huge pay cut she'd be taking, I'm going to beg Mar to work as my assistant for the Jackie and Hazel wedding, because as wonderful a photographer as she is, Hazel is going to require a whole team who've worked together before. Mar works primarily alone. She met her last boyfriend through photography, and she had him tag along as assistant for her contracted events. Since they broke up in the fall, she's been doing it solo and interviewing assistants from the photography program at city college, but none of them are ready for the scale of this wedding.

Sighing, I look at the clock. I have three more business hours if I want to make any headway on vendors. My absolute favorite rental company that I worked with under Whitney is the first choice for another couple I have. I don't usually get to work with Everlast Event Rentals because their prices don't match my clients' budgets, but Ashley and Davin want to splurge. I want to nail them down for Jackie and Hazel too.

I dial and hope that Vickie still works there. When I finally get her on the phone, we catch up for a bit about her kids, her mom, my mom. We haven't really chatted since I left WHW, and it's nice to talk to her.

"Okay, I have two weddings I want to get Everlast on the books for," I say.

"Hit me." I hear her long fingernails clacking on the keyboard. "We're really booked for the next six months so I hope you're early."

"I hope so too. I have the Dawsons on December second. They're looking for a standard package and a head table kit."

"Yep. We can do that. Plenty that day."

"Awesome. Pencil me in and I'll bring the couple in sometime this week. And then I have a really big wedding in October. FYI, it's probably gonna be covered by the media."

"Oookay, I will make a note. No chipped plates."

I laugh. "October seventh. We'll need a whole package, but I'm not sure about the details yet. I can bring them in this week."

"Hm." Vickie pauses. "October seventh is crazy busy. Ama, I'm not sure we can do it."

My heart stops. "Really? What am I missing? Why is that day so popular?"

"It looks like we have seven or eight that day already. We're going to be wiped out."

My mind is running. What if this is vendor-wide? What if I'm already behind on bookings because it's someone like Timothée Chalamet's birthday and all the Chalamaniacs want to get married that day?

"I... Wow. I've gotta check with my other vendors on this too. But Vickie, I wasn't kidding about high profile. Is there any chance of moving things around? Or...?"

She sighs. "Well, I would bring it up with the owner, but four of these weddings are Whitney. You, of all people, know I can't cancel a Whitney."

I blink at the wall, my mouth hanging open. "Four Whitney weddings? On October seventh?"

"Yep. Do you have anything else you want to get on the calendar now? Just in case?"

I shake my head, but she doesn't see me. "No, thank you so much, Vickie. Keep me on there for December second, and I'll call for a meeting ASAP."

I'm already reaching for my purse as I hang up, fumbling to grab my iPad. I pull up the notes app and search for the list I made in Whitney's office. The list she gave me of vendors she wasn't using on October seventh.

Everlast is at the top.

It's been four days since I was at Whitney's office. It's highly possible her calendar booked up in that time. But it's also suspicious.

I crack my neck, shaking off that thought. That wouldn't make any sense. Not with the way she treated me on Thursday. She was happy to see me, happy to help me. Now I'm worried I gave her the wrong date—that all of these vendors on this list are not being utilized by Whitney on a *different* day.

I look up the number for Freeport Bakery in a rush. I haven't talked cake with Jackie and Hazel at all, but I need to get these consults going quickly.

I call six bakeries. They all have weddings on October seventh. Two of them don't know who I am at all because I never worked with them under Whitney, and the others wouldn't tell me if it was Whitney Harrison Weddings that booked them even if I asked.

It's not the end of the world. They can still do another October seventh wedding, but scale may be an issue.

I text Jackie to get a read on what they're thinking for cakes. She doesn't get back to me until after four of the six bakeries have closed for the day, but it doesn't matter. She says, *No idea yet! What are you thinking??*

Well, I'm *thinking* that you've made a big mistake hiring me and that we might even have to do a San Francisco bakery at this point, and I have no contacts there.

Lady Cat-ryn jumps on my shoulder and tears into my skin as the sun is setting—a perfect reminder that I can't just sit here all day stewing. I unroll the sushi, put it on a plate, and drop it on the floor for her as I take my jacket and go for a walk.

I stuff my hands in my pockets, staring at the treetops billowing and thinking. Maybe I can call Whitney for help? Maybe I can ask if she'll talk to these bakeries on my behalf, or maybe give me the San Francisco names she's worked with? But that looks weak. And—

And unprofessional.

I should be able to do this myself, but it really feels like I've bitten off more than I can chew here.

My feet take me around the block and past the bookstore on the edge of the park. Then I'm headed for the Rose Garden. It's starting to get dark now, but I stand on the sidewalk staring at the spot where the arch usually goes during weddings. The unhinged people who can run a couple miles after a long day at work are now out, taking the dirt trail around the park. I almost get clipped by one as I step into the garden and plop down on the grass, imagining Hazel and Jackie getting married here in just under seven months.

The Rose Garden isn't really that great. It's beautiful if you love roses. And who doesn't? Except for angry florists who have endangered flowers tattooed all over their bodies, but I digress.

The Rose Garden...Well, it's not really Jackie and Hazel. Jackie and Hazel are wineries. Rustic barns. Old factories with flowers sprouting out of milk pails.

I hate that I don't have the reception venue yet, because it feels like I want the reception venue to make up for what the Rose Garden lacks. But maybe I just don't know what Jackie wants from this. Why the Rose Garden?

I used to ask these questions under Whitney, and she'd tell me later to try not to get carried away. But Whitney doesn't understand that in order to design someone's wedding, you *have* to know why. You *have* to know how they met. You *have* to know the proposal story, and how close the bride's mother is to her, and why she became a vegan, and *why she doesn't eat donuts*.

You have to know these things or else you might as well be designing anyone's wedding. And Whitney didn't like it when I crossed that line. But Whitney wasn't the one spinning out ideas like gold from straw.

I hear Elliot in my head. Something he said to me two and a half years ago that I buried and told him to drop.

Maybe Whitney did blacklist me from her vendors for October seventh. I don't know why she would, but maybe she did. And maybe that means I don't have to be her kind of professional anymore.

I pull out my phone and call Jackie.

"Hi, Ama!"

Her enthusiasm is seriously so cute. She really thinks that I can actually pull a wedding out of my ass. And maybe I fucking can.

"I'm sitting at the Rose Garden. Are you free?"

Jackie meets me in fifteen minutes. The streetlamps are starting to flicker on around the park, and the neighborhood dogs are on their evening walks. When she walks up, Jackie is bouncing in excitement, like I'm about to cast a spell and all her wishes will be granted.

She sits next to me on the grass. I ask, "Why the Rose Garden?"

"Gosh." She sniffs and thinks about it. "I used to have soccer practice over there." She points across the park. "And sometimes there would be weddings on the weekends. I feel like I've always wanted my wedding here."

I nod and twist my necklace through my fingers. "So there's a sense of nostalgia for you. Being young and dreaming."

"Yeah. Oh god." Her eyes pop wide. "Is that not good? Is it not a good enough reason?"

"Stop!" I laugh and nudge her with my elbow. "Of course it's good enough. It's what you dreamt of. I'm just trying to visualize Jackie and Hazel in the Rose Garden as twelve-year-old Jackie did."

I stand and help her to her feet. We trace the pathway we've seen dozens of brides take through the rosebushes. We frame the wedding party on either side of the main entrance. I still don't see this. She starts to sense my hesitation, I think.

"What's wrong?" She's wincing.

"I think you and Hazel are special. Not just high profile, but endearing and fun. So I want to utilize the Rose Garden in that same way, and it's difficult. Not to mention"—I sweep my hand over the grounds—"there's no way two hundred people are fitting in here."

It's something I've had in the back of my mind for a while. While permits for the Rose Garden are for up to two hundred, the seating really only fits one hundred before the views are obscured. I turn to look out over the whole park and the busy street attached.

That was the other problem. There's always a car horn in the middle of the wedding video when you're at the Rose Garden.

And that's when it hits me. I've never had this much money to play with at the Rose Garden. I haven't had this kind of budget for over three years. When you have money, you can think outside the box.

"What if the altar is over there?" I point to the opposite side of the garden, where the guests usually sit.

"Okay . . ." Jackie stands next to me. "Where is everyone else?"

"What if . . ." I take a breath. I know this is a little crazy. "What if we rent out this entire section of the park? We block the street. We hire security for the perimeter." I look at her and her eyebrows are in her hairline. "You guys want a showstopper. Let's stop the town."

I see the moment she realizes that I can do what I'm suggesting. She blinks quickly against the fading sunlight and says, "That's . . . that's amazing. There wouldn't be any concerns about seating."

The ideas are coming fast to me now. I spin toward one of the houses lining the street. "That two-story? That's an Airbnb. We can rent it for the weekend and have the wedding party stay there. Then when it's time to call Hazel to the altar, she goes around that way"—I point out the path around the edge of the garden—"hidden, and you come straight from the house, across the street that we've blocked off, and immediately down the aisle. You *both* walk down the aisle from opposite sides, to meet in the middle."

Her fingers come to her lips, watching the path I've laid out. "Can you actually do that? Can you block off the street?"

"I've done it before. It'll take some money, but we have that. Not to be crass . . ."

"Be crasser." She snorts. "What about the reception?"

"I still think that's elsewhere. I think we pull up our transportation along that side street, and file the guests in. We could—" I cut myself off. I think I'm moving too fast, but Jackie's hanging on my every word. "We could do something in the same style. Pop-up wedding—but permitted, of course. There's a lot of abandoned buildings in Midtown. And before you say 'yuck'—" I say, but she's bouncing on her heels.

"There's one next to Weatherstone, the coffee shop we met at. It used to be my dance studio when I did ballet."

I hold up a finger. "Okay, we're coming back to you being a ballerina *and* a soccer player, but first of all, if you're telling me there's an abandoned dance studio next to Weatherstone, then I think I'm calling the city tomorrow to make sure it's not condemned. It's the building on the left?"

"Yes! There's a studio where they used to rehearse for *Nutcracker*, so it may fit the guest list. High ceilings and everything. We used to sneak up to the roof, and I think it was at least three stories high."

I file that away. A possible rooftop wedding venue in Midtown Sacramento? That's a wedding planner's dream.

I'm biting back a smile as I look up and down the street. "You know, it's technically walking distance, but...we could do something really cute with the transportation to the reception, especially since this street will be closed off."

"Are you giving me a horse-drawn carriage at my wedding, Ama?" Jackie squeals, and I take her arms and shake her.

"I can't believe you stole my super exciting thing I was going to say! How dare you!"

She laughs and throws her arms around me. My mind is racing

as I think of all the permits I need to look into, but hanging over all of this is the knowledge that whatever I dream up...it can be done. I have Elliot Bloom working it.

I'm finally looking forward to this design. Tomorrow can't come soon enough.

10

Elliot

I'm addicted to my phone. One day we will have support groups for this—our backs curved like croissants, our thumbs twitching with the need to swipe, all blinded from the blue light.

I posted a picture of a deconstructed floral arch ten minutes ago, and I'm already checking on Twitter to see if Instagram is broken. After five minutes, I finally get a set of likes. But because my self-worth is now intrinsically tied to this picture, I'm thinking of deleting it, then myself.

The shop phone rings, and I thank god I have something else to think about.

"Hello," I mumble.

"Are you serious? Delete that."

I recognize the voice. "Emma Torres?"

"You know it's Am—forget it. That's the most hideous thing I've ever seen. You have a bag of potting soil in the corner of the image."

I fumble my phone out of my pocket and open Instagram. Damn it. I'm no better than my father.

"Yeah, I guess it's not that good." My thumb wistfully taps the delete button.

"Well, I mean the arch is gorgeous. Are those hydrangeas?"

I watch the picture disappear with its four likes, and something spins in my chest from her compliment. "Yeah. Hydrangeas and white roses. It's basic. And been done before."

"Not by you." She scoffs with it, like there's something I'm missing. "What are you doing this afternoon?"

The spinning in my chest stops, and I'm all vibration. My mouth opens to say *nothing at all*, but just before I do, I catch myself. "The shop—" I clear my throat. "We're open until five, but afterward..."

I let it hang awkwardly, but she jumps in. "Cool. I'll come by around two. Don't do anything with that arch!"

The line disconnects. Shame burns in my gut that I even suggested seeing her after business hours. She's probably bringing a couple by to look at the piece. I go into the back and start moving things around, getting the soil out of there and back into the cupboards. I smell like I've been working, unfortunately, so at noon I close the shop for ten minutes, run to the twenty-four-hour gym I belong to, and take the shortest shower of my life. I have one spare shirt in the back of my car. It's wrinkled, but it doesn't smell like I just spent four hours building a deconstructed floral arch just to get rejected by Instagram and Ama Torres in under an hour.

When two rolls around, the door swings open, and I pretend I wasn't waiting for it. I turn to greet her with my usual scowl, but instead, the most beautiful girl I've seen in my life is standing in the doorway. She's tall and long-limbed with dark hair and big eyes. She's the kind of girl that guys fall over themselves for, but who I decided long ago isn't for me. I don't like falling over myself.

Ama squeezes through the door behind her, and even in boots with heels, she's comically short next to this girl. Her eyes catch on me by the lilies, and even though I'm frowning at the pink box in her hand, her cheeks tug into cute little circles as she beams at me. Her hair's down, and she runs a hand through it, ruffling it to fall in loose tendrils.

I feel my fingers curl.

"Hi!" Ama chirps. "This is Mar! Mar, this is Elliot Bloom. He owns Blooming."

Mar steps forward with a demure smile on her full lips and shakes my hand. Just as I'm about to ask if she's the one getting married this time, Ama says, "I think you should get a shot of the front counter too." She's sweeping her hand through the air like painting a landscape.

Mar nods and reaches into a bag on her shoulder. "Totally. We can stage a couple of these." She pulls out a camera.

I stand in confusion as Ama moves to the counter, drops the donut box, and grabs a chocolate one before disappearing into the back. I hear "Oh my god, wow" around a mouthful of donut, as Mar starts attaching a lens and moving through the rows of bouquets.

My mouth opens and closes. I follow Ama into the back, where she's dropping donut crumbs on my floor.

"Don't eat back here. I'll get bugs."

"Yeah, this is beautiful," she says, taking another bite and ignoring me. "Mar will have to get some equipment from her car, but this will be great. Maybe we'll put it in the parking lot. Is there a fence back there? I forget." She starts moving to the side door.

"What's happening? Who's Mar?"

She spins to me with a huge smile. "My sister! Well, ex-stepsister. She's a photographer." She exits the side door like all my questions were successfully answered. The door closes behind her as she chatters to herself about the parking lot, and when she tries to open it again, I almost don't move to unlock it. She knocks softly in one of those shave-and-a-haircut patterns, and I roll my eyes.

I open it, and she pushes past me without a thank-you, calling for Mar to come see.

I stand in a corner as the two of them move around, rearranging flowerpots, moving paperwork from the front counter, and bringing in lights and screens. I'm not needed until it's time to move the arch. Ama tries to take one side, and I shake my head, lifting it by myself. She holds the door open for me, and it's the first time I'm glad I wasted all that time showering as I pass her closely. She smells like sugar.

Mar comes over to show me a few of the shots of the arch, and I agree, it looks better. Professional. I see Mar check my face for my opinion, and her eyes dart to my mouth, my collar. She's standing close, and I shift away.

"Hey!" Ama appears in front of us. "Let's get Elliot at the counter, in front of the Blooming sign."

I frown. "Why?"

"You can put it on the website! Or on Instagram," she says as she heads back inside. Then, under her breath: "*God*, the number of followers that would get you . . ."

I scowl at the floor as I hold the door open for Mar, trying to figure out her meaning. "I'm not going to post a picture of me holding a flower to the Instagram account," I yell after Ama.

She's already at the front counter, stealing an orchid to set next to the register.

"Oh, come on, I'll let you cross your arms and glare," she says, and I let my arms drop from where they were crossed. "Elliot, you'd be surprised how many people would like to see the man behind these stunning arrangements. And you look so good today."

The last part is so offhand and quick that I barely have a second to catch it before she's dragging me to stand behind the counter, under the old wooden sign that my dad painted himself. My limbs hang awkwardly and suddenly I'm back in school, forced into the back of every picture and asked to smile a bit less strangely.

Ama stands on the other side of the counter and tilts her head at me. "Lean on the counter." She shows me, pressing her palms against the top and pressing her weight into it. She looks ridiculous, like an angry mouse. But when I do it, she reaches up, and her fingers pull some of my hair forward. She's staring at the wave of black hair as her fingers try to twirl it, and I can't get over how close she is. It's not until the second click that I realize Mar is taking pictures already. I tear my gaze from Ama's focused expression and see a twist to Mar's lips that I don't like.

"Push your sleeves up."

I look down at Ama again. She mimes it, like I don't understand English. "Why?"

"So we can see your tattoos."

I hesitate. "I keep them covered so more conservative clients aren't prejudiced against me."

Ama snorts. "Trust me, we're going for a whole new demographic here." Her voice is sly, as if they have a secret she's not letting me in on. Behind her, Mar chuckles at the camera screen as she reviews.

I push my sleeves up, and Ama's eyes drop, catching on the flower on my right arm. "What's that one?" she asks.

I'm getting annoyed now, so I just say, "Look it up."

She flashes me a brilliant smile, cheeks round and teeth white. And then she bites her bottom lip with those teeth and I hear another click.

I look up to Mar, resume leaning on the counter, and Ama moves to Mar's side. "I won't smile," I say.

"I wouldn't dream of asking it," Mar says with a fake grin.

Mar takes a few shots. They talk lighting. Ama goes to fuss with my front window blinds. I'm aching for the phone to ring or a customer to come in. Mar shows Ama one of the pics and they both giggle, whispering.

Fuck. I *am* back in high school.

"Are we done?"

They look up at me, maybe shocked at my tone. Mar recovers first. "Yep! Let me email them to you, and then I should run across the street to Rite Aid, actually."

"Oh, okay. Want me to come with?" Ama grabs my business card from the counter and lets Mar type in the email address.

"No, no," Mar says, and the corner of her mouth twitches. "Why don't you help Elliot choose which one to post today."

I pull my sleeves back down and help Mar pack up her lighting equipment in silence as the two of them chatter. When I come back from setting the lights in Mar's car, Ama is sitting on my front counter, swiping through pictures on her phone. She's got one leg crossed over the other, like that's any better than not. Her dress is up to the top of her thigh.

"Off the counter," I say roughly, but she just jumps down, landing like a cat, face still focused on the phone.

"I sent them to both of you," Mar says. "Ama, I'll be back in ten or fifteen."

"What do I owe you?" I say to Mar.

She tilts her head at me, blinking. "Oh, no. This was fun. Just have Ama tag me in the posts as the photo credit."

And then she's gone.

And it's just me and Ama.

"Okay, there's like, enough here for two weeks' worth of daily posts."

I turn to her. She's leaning back on the counter, legs crossed at the ankles.

"I can't keep that kind of consistency though."

She waves her free hand, still staring at the photos. "Just get a gallery going, get some followers. The rest will come. I'd like to get the deconstructed arch posted first, so I can send it to a few clients."

I nod. I'm still standing at the door. It feels like I'm the customer and she's the shop owner, with how comfortable she is. For lack of anything better to do, I move into the back room to make sure everything is back in its place there.

While I'm resetting the things they moved around, her voice calls from the doorway, "Okay, go to your email."

Sighing, I pull my phone out and open the email from Mariana Jaswal.

"Download that whole album, and I'll help you post it."

"I know how to post to Instagram," I snap.

She snorts. It's still cute. I hate it. "Not really, no."

I download the pictures, I open Instagram, and I hand her my phone. Which immediately feels like a mistake. She shows me which filters to use, which hashtags, and how to properly credit

Mar, but none of it matters because she proceeds to schedule ten more posts the same way. I see over her shoulder the picture of me at the counter.

"Don't use that one."

She looks up at me for the first time in almost ten minutes. "Why not?"

I'm close enough to see where the dark brown of her irises meets her black pupils.

"It's ridiculous," I say, reaching for my phone.

She jerks it away. "*You're* ridiculous. Hey, what's this flower?" She points to the phone, where my right forearm is exposed.

"It's a Franklinia. Franklin tree, named after Ben Franklin." I feel myself reaching for my sleeve to pull down what's already pulled down.

"Are you like a Ben Franklin fanboy? Or . . . ?"

My eyes snap to her. "What the fuck is a Ben Franklin fanboy?"

She shrugs. "You tell me! Do you take a kite out in lightning storms? Do you work exclusively in hundred-dollar bills—"

"The Franklin Tree," I stop her, "is extinct in the wild."

I see her eyes sparkle. "So, you tattoo yourself with flowers you'll never see?"

My mouth opens to contradict her before her words register—before I hear how easily she explained it. I swallow, neither confirming nor denying.

"How many do you have?"

"What?" My voice is ragged.

"Tattoos."

"Six." I see her eyes scan me, searching for hints as to where they are. The blood that's been staining my face rushes *down*, and I clear my throat. "Do you have any?"

She shakes her head. Her lips are curved in a soft smile, and her eyes are impossibly big this close. "I've been wanting one, though. Where should I get it?"

I can feel my heartbeat in my fingertips. The restraint to keep from scanning her body like she scanned mine comes with such concentration. There's sand in my throat when I respond, "What do you want?"

Her lashes flutter so quickly I think I imagined it. I feel like she's closer, but I didn't see her move.

"Maybe someone could talk me into a flower." Her voice is low. Vowels round and slow.

"You already are a flower." I regret it the second it's out of my mouth. It's not smooth. It's not sexy.

But her mouth lifts, expression blossoming. "I am a flower," she agrees, teeth gleaming at me. Her tongue flicks out, and she must know. Madison Bailey must have told her to do that. She has to know that I'm staring at her mouth, that I'm half hard from just this conversation. That it's taking everything in me to not move closer.

The bell above the door to the shop cracks like ice over my body. "Ama?" Mar's back.

She steps away from me—maybe she *was* closer—and I run a hand through my hair, tugging hard at the roots to focus myself.

"Yeah, we're just scheduling posts!" she calls back. She finishes typing a caption for the picture of me at the register, hits Schedule, and hands me back my phone. It's warm. "Mark my words, that picture will get the highest engagement of them all."

I frown, and she beams back.

"I'll send my clients the deconstructed arch pic, and hopefully they'll want to swing by soon." She's walking backward to the door, sending me a little wave. "I'll call!"

The oxygen returns to the room, and I hear the two of them whispering as the bell chimes again, the door closing behind them. My phone is lighting up in my hands. The picture she posted already has one hundred likes. I have twenty new followers.

I spend the rest of my day puttering around the shop, and between phone orders and some drop-ins, I look through all the pictures attached to Mar's email.

She included the one where Ama is playing with my hair. Her body is stretched to reach my head, bent slightly at the waist over the counter's edge. Her dress is pulled high up to the tops of her thighs and settled perfectly over the curve of her backside. She has black nail polish on that I didn't even notice, but it matches my hair color as she threads her fingers through.

I'm so concentrated on her, that it's not until my third time looking at the picture that I see me—staring at her face, fascinated. Hungry.

And Ama is CC'd on all these photos too. I groan and drop my head in my hands.

Fuck.

11

Ama

Now that Jackie and I have talked, the designs run like a faucet. With the idea of a luxurious wedding inside an abandoned building, suddenly the inspiration is clear. It's going to be Industrial Luxe—with a shit ton of floral design.

Once Hazel is able to fly in next week to take a look at the Rose Garden ideas and ballet studio location, we'll be off. I'm already in contact with my friend at the city office to see how outrageous it is to block off the street around the park. Pretty outrageous, but it's a possibility, he says.

I'm headed to a cake tasting today for a different wedding, but I'm hoping I can sweet-talk the owner into considering a fifth wedding on October seventh. This couple is Michelle and Mitch. He proposed on a drunk night in Vegas, but what I love about them is that they ran around the MGM Grand that night telling everyone who would listen that they weren't allowed to get married that night—Michelle's dad had to walk her down the aisle, Mitch insisted. They went so far as asking workers which way the chapel was, just so they could avoid it.

Yeah, they'll do alright. It was me who suggested that they honeymoon in Vegas as a joke, but they ended up falling in love with the idea and dropped the Hawaii brochures.

I'd be lying if I said cake tasting day wasn't my favorite day. With my sweet tooth, it's easily the reason I became a wedding planner. Michelle and Mitch choose the three-tiered almond buttercream, and I set it up with the owner.

"Betty, can I ask again about October seventh?" I say, lowering my voice. "I know you're swamped with—I think you said—four Whitney weddings that day?"

"Hm, they're not all Whitney, but I'm sorry, Ama. It's going to be really tight."

I force myself to smile and thank her, but I just confirmed that Whitney either gave me the wrong day's availability, or she purposefully snatched up dates at all the high-end vendors. I don't know what to do with that information. She's only burning herself if she tries to cancel these dates with her vendors at a later point.

When I'm done with Michelle and Mitch, I see I have a new text in my chat with Hazel and Jackie.

> Ama remember the brunch at Jackie's parents' house the day before the wedding? We should have flowers there too, right?

I sit in my car outside the bakery, watching cars whizz by as I choose: email or call.

I'm a coward, so email it is.

Elliot,

Hazel is in town next week for some wedding prep.
Can we meet at the shop to start finalizing flower
type and colors?
Also, they are having a brunch at the parents' house
the day before (Fri Oct 6). They'd like to incorporate
it as a wedding event with full design.

To sum:

- Ceremony
- Reception
- Rehearsal Dinner
- Brunch
- Possible transportation design
- Possible Airbnb/hotel

I will schedule all these walk-throughs ASAP. For
next week, Jackie and Hazel's availability is open.
If there's anything you need from me, don't hesitate
to ask.

Best,

Ama Torres

Just looking at the list of locations is making me dizzy. It's not the amount of work; that's the fun part. It's knowing that there will be no safe space from Elliot for the next six months.

When the response comes in, all it says is:

10am Tuesday.

*   *   *

You'd think after getting the last meeting out of the way, I'd be better prepared for Tuesday.

While getting ready, I almost put lip gloss on my eyelashes.

Once I properly locate the mascara, things go downhill from there. I'm already in my car when I realize I didn't feed Lady Catryn. When I go back inside to grab her a can, she's already knocked my vase of fresh flowers off the counter, onto the floor.

She stares at me in arrogant feline disdain, tail twitching. I shake my head, wrench open the lid of a Fancy Feast, and leave it on the counter. She can figure it out.

After cleaning up the mess as best I can and returning to my car, every single warning light turns on—more than usual. Apparently my tires are flat, my oil needs changing, and my windshield washer liquid is low. The only thing going for me is the needle pointing to a half tank of gas, but even that is questionable with the low fuel indicator glaring at me. As my engine putters, I consider just how bad it would be to drive fifteen blocks in a car that is clearly screaming for death.

I look at the sky. It's clear enough. I grab my bag and hope I can get there in the fifteen minutes I have, but maybe that would be a blessing. I'm never late, but the idea of being early and alone with Elliot is worth the chance of tardiness.

Spring in Sacramento is lovely, if allergy-infested. We're not called the City of Trees for nothing. Branches of oranges, greens, and reds pop on every block, as do their pollens. I power-walk down busy J Street in three-inch heels, ignoring the strange looks from dog walkers and the two horns honked for no traffic-related reason.

Elliot used to tease me about the heels. When he finally saw me without them, he conceded that yes, I am short, and yes, I am more intimidating with them on. Of course I was wearing a pair of fuzzy frog socks at the time, so there was nowhere to go but up.

It's two minutes to ten, and I'm three blocks away. I shoot Hazel and Jackie a text that I'll be there shortly, and then stab the pedestrian crosswalk button. I don't love the sweat pooling in the center of my back or in my armpits. And I don't love the way my scalp is moist, flattening all the work I put into these beach waves. I thank the fates that at least I don't have lip gloss on my eyelashes as I finally arrive at Blooming.

I'm damp. And panting. If I didn't trust my Hazel Renee setting spray, then I probably would be checking my makeup before grabbing the door handle, but here I go

The bell rings above me, and I'm hoping I can just slip in while the three of them are discussing colors and centerpieces, but the shop is quiet. I look to the counter, and there he is, looming over the register, glaring down at today's newspaper, and ignoring me.

My heartbeat stutters and jumps. Did I get the wrong day? Did I miss daylight saving time? I tug out my phone and there's the text from Jackie—

we're late too! don't worry! be there in 10.

That was four minutes ago. I have six minutes. Six minutes that I could have spent in Rite Aid or wandering the alley like a stray dog. But now—*now*—I have six minutes alone with Elliot.

"They should be here shortly," I say.

He flips a page of the paper, dismissing me. I consider waiting outside, but I take a deep breath and move away from the front, looking at the flowers on display in the front window. He's got potted lilies and spring wreaths—always bestsellers—but also large bouquets in tall vases. Sunflowers and orange marigolds, wheaty pampas grass and dusty pink roses, crimson chrysanthemums and rusty calla lilies. He's really stepped it up. These are enough to make any person stop and think about flipping around to buy some flowers.

I look at him through a bouquet of hydrangeas. His focus is still on the paper. His hair is tied back again, and I can see how long it's gotten. The years didn't touch him. He's twenty-nine now, but he's always looked twenty-nine. He's always been on the brink of something. Always a hair's breadth away from a change, a definition. When I was twenty-two, I thought twenty-six was grown-up. You're a step away from needing your own health insurance. You've probably figured out what kale is. But now, almost twenty-six myself, I stare at him and wonder if I wasted a year of his life. He could be settled down by now. He could have children.

There's a pinch behind my eyes, and I have to look away. I bite my cheek to center the pain. I'm thinking of Jackie's friend—Kate? And I almost hope there *was* someone after me, someone who broke him differently. Because I'm not worth three years of someone's life.

Aside from a few hookups, I haven't dated seriously since him, but that's different. I don't date seriously. I could have been doing one-night stands if I'd wanted. He couldn't. He wouldn't be able to. I can match with guys on Bumble or meet one of Mar's friends for drinks one night and keep things light. Casual. That's not Elliot.

If there's one thing Elliot Bloom is not, it's casual.

I check my phone. It's been six minutes. When I still don't see a Prius pulling into the parking lot, I glance at him again. He's sitting with his arms crossed, staring at the counter.

If I were to talk to him, I wonder if he'd continue to ignore me. Maybe if it was about work, he'd have to.

"Do you have any questions or concerns about the locations?" My voice is small in the quiet shop.

His jaw tightens, and his eyes fall closed as he shakes his head once.

I suppose I could have made it worse. I could have attempted to apologize for what happened at his mother's wedding. *I'm sorry that your words had the same effect on me as a bee swarm. Was it terribly difficult to break down your mom's reception without me? Such a professional.*

The door opens, and I'm spared the insanity of my thoughts.

"Sorry we're a bit late!" Jackie says with a huge smile. Hazel is right behind her with a coffee cup in her hands, and I think I could scream, but I guess this is something I need to factor in for the future.

Hazel pulls me into a deep hug and all is forgiven. "I'm so excited for this week," she says, pushing her sunglasses up to sit on her head. "Jackie's been telling me that you are a genius, but not why. She wants me to be surprised."

I laugh nervously. "Well, I have some ideas, but if they're not clicking, then we'll move on to something else!"

Over Hazel's shoulder, Jackie is chattering to Elliot, dropping a folder on the counter and squeezing his arm in hello. He nods back at her with a smile that looks more like a grimace.

Jackie turns to me and Hazel across the room and says, "Are there donuts? Ama, I'm *craving* them."

"No! God, I'm sorry. My car was freaking out, so I had to walk today." I run a hand through my limp hair to fluff it. "But it's literally down the street. We can swing through after," I say with a wink.

"What's wrong with your car?"

His voice cuts through the room like a shark in a school of minnows. He's flipping through the folder Jackie brought, eyes down.

My throat is dry when I respond, "All the lights came on. It's fine. A sensor probably tripped." I roll my eyes at Hazel, like *Cars, am I right?*

"They wouldn't do that if you took it in for maintenance every twelve thousand miles like a normal person."

He's actually talking to me. Berating me, to be precise, but still it's language. Jackie must misread my shocked expression because she's shoving his shoulder and saying, "If you're an expert, then maybe you should offer to take a look."

That's horrifying. That's literally the cherry on top of my shit-tastic day. My mouth is open to suggest any other scenario when suddenly he shrugs and says, "Sure."

His gaze is still on Jackie's folder—a collage of flower ideas, I can see now—and it doesn't leave the pictures.

"That's okay," I say weakly. "Elliot has to run the shop, and we have to sit down for venue planning after."

"We can do it all," Hazel suggests innocently. "We can drive you back home to look at your car before we have lunch."

Jackie nods aggressively. Elliot flips a page. I slip into a small coma.

"Sure. Yeah. Let's get chatting, shall we?" Maybe we'll all conveniently forget about this conversation in an hour.

Jackie starts to talk Elliot through things that she wants and where she needs inspiration from him. She wants a consistency of design, but also for both their personalities to shine.

"Is it crazy to want a different kind of bouquet for each of us?" Jackie winces.

"Babe, I told you," Hazel says, taking her hand. "I can do pinks. I can do any kind of flower you want."

"I just want to feel like we're coming together," Jackie whispers. "I want you to want the colors and flowers I like."

I'm thinking of how to capture them both in something as large as floral design when Elliot says, "You want your wedding to reflect your partnership. There's Hazel, there's Jackie, and then there's Hazel and Jackie. It can be all three of those things."

Jackie turns her body toward him, like a flower looking for sunlight.

Elliot looks at Hazel and says, "What kinds of things do you like? What bouquets or centerpieces have caught your eye?"

"Muted fall colors. Cool tones. But at the same time, tropical. I love big leaves and exotic flowers. Maybe types that are hard to come by."

"We can order from other countries. That's no problem. What kind of tropical?" he says, moving around the counter toward the more exotic flowers along the back wall. "We have dendrobium orchids and calla lilies. They make nice bouquets. Hibiscus. There's the amaryllis"—he waves his hand at me noncommittally, and I feel my blood stop pumping—"and anthuriums."

I feel Hazel and Jackie turn to me, more than I see it. I've stopped seeing, in fact. Hearing the sibilant hiss and lulling Ls from his mouth again have rendered me senseless.

"Oh, wow! Is Ama short for Amaryllis?" Jackie asks.

I smile and nod, like a disembodied head.

"That's so unusual. I love it. Did your parents love the flower?"

"Um, my mom. And other connotations," I mumble, pushing my hair over my ear. "In mythology, Amaryllis fell in love with a—with a man who loved flowers…"

I think this is where I'll die. I think I'll just lie down and wait for death. He can use me to fertilize the flowers. I can't look at him, but Hazel is smiling at me with a romantic haze in her eye.

"What's the myth?" she asks.

"Well…" I hesitate. "She stood in front of his house every day, carving a golden arrow into her heart. On the thirtieth day, a crimson flower sprouted from her chest. And he finally noticed her."

"Oh, that's beautiful," Jackie says. "Gotta love the Greeks. All that unrequited love and sacrifice."

"Sacrifice?" a deep voice resonates. His hands are hard at work at a bouquet without our notice. "He didn't want her, so she carved herself into something he liked, something he wanted."

I feel that golden arrow now, carving, carving.

"Of course you would identify with the man," Jackie scoffs. It's supposed to lighten the mood. I force my lips upward.

The skin peels away under the sharp arrow at my chest.

He reaches for a large leaf, tugging the anthuriums out of a vase.

"What's an amaryllis look like?" Hazel says, turning to where Elliot pointed out the calla lilies.

"I don't keep them in the shop anymore."

The arrow hits bone.

He lets it hang awkwardly, so I say, "You're playing with the anthuriums?"

"Anthuriums come in several colors. They have a tropical feel that can be kept very classy. They can be a centerpiece, they can be a main event, but mostly"—he ties off the bouquet and hands it to Jackie—"they can be an understated piece of a larger bouquet."

I watch Jackie's eyes glisten. There are pink roses clustered among the bundle of anthuriums. They have a singular petal that is leaf-like and waxy-looking with a solitary stamen springing up from the center. Jackie's anthuriums are white with hints of pink seeping into the edges.

"I don't have them here in the shop—they'd have to be ordered—but anthuriums come in green," he says to Hazel. "They can be the complement to your bouquet, or the center of it. They also come in burgundy, for something more dramatic."

Hazel's lips twitch at dramatic. "I . . . would be interested in talking more about that." Her eyes slide to me, and I feel like I get a glimpse of truth. Hazel wants drama. She wants elegance and statements. But that's not Jackie, so she's been holding it back.

Elliot pulls his phone out of his pocket and opens Instagram. He shows the two of them a few anthurium bouquets he's done, and others tagged #Anthurium.

I have burgundy and pink dancing in my head as they start to talk about how centerpieces can be built around anthuriums. I see Jackie's pinks along the inside of the ceremony chairs, and Hazel's wine-reds along the outside. I see pink and burgundy every other table.

By the time we're leaving Blooming, I'm so focused on the design ideas in my head—so focused on *ignoring* the behemoth of a florist three feet to my right—that I don't hear Jackie right away.

"I said, should we drive you? Because of your car?"

I hesitate for only a moment, thinking of Whitney and how

unprofessional it is to be chauffeured by your clients. *If you have to drive anywhere with them,* you *need to be the driver.* But by the time my brain is working again, Hazel is grabbing Jackie's elbow, her eyes drilling brilliant ideas into her head.

"Isn't Elliot going to look at her car? Maybe we'll meet you two over there. Elliot, you can drive Ama real quick, right?"

"No, er, no." The words pour out of me. "No. I can... Elliot shouldn't leave his shop. I can take the car in tomorrow."

"It's super dangerous though," Jackie says, getting the idea. "Elliot, do you have a minute?"

"Elliot's not a car person, really," I'm mumbling. "He's—he's a florist, not a mechanic."

I see him cross his arms in my peripheral vision, and then there's an edge to his voice: "I can take a look. 'Car person' or not."

"Cool!" Hazel grabs the door. "Ama, text Jackie your address and we'll be there shortly!"

"I can—I can ride with you!" My voice is desperate. "Elliot doesn't need a *girl* in his car," I say with a laugh and an odd swooping gesture from my hand, that may be part pirate, part chimney sweep.

"It's fine!" Jackie says, fully on the inside of this scheme by now. "Hazel and I will buy *you* donuts for a change."

And then the front door is closed. And I wish I'd driven that death trap over here. Having it explode at a stop sign is better than this. To avoid looking at him, I text Jackie my address. Following instructions is easy.

He cleans up a few things and grabs the BACK IN 15 sign that his father painted by hand, and then I follow him to the door. I walk to his truck, because I know his truck. Just like I know that the door handle sticks, and you have to jiggle it. Just like I know how the windows fog up with every moan and the leather on the seats isn't comfortable when I'm kneeling on it.

I hoist myself up, slip inside, and put my seat belt on, all before he even opens his door. I can hear his heavy footsteps approaching. The yank of the driver's door. The *oomph* of his body.

He pulls out of the parking lot and onto the street, and I stare at the dash. I wish he had something ridiculous like a hula dancer—something I could focus on instead of the way my heart is pounding or his loud breathing.

"Did you tell them?" he asks, turning easily toward my street.

He's looking straight ahead. It's the first thing he's said to me.

"No. They're just... intuitive, maybe." I stare at my knees, mad that he won't look at me. "You'll have to be ruder to me to really get the point across."

He flicks on his blinker dismissively. "Noted."

I watch an older couple cross in the crosswalk. They start to blur in my eyes, and I bite my lip, tearing my gaze to the right so he won't see me. It takes a lot of concentration to keep my breath even.

He pulls up in front of my house and is out of the truck before the engine is fully turned off. I scramble in my purse for my car keys, hit the unlock button, and slowly exit as he lifts the hood. I lay the keys next to him and go sit on my front porch step.

Elliot fixing my car is normal for us. He isn't a "car person," but he's right: I could just—I dunno—change my oil or learn even one thing about engines, and I wouldn't be in this mess. It's my dad's car. The one thing he's really ever given me, aside from toys and sweets when I was a kid. My mom has offered to buy me a new one several times, but I can't get rid of this car. And I really think if I take it into the shop, this car will never come back.

But it's been years now since the last time this car has had an Elliot Bloom tune-up. No one has made fun of me for the nail in my tire for two years. No one has skulked out of my house one Saturday morning, dragged me down to the open engine, and shouted about oil levels. No one has commented on the exactly zero amount of wiper fluid I have.

I feel like this car now. As Elliot stomps around, turns over the engine, shoves the seat back a full foot, and shakes his head at my little Camry, I feel like maybe nothing's been working right for a while.

By the time the Prius pulls up, Elliot is closing the hood. I paste on a smile as Jackie compliments me on the house and the yard. She offers me the pink box, and I inhale a chocolate cake donut, desperate to have something to be doing.

"Can I use your bathroom?" Hazel asks.

I think of Whitney again. How entirely inappropriate this whole thing is. I nod and take my keys from Elliot. "Down the hall on the left. If there are towels on the floor, just pretend I have a terrible roommate."

She laughs and opens the front door with the key I picked out of the bundle for her. A furry demon darts past her legs as soon as the door is open, and before I can check the street for cars, Lady Cat-ryn is rubbing her head between Elliot's shins.

Hazel apologizes and I wave her off. Air leaves me entirely when Elliot bends down to scratch her head, clearly deciding for appearances to pretend that this cat isn't a menace. I scoop her up, and she starts to claw at me.

"Oh my god, she's beautiful!" Jackie says.

"She's okay. She's not worth the trouble." Lady Cat-ryn twirls in my arms, fighting me, and I straight up grab the scruff behind her neck and just let her hang like a doll.

"You need to take it into the shop," Elliot says, and after a moment I realize he's talking about the car, not Lady Cat-ryn. "Your oil needs to be changed, your power steering fluid is low, and there's a nail...in your back left tire." He says the last bit with effort. Because we both know it's the same nail I had two years ago.

"Thank you." It's strained, and not just because Lady Cat-ryn is fifteen pounds and currently being held *Lion King* style away from my body.

He pivots toward his truck. "I'll get you pictures of those anthuriums this week," he tosses over his shoulder.

Hazel is just coming out of the house when Elliot's truck pulls away. I grab another donut from Jackie's arms.

"How often have you and Elliot worked together?" Hazel asks innocently.

I swallow. "A couple times. He's great."

Lady Cat-ryn hisses, and Hazel and Jackie's lips curve into matching secret smiles.

12

Ama

APRIL

With Hazel in town, we burn through our to-do list quickly. I want to get a lot settled before my busy wedding season is in full swing. After our meeting at Blooming, we go to the Rose Garden to talk through my ideas about closing the street and renting the Airbnb across from the park. Hazel nods along with me, but her gaze keeps sliding to the Rose Garden.

When Jackie walks down the park to look at the area we'd be using for guest seating, I say to Hazel, "What are you thinking?"

She takes a deep breath. "The garden is beautiful. It's very Jackie."

I say, "Maybe we can add a flair of drama," echoing Elliot's comment about dramatic bouquets.

She fake-glares at me, and we share a smile as Jackie comes back to us.

The next day, I've secured a visit to the old ballet studio from my friend at the city permit office. When I say I have a friend at the city permit office, it's not as glamorous as it seems. His name is Hal. He has the keys, and I have the donuts.

I told Hazel and Jackie to meet at ten, but half an hour before that, I'm at Weatherstone getting an espresso shot and cold brew. I have a bag of donuts in one hand, and as soon as I open the rusted front door of the old ballet studio, I realize I should have left them in the car.

Something skitters.

I go sit in my car for ten minutes, eating my chocolate old-fashioned to calm down.

Jackie didn't say how long the ballet studio has been closed, but when I think about it, I've been going to Weatherstone for almost ten years, and I've never seen tutus or pointe shoes.

Maybe this is a mistake. Creating a reception hall from nothing is a *huge* task. Not to mention electricity and plumbing, all the catering, the sound system, the back-up generator—it's all brought in. It's *building* a new reception hall.

I take a deep breath, stuff the donuts into the bag, and go reopen the front door. I prop it open so they'll know I'm inside.

Now that I'm prepared for rodents and roaches, it's easier to just stand still and look around.

And it's not bad. Truly.

There's no indication that anyone's been squatting. There's no trash or toddler's forgotten ballet slipper lying dramatically as a symbol of the dying arts. Hal told me that someone bought the lease five years ago but never did anything with it. It expired a few months ago, but clearly in that time they'd cleaned it at least once. I don't expect the lights to work, but I flip the switch uselessly anyway.

Along the side wall, there are six or seven windows covered with a velvety curtain meant to resemble a grand drape at a theater. I start tugging them back, and light and dust spill into the room in a haze. My eyes travel up the tall walls. There are marks where the ballet mirrors and barres used to be, but above that, there are dancers painted along the wall—a strong man performing a split jump; a girl in a white tutu mid-pique, a woman in a simple rehearsal leotard and skirt standing in fourth position, fingers delicately reaching.

It's enchanting. I smile at the silhouettes of them all, wondering who I could call to clean and restore them.

There's a room at the back, and I make my way toward it, opening curtains and letting the light in as I go. The door is ajar, and I turn on my phone's flashlight to make sure I'm not disturbing anything as I enter. It's a smaller dance room; still, probably three hundred square feet.

I remember Jackie mentioning a rooftop and go looking for the way, hoping there are stairs and not a fireman's ladder. When I open the door to what I thought was a closet, I find stairs, thank the heavens. The venue needs to be ADA compliant to clear permits, though, which is a problem. For now, I focus on climbing up to see if this is even an option. Without finding any rickety steps or broken floorboards, I make my way to the door at the top and heave it open.

The wind floats across my face. The sun shines like I've found nirvana. My mouth opens in a huge smile when I see a flat industrial rooftop with brick half walls around the edges, primed and ready for a party. There's nothing here, but I can see *everything*. The LED floral dance floor in the center, twinkling as dusk falls on the party. A bar to the right. High-top tables scattered. Boxwood hedges lining the perimeter. And some kind of magic Elliot can create. Maybe added height?

And along with all of this—the Sacramento skyline is right

there. I prop the door open and check every angle, making sure there isn't anything unsightly. All I find is my hometown. *Jackie's* hometown.

This is the kind of venue people would kill to have.

I see a Prius pull up on the street, and I head downstairs. My mind is spinning with ideas as their footsteps patter to the door.

"Oh, *wow*," Jackie says, stepping through the threshold with Hazel behind her. "This is wayyyyy worse than I thought it would be." Her eyes are on the floor and the dirty windows. "I'm so sorry for suggesting it."

"I love it," I say, and she looks at me like there's a rat on my shoulder. Which, there could be. "So, listen to this."

Hazel steps inside gingerly, like maybe the floor could give in. I come to stand next to them in the entrance, fanning my hands and painting a picture.

"We create something here." I point to where the small lobby used to be. "Some kind of welcoming area. A separation between here and the main hall. Maybe a photo booth, but sophisticated? Elliot could make a rose wall that says *Jackie and Hazel* and the wedding date. A sign here reminding everyone of the hashtags." I don't even have to consult with him on what's possible. We have money to throw around.

I see their eyes following my hands as I weave a story, not looking at the dust or possible vermin droppings.

"So the flow through the door is here"—I push my hands forward—"around the flower wall, and into the dining area." I walk Jackie to the center of the ballet floor, and Hazel follows. "We can use the entire space for round tables to really open it up. We set up a bar in one of the corners. Caterers station in the small room back here."

Hazel lifts a doubtful brow at me. "And we break everything down before dancing? I don't really like that."

"Neither do I," I say, grinning broadly. I gesture for them to follow and lead them carefully upstairs.

"No way." Jackie laughs as she steps onto the roof. "No *way*. Can you really do this?"

"I don't know yet, to be honest. But I'd like to try." I watch Hazel move to each of the corners. I can't read her face. "Elliot's dance floor is center here, looking *amazing* at night. A second bar over there."

Jackie is nodding, looking around, but it's more of a jerky, nervous thing. Hazel turns and she's smirking at me. "I love this," she says.

I breathe in the spring air and launch onward.

"I need to warn you that building a space from nothing can get expensive. Plumbing, sewers, checking for mold, rewiring electrical, ADA compliance. The food will now be one hundred percent off-site catering, which is never a bad thing, but just not all inclusive like other locations could give you."

I give them all the warnings and fine print, but Hazel is floating across the rooftop, hardly listening. "Let's look at downstairs again," she says. She takes Jackie's hand, and I see Jackie's shoulders relax.

Once we're down in the dance studio again, I point out the exposed beams, the height, the brick walls. This space might have been a dance studio, but it was never built that way.

"Do you think Elliot could do something nice with these ceilings?" Jackie asks.

"Absolutely. He has beautiful chandeliers. You could have flowers above down here, and below on the rooftop dance floor."

"When can he come see it?" Hazel says. "I'd love to start seeing this whole thing come together."

"I can definitely bring him in the next time we visit—"

"Can he come by today, do you think?" Jackie interjects. "I mean, we're already here. We already have the key."

I stammer a bit before saying, "Last minute may be tough with the shop. But I can offer it."

They nod—annoyingly—and there's nothing left for me to do but pull out my phone. After yesterday's disaster, I really hate that I'm bothering him again. I want to just text him instead of calling the shop phone, but that would be admitting that I never deleted his number. And I really don't want to see the last messages he sent me again.

I hit the button to dial, and listen to the ring. He picks up quickly. Too quickly. Like maybe he's at the register already and he's busy?

"'Lo?"

"Hi, it's Ama Torres. I'm here at a possible venue with Jackie and Hazel, and they wanted to know if you had some time to spare to come down." My voice is pitched way too high, and my fingers are like claws around my phone. "Totally understand if it's too short notice."

The line is quiet. I pray it's an easy no. Cut and dried.

"I can't go to every potential venue. They do know I'm the florist, not the designer, right?"

Breath puffs out of me like I've been punched in the stomach. God, it's so much worse than just hanging up on me. I feel like I'm nineteen again, and Whitney is scolding me for being too passive at the setup. *Are you in charge, or aren't you?*

"Of course. I assume you'd want to be looped in later, at a more appropriate time. When we've finalized, I'll send you the initial designs, and we'll work over email from there."

My face is burning. I can hear Jackie and Hazel chatting behind me about tables and layout and all the things *I'm* in charge of. I wait for the line to click dead, but I don't hear it. He's rustling papers around. Maybe I'll hang up first.

"What's the address?"

The embarrassment from the last two minutes has clogged my ears or something. My first thought is that he's got a customer at the counter, and he needs their address for the delivery.

"Emma?"

My eyes squeeze shut. I know he didn't mean to say it like that. I know that's just how he talks. But it sends needles pressing into my chest, puncturing everything.

"It's on Twenty-First Street, next to Weatherstone."

"I'll be there in ten. I can only stay a few minutes."

I nod to myself until I realize he can't see me. I say, "Great," but the line is already dead. For Hazel and Jackie's benefit, I add, "See you soon. Bye." I turn to them with a pasted smile. "Ten minutes."

Hazel and Jackie are happy, and that's all that matters. Hazel asks if I need a coffee, and before I know it, I'm alone in an abandoned building, while my clients wander over to Weatherstone.

I take the opportunity to center myself. He's partially right. If it were any other clients besides Jackie and Hazel, I would have told them we don't bother the vendors before a location is secured. If it were any other vendor, I wouldn't have called. And the idea that Hazel wants Elliot's input on the overall design instead of just the floral aspects is concerning. I should be taking more control of these meetings, but I've been far too underinvolved at the only meetings she's been to—the ones at Elliot's shop.

I pace the ballet floor, taking pictures of everything and getting my thoughts together. I'm lost in my own imagination of design by the time a shadow darkens the doorway. He steps inside without a word, taking in the scope of the work to be done. I'm standing across a dark ballroom, holding my breath, waiting for him to scoff at my idea, mock me for thinking I could create a reception hall from nothing.

I watch him tilt his head back to the ceiling. He says nothing, but pulls a measuring tape from his back pocket.

I breathe in relief. His mind is working, and that's all I need.

I find my voice and explain, "There's a rooftop. I have no idea if it can work, but the goal would be dinner down here, dancing upstairs."

"Who's your rental company?" He barely raises his voice, but I can still hear the clatter of consonants across the wood floor.

"I don't have one yet. Everlast has four other weddings that day, so I might have to work with an out-of-town company and ship it up."

"Whitney has four weddings on October seventh?" He scoffs. "Did you give her the date?"

I hate that he's pinned down my exact fears, but he's talking to me for once. "She doesn't have to work around my schedule—"

"But you have to work around hers." He's stretching the measuring tape down the long wall on the right, making notes on a scrap of paper.

"She's Whitney Harrison," I argue.

He looks up at me for the first time. The first time in two years. I want to fuss with my hair, my jacket, my makeup. He actually sees me.

"And you got the Hazel Renee wedding," he says.

A light, feathery feeling fills my chest. It's like a compliment. It's like a reminder that I'm also amazing.

But then I hear it again, as a whole sentence, as a cause and effect.

She's Whitney Harrison, and you *got the Hazel Renee wedding.*

I'm suspicious again if Whitney did this on purpose, like he's implying.

His eyes leave me, and he looks down to his notes. "What about Michelangelo's?"

"They're blacklisted."

The words are out of me before I can stop them, and I see him shake his head in disdain.

They *are* blacklisted. By *Whitney.* They work on baby showers, graduations, and quinceañeras, barely scraping the wedding circuit because Whitney Harrison owns the wedding circuit.

"That's a great idea," I say. "I'll call them today. Thank you."

He doesn't say you're welcome, like a normal person. But he never did.

Jackie and Hazel step into the doorway, and I feel like I can breathe. They greet him, and I launch into my spiel again. I focus on project-ing confidence, laying out *my* vision before Hazel can turn to Elliot and ask for his. I watch his face, searching for resistance, waiting for that curl of his lip that means he's feeling put out. It's not there.

I see a familiar intensity behind his eyes when we get up to the roof. He's measuring the square footage and checking the height of the side walls while I talk. But I know that look. He's inspired.

He interrupts me once. "The dance floor. It's going to be raised about a foot off the ground. I can make it as thin as I can, but you'll lose the depth of the piece. If it's above eight inches, then we need a step all the way around it, to pass inspection."

"Can we raise the floor everywhere?" Hazel asks, like raising the floor is an everyday thing.

"I . . . I suppose Elliot and I can look into creating a full artificial floor for the roof."

"What do you think, Mr. Architect?" Jackie asks, nudging Elliot's arm.

I wait for him to correct her, to say that he never finished his degree. He was always so sensitive about that. But he just adjusts his watch.

And I blurt out, "Did you get your degree?"

His eyes snap to me for the second time today before quickly darting away.

"Yeah," Jackie says helpfully. "Last year, right? *And* his license. He's a fully licensed architect now!"

Hazel says something—something about how nice that'll be for our purposes. But I can't hear anything but white noise for a moment.

I relaxed back in my chair, staring at him across a table set for two. "I think you could go back, if you wanted. They have a bunch of online options for degrees. It's up to you, but . . . you just said it yourself—your dad wanted you to get your degree. And who knows? Maybe it would give you a leg up in some way, when you inevitably open a showroom." I winked at him slyly, and his eyes dropped to my lips as I brought my wineglass to them.

"Yeah, it's possible." His voice cuts through my memories. I blink, and he's telling Hazel what the options are. I blink—and he's finished his degree. There's a pulsing pain in my stomach, like an old wound that never quite healed right, but I refocus.

"It won't be cheap," I add.

"Well, run it by me. Maybe we can wiggle the budget," Hazel says.

Jackie turns to Hazel and whispers so low I can barely hear

over the breeze. "Are you comfortable with that? I mean, we can see other places too."

"Other places won't be your old dance studio in your home-town," Hazel says, and kisses her softly.

I feel my armpits start to sweat. It's always amazing when the couple likes something so much that they want to make room in the budget for it, but you never want them to regret giving you so much money to play with. It has to be spectacular.

When we go downstairs again, I say to Elliot, "We wanted your thoughts on the ceiling."

I watch as his throat tips back, eyes moving over the beams. "Do you want a full floral wonderland? Above in the downstairs, below in the rooftop?" he asks.

It's remarkable how well we finish each other's thoughts. My stomach twists with the nostalgia of it all.

"Chandeliers is what I was thinking. But tell me what you see," I say.

"We have the pink roses in the design already. We can do chande-liers. Add in baby's breath. Make it cloud-like, like your mom's was."

He says it casually. Like that wasn't the beginning. Like it was just a job to him, not the first time I was in the back room, or the first time I asked him about his tattoos.

Hazel looks at me hungrily, eyes leaving the ceiling. Jackie says, "Elliot did your mother's wedding? That's sweet."

"Yeah, one of 'em." I clear my throat. "What's your other idea? If not chandeliers?"

He points to the tall beams running up the brick walls. "Structures. Tree-like. Large columns that pull the eye upward, with large pieces on top. Maybe you don't want to give up space, but there's also the option of renting white curtains or tent pieces from Michelangelo's."

"A faux outdoor tent," I say, looking over the room. "With lights above, it could feel like a night sky."

"I think I may pass out." Jackie laughs. "You guys are describing such beautiful things. I feel like I need to see it."

"Of course," I say, squeezing her arm. "We'll let Elliot get going, but I'll mock up a few designs and send them to him, then he'll add the floral design to them. It's rough, but we can see it all together that way."

I look at him to make sure our old way still works. He's looking up at the ceiling, his fingers scratching at his collar.

That's when I see it. Ink. My heart stops. I can't tell if it's coming from his chest or his shoulder, but there's a tattoo creeping out of his collar.

A new one.

It's barely a glimpse before I have to look away. My mind is running a mile a minute as Jackie says something to him.

It hurts to know that there's a tattoo I can't look at or touch. That I can never ask which extinct flower lives on his skin.

I swallow down this ache in my throat, agreeing with them that it's time to go. I feel empty. I wish I'd never known.

I'm digging through my bag for the key to lock up, and there's a touch to my elbow. My head snaps to the side, and it's Elliot's fingers stopping me. He lets Hazel and Jackie walk out into the sunlight, before tilting his head back to the ceiling. I wait, hanging on a string for him. For whatever he'd need to say to me in private.

"You'll need to do something about the bats," he says.

I stare at where he's staring. And yep. Those are bats. I take a deep breath and thank him.

Forget tattoos and feather-light fingertips on my elbow.

I have my work cut out for me.

13

Elliot

She might have outdone herself. I've done a fair number of weddings and events at the Old Sugar Mill, but none quite like this.

She's rented tents and silks that seem to add to the height of the room instead of limit it. There are lamps hidden somewhere that are casting enough light over the ceiling to draw your eye up. She did farmhouse tables instead of rounds, and I'm just here to sprinkle some magic in.

I'm dragging the dolly into the reception venue when I finally catch sight of her. She's got a Bluetooth in an ear, and she's distributing a stack of name cards onto the table. She waves at me but doesn't move to come say hi.

Which is fine.

Whatever.

We're working.

I take my hand truck back to the parking lot to load up more flowers. I'm just stopping at the fork in the path where a basket of flowers will sit next to a sign directing the guests, when she appears out of nowhere, moving quickly.

"Oh, good! Can you grab the sandwich board and set it up? It's against the wall." She points and runs.

Before I can say no, she's gone. Sighing, I heave the basket into one arm and grab the top of the sandwich board with the other. When I flip it over, the name of the wedding and the date are beautifully drawn in chalk, along with the social media hashtags. I kick it open and set it on the path, positioning the basket in front of it. I'm fixing the arrangement as I hear her heels click back from the parking lot.

"Great! Move it to the right of the path?"

I glare at her over my shoulder, but by the time her short legs have reached me, I've dragged it all to the other side.

"Awesome. Can you come be tall for me?"

And then she's gone again.

"Be tall?" I call after her.

"Yeah! Two seconds!" She spins in a circle to respond, but continues her pace inside.

"Ama, you need an assistant!" She waves her hand over her head like she heard me. "Preferably a tall one," I mumble.

I follow her back inside, catching up with her quickly. She snatches a poorly folded napkin from the table as she walks and, without breaking stride, hands it to the setup crew with the exact seat number she took it from.

"Whitney would be proud," I say with a bit of a mocking tone.

She doesn't pick up on it. "Really? You think so?" Looking me over, she says, "You look nice."

And so dies my focus and confidence, in one fell swoop. I run a hand through my hair nervously. It's just a plaid button-up and my best jeans, but the fact that she noticed anything means it's too much. I knew I didn't need to construct anything here, just bring the dolly back and forth to unload the centerpieces.

"Okay," Ama says, pointing upward to the canopy. "This strand of lights got tugged and unplugged."

"Ama...Not even I can reach this. It's like, ten feet up."

She nods jerkily. "Right. Okay. So maybe you can lift me and I'll..."

"Get out of here." I wave her off. "I'll find a ladder."

"Thank you, thank you, thank you," she says. She squeezes my arm, and before I can wonder what she's doing so close to my face, her lips peck my jaw.

She's gone before she can see the heat spread across my neck. I run my knuckles over the spot, hoping there's no lipstick there now, and watch her snatch two more napkins on her way outside to the ceremony seating.

By the time I find a ladder, fix the plug, and carry it back to the storage closet, she's hot on my heels.

"God, Elliot. I fucked up."

I look at her over my shoulder as I walk the ladder back into the closet. "Fucked up?"

"There's not enough of them." She's frazzled, her eyes wild and her voice bubbling. "The centerpieces."

My eyes move past her to where I can just make out the edge of the tables. "You can't spread them out?"

"They're *too* spread out." Her hand drags through her hair, and I try not to watch the way it falls over her face again. "It's not the floral. Honestly. It's the rental. The globes and lights. I needed three more per table."

I shut the closet door and move to get a better look at the

reception area. It's something I would see only if she'd pointed it out to me. Which she has. And now it's all I see.

"I just didn't want to overwhelm the tables, since this is much more minimalistic. Let the room shine, you know?" she says. "But now I think I should have just gone with floral. Do you have any spare vases in the truck? To hijack some of the arrangements and spread them out a bit?"

"When they're glass, I bring spares, but these are buckets, so . . ."

She bites her lip, staring at the room in displeasure. "Can you run back to the shop and whip something up?"

"Whip something up?" I repeat drily. "Doesn't the wedding start in an hour? It's thirty minutes back to the shop alone."

"The ceremony will take about forty-five minutes." Her eyes are wide and begging. "Please, Elliot. This is so embarrassing. I thought I nailed it. I really did. I've been dreaming of designing this venue for three years—"

"Yeah, yeah." I grab the dolly and wheel it to the parking lot. She's yelling her thank-yous and apologies after me, and some sick part of my brain wonders if she'll kiss my face again when it's done.

The Old Sugar Mill is on a narrow road that runs along the Sacramento River, so there's not a lot of wiggle room for speeding. I get back to the shop with ideas spinning in my mind already. I drag a box down with the rest of the buckets and take another box that has smaller versions. She had good instincts about minimalism, so I think peppering in the smaller versions along the empty spaces actually complements the original idea well.

My hands work on autopilot for twenty minutes, pulling white roses and eucalyptus stems from all directions. By the time I'm loading up the truck again, the wedding is ten minutes from starting.

When I arrive back, I can hear someone reading "Love is patient, love is kind" over the mic in the back garden as I load the cart. The rusty wheel isn't meant for sneaking into a wedding that's already started, so I move slowly to the side door of the reception. Once I'm indoors, I see Ama notice me from her post outside the glass doors, watching the ceremony. She slips inside and speeds to me as I pull the cart up to the first table.

"Smaller versions. They won't overwhelm—"

"This is so perfect. God, it looks like I had a plan all along." She takes two from me and crosses to the other end of the table.

"You did have a plan. It was good," I say.

She tosses me a smile. "Throw these on a separate invoice? I may have to pay it myself."

I'm about to do the very gentlemanly *no charge* thing, but then I see her fingers rip out a petal from one of the roses. Then two more.

"This one's dead," she says, yanking the whole bloom and stem out of the bundle.

"It's not dead. It's a fungal disease—"

"You want me to leave the disease-ridden ones?"

"I'm *saying* they're leftovers."

"And I'm just making them not look like leftovers," she says matter-of-factly. Her eyes jump to the ceremony on the lawn and her hand comes up to the Bluetooth in her ear. "Got it," she says. "I'll be there in thirty seconds." She spins to me. "Can you spread them? Get the smaller ones in the middle, larger on the ends?"

She pushes open the door and is gone. I move through the tables, respacing. When she ducks her head in again, I'm just about done, but she says, "Do you have two double-A batteries?"

I blink at her. "No."

"Can you ask the staff? The remote for the slideshow isn't working. I used all my AAs last week and forgot to restock."

I scowl and say, "Ama, you need an assistant."

"I have two today!" she says cheerfully, as if that answers my problem, then shuts the door again.

I roll my shoulders back and head into the catering room, asking all the workers what they might have with them or in their car. Finally the venue manager takes pity on me and opens the small flashlight she keeps in her purse. She pours the used batteries into my hand and I meet Ama at the door with them.

"Okay, is that it?" I ask with as much sarcasm as possible, but she just smiles and thanks me.

When she shuts the door on me, I jog to drag the cart around the side of the building, making as much noise as I want. I get to the back lawn just as the guests are coming to their feet for the walk down the aisle, and I barely wait for the last person to clear the chairs before starting to break down the ceremony floral. Some of it gets repurposed, some just gets donated.

Once it's loaded in the truck, I pause in the parking lot. I should just jump in and head back to the shop—come back for cleanup. I get some guys in the afternoon coming in for flowers for Saturday night, but generally it's slow. No phone orders until weekdays. I'd only be missing the vendor meal, as good as it is, but getting away from Ama's insane requests and burgundy-tinted mouth seems like a bigger priority.

I'm closing the tailgate when my phone buzzes. It's a text from Ama.

I saved us some canapés

I could leave right now. I should leave.

But instead, I'm texting Ben to ask if he can swing by the shop. I'm walking back to the side door and trekking through the now swarming winery as the guests run to drink as much free wine as they can.

She's just beyond the door to the kitchen and has a napkin with a few quiche-looking things. Her eyes light up when she sees me, and maybe that's worth it. I eat the appetizer and hum in surprise while she talks to someone on her Bluetooth.

"So good, right? There's more, too. I'll grab them."

I'm still chewing when she disappears, trying to figure out if I'm her plus one to this wedding.

I hover in the kitchen and look through the window to the main hall. It's gorgeous. Once the happy couple have made their way into the reception, Ama moves back toward me, jerking her head for me to follow her down a hall. She's carrying a large tote bag.

"Do you think it looks nice?" she says, opening a door to a room where they store the wine. It's huge and empty, except for the barrels stacked in pyramids against the wall.

"Yeah. You were right about the centerpieces. What's...what's this?"

"I need to put votive candles"—she takes a Walmart-sized bag of candles and a bundle of paper bags out of her tote just then—"into these paper bags. Kinda like a lantern thing. They'll be outside when the sun goes down."

"Why don't you have an assistant for this?"

She rips open the bag of votive candles on the flat top of a barrel. "They're monitoring the catering. And they're mostly my younger stepsiblings, so I don't fully trust them with fire."

I feel wrung out, like all my energy got sucked from me. And I feel incredibly stupid for some reason. Even though I was contracted to be here, as her vendor, I'm not acting like her vendor.

"I can't help with that." My voice is gruff. Her eyes snap up to me.

"Okay. You need to get back, huh?"

Her hands are still moving quickly to open bags and tilt up wicks, and I'm irritated that she can't just pause for a second and hear me be mad at her.

"You need another assistant. Probably a tall one. Because I can't show up on Saturdays and help you run things."

"No, yeah. Of course!" She smiles brightly, and that pisses me off more.

"And bill me for the publicity and marketing lessons you and Mar gave me last month. I appreciate the new shots I got for the website and Instagram, but I can't have you just dropping in and taking over my store like that."

My words are sharp, and she finally stops with the candles. "Okay—"

"And stop bringing goddamn donuts to my shop." I point my finger in her face. "I don't eat them. They're disgusting. And you leave the box every time—"

"Maybe you need to try one to know if they're disgusting!" She plants her hands on her hips.

"They're unprofessional, Ama. I don't want them in my shop."

Something clicks behind her eyes. Her jaw tightens.

"Well, you won't have them *or me* in your shop anymore," she says hotly. "There are plenty of florists—"

"Oh, please," I snap. "You think they'll bend over backward for your attitude at Relles? Run errands back to the shop and let you slide into their DMs at eleven o'clock?"

She laughs, and there's a sparking of flint behind her dark eyes. "If you don't want me messaging you in bed, Elliot, you can just respond in the morning." My eyes narrow at her, but she cuts me off. "What you do isn't that special. I can get wedding arches and chandeliers made in San Francisco with much less fuss."

"Fuss? *I'm* the fuss? *You're* the fuss."

"I don't fuss!"

"You're fussing right now!"

She steps around the barrel, poking her own finger back at me, and I want to grab her. "You're the one who's throwing a tantrum about a few votive candles. Just go. Send me a fucking bill for all the time you wasted today."

I'm about to pivot and stomp off, but I find myself stepping toward her instead. "Get a fucking assistant. Don't ask whatever chump you can bat your lashes at to grab ladders"—she gasps, outraged—"or redesign *your* reception tables."

"Oh, boo-hoo. Add your emotional damage to your invoice. I'll pay you one hundred dollars for skulking around to look for batteries today. And hey," she snarls. My blood is pounding in my ears. "Here's a pro tip. Don't give every girl who 'bats their lashes' at you a rare South American flower. You'll go out of business."

My breath is heaving in my chest. I'm so close to her, I could kiss her if I only stepped forward—

And I guess she's thinking the exact same thing because her hands reach up for my shoulders as I grab her waist. Two arms wind around my neck as she pushes herself against me.

The press of her lips on mine sets everything in my chest on fire, and my fingers curl into her hair like a lifeline. We stumble backward, and my shoulders land on the brick wall. I hear myself groan.

She's tugging my head down to hers greedily, pressing herself close and keeping my back against the bricks. Her lips puff air against mine between rough kisses, and I want to pause and ask her—*Which of us did this?* But her fingers are in my hair and her tongue is slipping into my mouth, and my head spins.

I hear a soft sound from her throat, a mewl, a moan, and my hand tilts her head back, angling to kiss her deeper. It happens again when my other arm slips over her waist, our tongues dancing and lips nipping.

Her breath is hot against my mouth when she pauses, and as I open my eyes, I prepare for the worst—for her panicked expression or even laughing at me. But before my eyelids flutter open, her mouth is on my jaw, just where she kissed me earlier today.

My cock twitches, and I know she can feel it. She can feel *everything* with how close she's pressed.

When her teeth run across my pulse, a groan pours out of my throat, and my arms wrap around her back, pulling her impossibly closer. She starts sucking on my neck, just above the collar, and I may pass out.

"Ama..."

Her fingers curl into my shoulders, and a whine pops from her throat. My hands move along her spine, lower and lower, and when her backside curves perfectly from her low back, my hips roll into her without permission. She gasps against my neck, and quickly forces our mouths together again.

I can't bring myself to slide my hands down to her ass—her spectacular ass that she doesn't even know I want in every way. I'm kissing her back with little to no finesse, completely overwhelmed by her body on mine, her mouth on mine, her tongue everywhere. Her teeth are becoming rougher, her mouth more insistent. I can hardly breathe.

Her hands disappear from my shoulders and start rucking up my shirt, pressing it higher until she has her fingers on my stomach.

I'm so fucking hard. My hands slip lower, and just my fingertips are curving over her backside, and then I feel I might dissolve into syllables and moans for the rest of my life.

I feel her hands dancing against my waist. And then the harsh click of my belt opening.

I grip her hips and push her back. Her mouth tugs from mine, and I swiftly turn to the side. "Okay, okay, okay," I mutter. "Yeah, okay."

"What's wrong?" She's breathless. And I wish I could see her face—see if her eyes are bright, if she's flushed, see what her lips look like after I've kissed them. But I'm gonna come if I look at her. If I have my hands on her body for one more second, I'll be done for.

So I say the first stupid thing that comes to my mind.

"Are you in charge of this wedding or what?"

I'm trying to catch my breath when I hear her scoff. "Excuse me?"

"Don't you have to get back?"

Fuck, my dick is hard. Pressing against my zipper. My open belt mocks me.

"Are you joking?" Her voice is sharp. Angry.

I press my eyes shut and twist back to her, leaning back on the wall for support. "I'm sorry. I'm just...I'm gonna come."

I'm back in freshman year, finding out from Madison Bailey and a room full of her friends that completion during Seven

Minutes in Heaven is not impressive at all. Fuck, I really gotta get over this Madison chick.

She shifts, and I'm half hoping she's leaving. I feel her warmth before I see her.

"That's kinda the point." Her breath is hot over my neck.

My eyes flutter open to her, and it's worse. She's flushed, she's electric, she's beautiful. Her lipstick isn't even smeared, but there's something about her mouth that makes it clear I've kissed her.

Her hands rise to my button and zipper slowly.

"It's gonna be real quick," I warn her.

She smiles. "Good. 'Cause I have a wedding to get back to..."

She tilts her head up to kiss me again, and my zipper slides down in the silence. My breath is quick and heavy, but I kiss her slowly, maybe a bit sloppy. She reaches down into my jeans and my air stutters out of me.

"Oh," she whispers. My eyes can barely open with the soft press of her fingers over my briefs, but I panic now.

"What? What is it?"

Her gaze is aimed at my chin, but out of focus. Her lips are pulled into a beautiful *oh*, and if I wasn't afraid she's about to tell me something is wrong with my dick, I'd be kissing her again. Her fingers stretch, gliding down the length of my shaft, and I see her eyelashes flutter just as mine need to do the same.

"Everything's good," she says with a smile. "Everything's *really* good."

She looks up at me with some kind of secret smile, and I must be telling her I don't get it with my expression.

"You're a good size," she clarifies, a blush staining her cheeks. She starts to rub me through my briefs, soft but firm. She's staring right at me, and I can't look away. Not while her hand is doing that to me.

"Oh, good. Yeah. Great," I stammer.

And then she reaches into my briefs, and we're back to the edge of climax. I grab her face and pull her to kiss me. I can feel her smile against my lips. She wraps her fingers around me and starts to pump.

I'm gonna fuck her. I'm gonna fuck her one day, and I'll drive her just as crazy. She's got her mouth open, accepting me as I taste her over and over. My hips are starting to jerk. She hasn't even begun and I'm gonna pop. I moan into her mouth and she squeezes me harder—faster—

"Elliot," she whimpers, and that's the end.

White flashes behind my eyes. My mind bursts with color and sound. I'm emptying myself into my jeans with her hand pumping me quickly, her sweet breath on my face, her lips brushing softly over the corner of my mouth.

When I can open my eyes, she's pulling her hand out of my jeans. I grab her wrist and clean her fingers on the inside of my shirt. Before she can say anything, I turn us around, press her into the wall, and push my tongue into her mouth. She gasps, and I kiss her deeper. My hands reach for the edge of her dress and roll it up her thighs.

She smiles against my cheek as I move to kiss her neck. "I have to get back." She sounds wistful, undetermined.

"I can be quick," I whisper into her ear. I slide her dress up to her waist, and finally fill my hands with her ass. She groans, and I suck at her pulse, slipping my fingers around to dip into the lace.

A soft *beep beep* sounds from somewhere, and before I can put together what it is, she reaches up to the Bluetooth that's magically still in her ear, and taps it. "This is Ama." I can't hear what the other person says, but she replies, "Great. I'm on my way."

"No, don't," I say once she ends the call. "Let me be quick."

"I have to go. Catering needs to move their asses, apparently." She smiles and brushes her hand through her hair.

I run my fingers over the band of lace across her belly. "I promise I can—"

She grabs my jaw and kisses me deep. It's goodbye, but I have to try.

"I need to know how wet you are," I whisper against her lips. "I need to know..." My fingers dance over the lace.

Her eyes are warm, and her lips are mischievous when she says, "Next time."

She pushes my shoulders, and I step back reluctantly. There's a mess in my jeans I need to deal with sooner rather than later, but I don't want this to end.

With barely a tug to her dress, she's ready to go back out. And I'm suddenly ashamed how different our experiences were. I shouldn't have let her hand in my pants until I'd gotten her off.

But the echo of *next time* hums in my blood as she tosses a smile over her shoulder, tugs the door open, and waltzes out.

I stand alone for a few minutes, trying to figure out what just happened and how to make it happen again. I set up twenty of her votive candles before gingerly walking back to my truck, hoping my gym clothes are still under the seat.

14

Ama

MAY

I jerk awake from a very pleasant dream. Elliot and I were back at the Old Sugar Mill for the Robinson wedding. But instead of me getting him off, he'd gone to his knees faster than a bullet. My fingers are still clenched around the bedsheets that I had been substituting for his hair.

I slap my cheeks with both hands, then rub my eyes. Maybe it's because I haven't seen or heard from him in three weeks. Reintroducing him to my life in such a stressful situation like the Jackie and Hazel wedding really didn't give me time to process my emotions. Or my libido.

I always thought he was attractive. Even when I was twenty and following Whitney like a puppy. He would unpack all the centerpieces while his dad chatted with everybody, and sometimes I'd get in his way on purpose just to force him to say "Excuse me." I didn't know him well enough back then to know those words aren't in his vocabulary. He usually just said "Move."

But now—being near him again, hearing his voice, smelling

his aftershave or body wash or whatever—it feels like it did back then. He was back in my life for a handful of weeks and then gone again. And it will never be the same, clearly. I'll have to live with the fact that I'll never feel his fingers in my hair again, and that there's ink on his skin that my mouth will never touch.

None of this is helpful, I remind myself. I see him again this morning, and the spectrum of horny to mournful is an absurd way to start the day. I throw back the covers and jump in a cold shower.

Today is venue day. I have a few of my top vendors meeting me first at Jackie's parents' house, where the brunch is planned, then to the Firehouse Restaurant in Old Sacramento, where the rehearsal dinner will be, and then a quick stop at the reception venue just for me and George from Michelangelo's Event Rental. No need to scare the others away with the state of the building.

I got the permits settled with Hal already. The only thing he's giving me trouble on is blocking off the street around the park, but I'll work it out.

I'm getting in my car when my phone rings, so I pop in my Bluetooth and answer.

"Hi, Honey Bear," Mom's voice sings, soft and sweet.

"Hey! How's it going?"

I can already tell what this is, seeing as the shit show that was Easter at her husband's house still has me reeling.

"So I just wanted to let you know that me and Carl aren't gonna work out."

As I back out of my driveway, I slip into a script I've perfected over the years. "What? Oh, no. Mom, that's too bad. What happened?"

"You know, something just wasn't right. I was struggling to see it, but I feel a lot better now that we've talked it out."

"He was one of the good ones, but ya know what? So are you," I say by rote.

"Yeah, yeah." Her voice is a bit wistful. "And Jake really liked you, too. He said he'd like to help with more weddings if you ever need him."

"Sure," I say, rolling my eyes. He'll go in the Rolodex with the rest of the stepsibs.

"So, listen," she says, "I'm moving out today, just taking a few things. Can I come over for a couple days until I can find a new place?"

I take a deep breath. This is the pattern. Mom moves in with me for a week. Mom buys a new house. Mom meets a new man and abandons said house. Mom marries new man and sells house. Mom divorces new man. Mom moves in with me. Et cetera. On and on.

"Of course. I'm swamped today, but I'll be home around dinner. We can do Chinese together."

"I'd love that. I'm going to come by in about an hour. I have my key," she says.

"Awesome. Don't...clean my room. And when you ignore me and do clean my room, don't hide my vibrator again."

"I didn't *hide* it, Ama. I put it in the closet where no guests could be offended—"

"Okay, please don't touch my sex toys, love you, bye!"

I hang up on her. Cynthia Jones, the woman who needs no vibrator. Because she's been with a man for ninety percent of her adult life. And a *new* man at that, so there's no space to get bored with a person.

I pop in to see Mr. Kwon at J Street Donuts, and he plies me with a baker's dozen before the door swings closed.

Jackie's parents live about twenty minutes from the Rose Garden in a rather classy borough of Sacramento called Carmichael. I pull up to a lavish two-story and remind myself to ask Jackie what her parents do. Yowza.

Her mother, Kim, drags me into a deep hug and complains about processed sugar as she selects a Boston cream. Jackie greets me in the kitchen.

"Beautiful house, girl! You grew up here?" I select a donut hole and lean on the kitchen island.

"Yes! But I'm sure it's nothing compared to where you grew up, Miss St. Joseph's."

I shrug. My childhood home wasn't anything like this, but it was nice. Kim sneaks another donut as she takes my elbow and thanks me for everything.

"Jacqueline is absolutely enamored with you," Kim says with a smile. "I hope you don't mind, but I just have one teeny, tiny request?"

"Of course. Please!"

Kim places a hand over her heart. "We have a family heirloom that I'd love incorporated somewhere. It's a tub that I was thinking could be used as a basin of sorts?"

Jackie pipes up, "I think maybe the reception? We fill it with ice and place the drinks in it?"

"That sounds...so much classier than a plastic barrel. You're on." I laugh. "Hazel was already talking to me about craft beer bottles, so maybe we display them in the basin."

Kim claps her hands together and looks like she might almost cry. "That would make me so happy. My father passed just a few years back."

I squeeze her hand and let her tell me a few stories about him.

When the oven dings, Kim goes to grab the cinnamon rolls she went to the trouble of making. I turn to Jackie.

"Okay, walk me through what we're thinking before everyone gets here."

I ignore the stab of anxiety in my chest when I remember Elliot is part of that everyone and follow Jackie back to the entry hall.

"I was thinking we station everything in the living-slash-dining room because we have French doors that open up," Jackie says, leading me into a room with tall ceilings and furniture that looks like it just had the plastic taken off.

"Wow. Gorgeous." My eyes drift over the brick fireplace and the perfectly primped throw pillows. The French doors do indeed open into the formal dining room, which in turn connects to the kitchen. "You're spot on. Long table down the center of these two rooms."

As we're talking parking and number of people, there's a knock on the front door, and it swings open hesitantly. I see his large hand curled around the door and look away into the dining room before the rest of him appears.

Ten minutes early, just as his father taught him.

Jackie leaves my side to greet him. I can hear Kim asking after his mother, and before he can even respond, she's steering him around the house, talking about where *she* would like flowers.

Jackie comes back to me, shaking her head playfully. "Whatever she's asking for, give her half," she says. "Okay, where were we?"

"I'm loving your mother's taste. The flow in here is great. I just need to speak with the rental company about what to bring in."

Elliot chuckles at something, and my attention is stolen. Kim is walking him through the full tour, and I can finally see him over Jackie's shoulder. He smiles so rarely. It's been forever since

I've seen it, and I ache for it to be directed at me. I clear my head and move to the back window to see what options there are for the backyard.

Jackie sidles up to me. "So... are you dating?"

My head snaps to her so fast I can hear a crack. "Us? No. God, no." I laugh manically. "Why—why would you say... Nope. Not us."

Jackie blinks at me, her mouth opening. "Uh, no, I mean—are *you* dating. Like as in the concept of the word."

My shoulders droop with the loss of adrenaline, and I rub my brow in embarrassment.

She says, "But if that's where your mind goes, then I'd be super on board with that. He's single—"

"Sorry. I'm..." I wave my hand, searching for which neurosis to blame this on. "Tense, I guess. Uh, no, I'm not dating right now."

"Bad breakup?" she guesses.

I give her a half smile. "Something like that. I don't do long-term relationships."

"Well, ya know something that could help with that 'tension,'" she says joshingly, and I follow her eyes as they comically slide to Elliot listening intently to her mother go on about chrysanthemums versus carnations. He feels our gaze and glances over. I snap my eyes away, and Jackie waves. "Sorry, if I'm being ridiculous. Hay and I have a bet on when you two will bone."

Lovely. My abject horror and petrified silence over the past few months has been mistaken for flirtation. I hum weakly. "You will both lose. I guarantee it."

"Not your type?"

My very unhelpful brain supplies memories of my dream this

morning, with my knee over his shoulder and my back against the brick wall of the Old Sugar Mill. And then, not to be outdone, my very real memories surface—crushed rose petals sticking to my skin, leaves in his hair, his tongue everywhere.

"I don't have a type," I say perkily, turning on my heel and ending the conversation. It's inappropriate anyway. If Elliot or Kim notice the flush to my cheeks, they don't say anything.

After George from Michelangelo's has seen the layout of the house, and I've heard some thoughts from both him and Elliot as to what they can offer, we leave the Nguyen home, and jump in our cars, heading to the Firehouse Restaurant. I offer to drive Jackie, and I can tell she's looking for a good reason to put me and Elliot in the same car again, but she just can't find one.

George has done one event at the Firehouse and knows the basics of what the restaurant will provide. Elliot has dropped off centerpieces before, but not worked installations. He's ready with his measuring tape for doorways and corners.

I love a cut-and-dried rehearsal dinner. Fewer guests, fewer once-in-a-lifetime moments, more alcohol. In fact, both the brunch at the Nguyens' and the rehearsal dinner are shaping up to be lovely because they do not include Hazel's agent's list, which is already giving me a headache, despite my excitement at the possibility of meeting Anya Taylor-Joy.

The rose wall Elliot is building for the reception will be brought here the day before, and he'll bring in centerpieces. George will bring in black and gold balloons and signage. It's easy.

Now comes the hard part.

We're standing in the parking lot of the restaurant when I turn to Elliot. "Okay, the three of us are headed to the building on

Twenty-First to show George what we're working with." I blink against the sunlight, bringing my hand up to my eyes. "So you're free to go. I know you've seen it."

"Oh, but you're welcome to stay with us!" Jackie adds helpfully.

"Uh, yes, of course. You're welcome to come. But I know you're busy." I move to the cars before Jackie can wheedle him any further. "George, do you want to drive together? Parking's a little rough, and I can drop you back here after."

"Yeah, I'll come," a deep voice says, cutting off George's response.

My keys fumble in my fingers, scratching the car door. I glance over at Elliot. He's shrugging with his hands in his pockets. Jackie looks like she's going to burst. George has his mouth open like he's ready to respond, if only someone will pay attention to him again.

"Great! Awesome." I sound like a cartoon mouse. My keys finally open my car door, and I watch in horror as George and Elliot try to out-gentleman each other for the front seat. George is a rounder man, but Elliot has longer legs, so really it was going to be fifty-fifty. George takes the front, Jackie slips in the back seat on the passenger side, and I see Elliot reaching for the door behind me.

George and Jackie are talking about radio stations, and I'm just waiting for the fourth click of a buckle so I can get this the fuck over with. I can see the edge of his jaw in my side mirror.

"Whoa, you got a lotta lights on your dash!"

Shut the fuck up, George. My eyes squeeze closed, hoping I can just laugh and say, *Yeah! Crazy!*

"Are you fucking serious?" his voice comes from behind me, and I can feel him sitting forward, looking over my shoulder. The hair on my neck doesn't know we're in trouble, so it stands on end when he says, "What the hell, Ama?"

I put the car in reverse, and back out of the parking lot. "The shop says there's nothing they can do!" I squeak in the *I'm only a girl!* voice I use to get out of things.

Jackie is laughing at me, but in every glimpse I get of Elliot in the rearview, his eyes are glaring into the back of my skull. George is quite offended to hear that a shop told me they couldn't do anything and wants to know which shop it was, because he'd like to avoid it.

We get to the building without dying in a fiery wreck, thank you very much, and aside from the way *someone* refuses to look at me again, it goes smoothly inside. George is very worried when he first sees the state of the place, but I tell him the plan about the permitting and the health inspections, and he's starting to smile by the time we leave. He does the same thing Elliot did and quietly makes sure I know about the bats.

The hard thing about today is that while this is the first time I've had to be in his presence in several weeks, it's also the last time we'll need to see each other for almost two months. Now we just go our own ways for a while. It's May, and the wedding is in October. As I drive the four of us back to the restaurant parking lot, I can't help but check my mirrors more often than necessary, searching his stoic face for some sign of life.

He doesn't say goodbye once we're back to the cars, and I'm still firming things up with a very talkative George when his truck starts. He pulls out of the parking lot as I'm settling Jackie and me back in my car to drive her home. And then he's gone. I don't know why he came to the building on Twenty-First again when all he did was scowl.

If all goes well, that's the last I'll see of him for a while. I feel like an addict, starting to mourn him even as his scent lingers in my car.

I have an upcoming wedding that I know he'd be perfect for, but I'm afraid to ask him about it. Are we back to partnering on weddings after this one? Or is Jackie and Hazel's wedding just special circumstances forcing us together? And which would I prefer? I know I'm at my absolute best when working with him, and I'd like to say the same goes for him, but that doesn't mean it's worth it.

We can't go back to before—not even before the sex. Because there was always sex between us, even in those months when he refused to make a move. It was my mistake thinking there could *only* be sex between us.

I don't know if there's a future where we can work together while forgetting the rest of it.

I just know I don't want this wedding to be over anytime soon.

15

Elliot

Toward the end of their marriage, my father and mother were clearly not seeing eye to eye on much anymore. He wanted to send me to science camp; she signed me up for a set-building apprenticeship at the local theater. He wanted to buy a larger house in the suburbs; she had a political career taking off and needed to be close to the capitol. He liked scrambled; she liked over easy.

But the one thing they would have agreed on is that I should have called Ama on Sunday.

Dad would have argued Saturday night on her way home, just to be ornery. And Mom would have countered that I never should have left—I should have been there to walk her to her car.

Even with Dad dead and Mom clearly not being told about the hand job I got at a stranger's wedding, I am their son enough to know that by Monday morning, I've fucked it.

I drag myself into the shop early to try to get my head on straight. Calling her today is better than calling her never, so that's on my to-do list, but there's a message on the shop voicemail already. It's eight a.m.

Hi, it's Ama.

My muscles freeze, and I turn to the black box that holds my fate.

I have a couple who wants a chandelier for their wedding in June. It's short notice, again, and I'm sorry. I'm bringing them in today to hopefully sweet-talk you into it.

I can hear the smile in her words before the message ends. I run my hand through my hair, looking around the shop a bit helplessly. I look up at the chandelier I have hanging above my head. Should I refresh some of the flowers?

Instead, I replay the message, hoping to get a read on how she feels about what happened on Saturday. Maybe the lift in her vowels says she can't wait to see me again. Maybe I'm not imagining the hum of *sweet-talk* pouring out of her smiling lips.

It's only five minutes past opening when the door tugs open and my father's bell announces visitors. A young couple enters, looking around, and Ama shuts the door behind them. They're commenting on how "cute" the shop is as I meander back to the counter.

"I know, right?" Ama says to them. "This is Elliot Bloom. It was his father's place before he took over, and he's transitioning into custom installations too."

I'm almost annoyed that she's talking about me instead of to me, but then she steps up to the counter and produces a pink donut box with a sly grin to meet my scowl. Like she knows the donuts push my buttons, and she brought them anyway.

I meet the couple, decline a donut, and try to have a normal conversation with the bride about a baby's breath chandelier while

Ama leans against my front counter, doing suggestive things with a cinnamon twist bar. Either that or I've completely lost my mind and she's just eating a donut like a normal person.

As the bride tells me how much she hates baby's breath and can we find an alternative in the chandelier, my eyes catch on Ama as she looks me dead in the eye, parts her dark, full lips, and slips the long donut between them slowly—way more of it than necessary.

"Do you think that would work?" the woman asks me, and I have to trace back the last words I heard before Ama decided to deep-throat a donut in front of me.

"Absolutely," I croak, then clear my throat. "There are options besides baby's breath." I take her through a few possibilities before we settle on hydrangeas in white.

Once I confirm that the chandelier is all they need, Ama starts walking them to the door, and I feel my moment slipping through my fingers. I see the pink box still open on the counter.

"Take your donuts," I bark after her.

She spins to me at the door. "Oh, I know how much you love them." Her lips curve and her lashes flutter. And then she says, "I'll be right back," and lets the door swing closed behind her.

I glare at the offending box, tempted to just throw it in the trash and lock the door behind her. It's not that I have an irrational hatred of deep-fried dough; it's that Laura Gilbert didn't keep sugar in the house. Therefore, I don't drink soda, eat Halloween candy, or order ice cream. It made me a real popular kid, clearly.

I pick up one of the frosted monstrosities, and I can feel the sugar seeping into my skin through osmosis. I'll try it so I can tell her I hate it, and that will be the end of that.

I shove the dough into my mouth, and the second I chew, I know it's a mistake. I see the virtues. I do. But for someone who doesn't put cream in their coffee because it makes it too sweet, I can barely get it down. I throw away the rest of the donut and do my best to swallow. It was filled with something too, and now *that's* on my tongue. I close the box, push it toward the edge of the counter, and hope she just takes them with her.

I start cleaning up. I'm not just gonna stand around and wait for her to come back in. I'm in the back when I hear the bell over the door, and it should irritate me how she just waltzes into the back room.

"You should consider a showroom."

"Mm-hmm."

"I'm serious." She moves to the solitary worktable and pulls herself up on it. "If you want to continue doing custom installations, you'll need a studio, Elliot."

I look away from the flutter of her dress on her thighs and grumble, "I made a couple of things. I'm not converting the shop just to play ball with Whitney's high-end clients. My dad would never have wanted that."

She seems to think about it. "Why not both? What about the back room?" She looks around, and I can see her designing the space like she designs a reception. "If you had some clever storage in here, you could have whatever you want while still using the walls and floor space for a showroom." She turns back to me. "Does Whitney even know what you've been making? She really should contract you more."

"Whitney Harrison Weddings follows me on Instagram, but I know—"

"That means nothing," she finishes for me, nodding. "It's all assistants. You can reach out? Tell her what you're intending to do more of in case she ever wants more than just centerpieces."

I reach for a leftover bundle of astilbe next to where she's sitting on the table. "You're still really loyal to her, huh?"

Her eyes glitter back at me. "Yeah. She made me everything I am today."

I have to disagree with her there, but that's for another day. "What have I told you about walking around my shop like you own it?" I say softly, looking down to where she's sitting in the middle of my workstation.

Her lips press together. "Hm. That you love it?"

I shake my head and step closer. She parts her knees, and I almost drop to mine.

She hums again, tapping her chin. "Was it along the lines of 'Thank you for bringing donuts to my place of work, and thank you for the free publicity you and your photographer gave me'?"

I place my hands on the table on either side of her hips and lean forward. She's taller than me like this, and I think she likes it.

"You'll have to forgive me forgetting," she says, reaching forward to finger the button at my collar. "You were in those skinny jeans and that plaid shirt. It made you look like a missionary come to save my filthy soul."

She presses forward, and her lips brush over my temple.

"Those aren't skinny jeans," I argue.

"I could barely get my hand in them," she whispers against my cheek.

I swallow, and I know she hears it. I lift my hands from the table and place them gently on her knees. They open wider.

"Tell me where another tattoo is," she sighs into my neck, feathering kisses along my jaw. "One of the other four. I'm desperate to know."

My eyes flutter closed as her teeth skate over my ear. "There's a cry violet on my ribs."

"How endangered is it?" Her breath hitches as I glide my hands up her thighs.

"Very. Extinct."

"I want to see. I want to see them all," she whispers, and the air sends shivers across my shoulders. "I want to put my mouth on every last one of them."

I'm half hard again. I grip her thighs, watching my hands as I drag the edge of her dress up to her hips. She's sucking at my neck now, whimpering puffs of air as I reach the lace of her underwear. I skim over them, round her hips, up to her waist. I can almost touch my fingertips around her back.

My hands stretch upward, spanning over her stomach. I push the padding of her bra aside and find her nipples tight and hard. She whines and grabs my neck, pulling my mouth to hers. I can feel her shifting forward, bringing her center closer to mine. My tongue sweeps through her mouth, and my cock has gotten the message that yes, I'm going to fuck her on this table.

I flick at her breasts, rubbing softly over the tight skin. She gasps, and her knees bracket my hips. She's panting into my mouth, wheezing. Her fingers curl into my collar, and just as I get the idea to pull her panties down and taste her, she pulls back from my mouth.

Her eyes look between each of mine quickly. "Did you . . . You had a donut?"

I laugh, sliding my hands down her stomach to hold her waist. "Caught me. It was disgusting. I hate them."

She's breathing hard, and there's something behind her smile. "Okay, okay." She looks down at the ground. "Okay, so——" There's a rattle in her throat. "Everything's good. But you need to call 9-1-1 and grab the EpiPen in my purse."

I blink at her. And before I can ask if she's joking—or take my fingers out of the waist of her panties—her eyes roll back and she slumps against my shoulder.

I'm frozen. Is she joking?

"What the fuck?"

I shake her. I tip her back and pull her eyelids back to check her eyes. My heart is struggling to pump because all the blood is still in my cock, but I think she said something about an EpiPen? I lay her on the table as gently as I can and search the room for her purse. My phone flies out of my hands as I yank it out of my pocket. It clatters on the floor and I have to go digging for it under a storage shelf. I come back to her and check her pulse while I dial 9-1-1.

"What's your emergency?"

I stare at this beautiful girl I've clearly killed and say, "I don't know, but she's passed out? She said she has an EpiPen?"

"Does she have an allergy?"

"I don't know! I don't fucking know her!" I start digging in her purse, victoriously grabbing a tube before I realize it's a tampon. "What do I do with an EpiPen?"

"Sir, what's your location?"

I tell her the address as I finally locate the EpiPen.

"And this is her EpiPen? She indicated she had an allergy? Maybe peanuts?"

"She didn't eat any peanuts! I was kissing her—"

I jerk my gaze to the front counter, where a purely innocent pink box sits.

"Did I just kill her with a peanut butter donut?"

"Sir, I'm sure she's not dead, but she needs your help. Can you follow instructions?"

I'm thinking of Mrs. Tarico in third grade, who told me I have a terrible time following instructions.

"No. Probably not."

Maybe this is shock. Maybe this is a dream. Has she been passed out for too long?

"Do you have the EpiPen, sir?"

"Yeah, what do I do with it?"

The woman talks me through some bullshit about orange to the skin, blue to the sky. I pull back the tab, shove it against her thigh, and listen to a hiss.

Ama sucks in air like a Disney princess waking up from a curse. And then promptly turns over and vomits on my workbench.

The hospital is only eight blocks away, so there are paramedics in my shop before I can properly react to the vomit and the shaking.

She won't look me in the eyes as the EMTs load her up on a gurney, and it's probably because I just tried to kill her. It may put a damper on what was turning out to be a truly incredible first date.

They have her wash her mouth out once they learn it was her tongue that came in contact with another person's tongue that came in contact with peanut butter. I stand stupidly as they wrap her in a space blanket and wheel her out.

"Are you coming?" one of the guys asks.

"Uh, yes. Yes." I grab my keys and her purse, flip the sign to CLOSED, and follow them into the ambulance.

When the nurses ask me to fill out forms for her, I can't explain that I only just started touching her tits and I'm not really her boyfriend, so I spend twenty minutes in her purse, looking for information. Once they have her medical cards and driver's license—*birthday May 10*—I sit in the waiting room until a blond woman approaches me two hours later. She doesn't look like a doctor, but I stand when she says, "Are you Elliot?"

"Yes, ma'am."

She extends her hand with a wide smile. "I'm Cynthia, Ama's mother."

Well, fuck. "Hi, good. I mean, good to meet you."

I shove my hands back in my pockets as soon as possible— the hands that had only hours ago been rubbing her daughter's nipples—and say, "Is she better?"

"Yes, she's good. They'll release her momentarily." Cynthia's smile is sweet as honey, and I'm staring at her trying to find the pieces of Ama. She gets her dark hair from her dad, but I guess I can see her mother's nose and the shape of her jaw. "So, you're the florist that did my wedding in April!"

"Yes, uh-huh, yes, I am." Good. That's safe.

"And you're also...dating my daughter?"

Not safe. "Um, no. Not as far as I know."

"But you were kissing her..." Cynthia rolls her hand in the air as if casting a spell to make it so.

"Yeah. Yes. That's...a medical fact."

"On her chart, actually!" She laughs.

"Wonderful."

"Mom, please don't marry him," I hear behind us. I turn to see Ama being rolled out in a wheelchair.

I've paralyzed her.

And before I can start mentally drafting up plans for widening doorways at the shop and installing ramps at my house, she stands up gingerly with her mother's assistance.

"So, thanks for that EpiPen," she says with a tight smile. "Nice to know you can keep a cool head under pressure."

I feel like today was anything but "a cool head under pressure," but I guess we'll leave that between me and Josephine, the 9-1-1 operator.

"Yeah." I nod. "So you're allergic to peanut butter, but you buy a peanut butter donut anyway."

"It's wrapped separate." She shrugs. I bristle at that. Like today's events could be shrugged away. "Sorry I threw up on you."

"Right. Well, I should go—clean that up." I hand her purse to her and step back toward the sliding glass doors. There's no formality here for ending a conversation in a hospital after your mouth has given the girl you like anaphylactic shock, so—

"Elliot, would you like to join us for lunch?" Cynthia asks with the sparkle of grandchildren in her eye.

I'm about to stammer a response when Ama cuts me off: "He's gotta run the flower shop, Mom. And it's not like I'm quite ready to head over for a martini at Bistro 33." She heaves her purse up onto her shoulder and smiles at me. "I'll see you at the Gordon wedding next Saturday."

"Right. See you next Saturday." I watch them walk toward the parking lot. Ama looks back at me once with a soft smile.

Once they're gone, I turn in a circle a few times until I realize I came in the ambulance with her. I stick my hands in my pockets and walk back to the shop in the May breeze.

16

Elliot

T he problem with saying "see you at the Gordon wedding" was that it left me in the same position as before our almost mouth-murder incident. I still should be calling. I still should be taking her on a real date (preferably someplace they haven't even heard the word *peanut*). I still should be trying to tell her that playing grab-ass in my back room is nice and all, but I'd like to escalate this.

Because I do. Want to.

Sometimes I feel like she blew into my life like a hurricane and barely left me a second to catch my bearings, but in reality, I've known her for almost half a year now. And she's been running in my circles for a few years before that. My dad even knew her—which is a strange thing to think about as I'm trying to narrow down my exact feelings for her. She knows a piece of me that's gone. When I think about spending more time with her, about *escalating*—there's something oddly *right* about Dad having met her.

So I put on my (very well washed) jeans that she called "skinny," I pull on a different plaid shirt, and head to the Gordon wedding like it's a second date. I remind myself that I accidentally got my expectations up the last time, so don't count on this being different, and don't get frustrated if it's the same.

The Gordons are having a church ceremony, so right off the bat, I tell myself there won't be any flirting in a church.

But as I'm unloading the garlands to string along the pews, she catches sight of me, and even from the distance to the altar, I see her eyes drip over my clothes, my body. She smiles in a way that tells me she knows exactly why I dressed like this, which immediately makes me feel too eager and like I should go home and change.

When I bring in the garland to drape over the easel for the front of the church, small warm fingers touch my wrist. She's at my side, so close I can smell her hair.

"Looks great. Can I get your opinion on something?" She cocks her head toward the right, and I nod and follow her. She leads me to one of the corner alcoves and asks over her shoulder, "You haven't had any donuts today, by chance, have you?" She pushes her hair behind her ear and glances back at me.

"Nope," I respond a bit shamefully.

"No PB&J for breakfast?"

I roll my eyes at her. "No."

She spins on her tall heel and says "Great" before wrapping her elbows around my neck and planting her lips on mine.

I hum in shock. My eyes are still open, and I search around us, realizing she's taken me somewhere secluded. *In this church.*

Her tongue teases my lips, and I lay gentle fingers on her waist as I open my mouth to her. Her hands fist in my hair, and she angles my head to kiss me deeper. My hands flex on her hips.

I pull back as far as she'll let me and say, "Is this weird? Are you Catholic? You're not like…getting hot because we're in a church, right?"

She laughs against my lips. "I grew up Catholic, but over the years I figure my mom and I side pretty well with that British church. The one created for divorces."

"Um, I wouldn't say it was *created*—"

She kisses me again, and I allow myself to just feel her body pressing against me. Before my brain can chant *church, church, church* at me, she pulls back.

"I have stuff to do, but I wanted to say hi." She smiles so prettily, and her fingertips graze the back of my neck so softly, my body starts to react. "Is your cousin all set at the reception venue?"

Mind struggling to catch up, I say, "Yeah, Ben's there with the centerpieces. I'll check on them once I transfer the ceremony floral."

"You should stay during the reception," she says softly, imploringly. "I promise I won't send you looking for batteries."

Her lashes flutter as she looks up at me, and that's all I really need. "Yeah. When I'm done setting up, I'll stick around."

She kisses my cheek, straightens her dress, and walks out of the alcove with that sway to her hips that I've grown to adore.

And that's how I find myself standing uselessly, getting in the way of the catering in this historically preserved mansion in Midtown. My job is done. Floral has been transferred, and Ben has been excused. And I'm just shuffling my feet, waiting for the couple's entrance. In a normal situation, I would go home now and come back for cleanup. But I'm learning that nothing with Ama is normal.

It's not long before Ama smiles at me and makes her way over.

She squeezes the elbow of the photographer—Mar—and jerks her head in my direction. When Mar looks over at me with a coy smirk, I pretend to examine the pattern on the ceiling.

Ama walks by me, brushing her fingers over my hip, and after a moment, I follow. Surprisingly, she leads me into the kitchen.

"Do you want an app?" She grabs a canapé and gestures to the tray. "They just started dinner, so these are going to be tossed. Or eaten by me." She turns and grabs one from a far tray, and I'm struck wondering at how cool, calm, and collected she is.

Maybe she regularly hooks up at weddings. Maybe she sneaks her boyfriends in the side door all the time, and no one needs to ask further questions about where she disappears to during the reception.

All that is swirling around my head as I decline an appetizer, stuffing my hands in my pockets.

"Do you want champagne?" She gestures to the trays being filled.

"Um, no. Do you usually drink during the reception?" I ask.

She flashes me a smile and brings another canapé to her lips. "I stay sober. I was just offering you a glass. You look…tense." Her fingers bring the crostini to her wide, soft mouth, and I know she wants me to stare and imagine filthy things.

I'm ten steps ahead of her.

I grab her hand and lead her out of the kitchen, into the hallway bustling with servers. There's a small holding room for the bride and groom to wait in before they're announced. I've done weddings here enough to know where it is. I don't look back at her, but I know she's moving quickly to keep up.

The room is empty, and as soon as we're inside, I shut the door and push her against it. She's already smiling as my mouth slants over hers. I feel like she's been in charge this whole time. From the moment she asked about the tattoo on my forearm. Even before that, she's been calling the shots.

I brace my hands around her face, my thumbs on her cheekbones and my fingertips sliding into her hair. She moans into my mouth, and I've hardly done anything to warrant it. My tongue slides against hers, pulling whimpers from her throat as my hips press forward against her stomach. Her hands are on my upper arms, and I feel a flash of arousal knowing that she's just barely hanging on for the ride.

"When do you have to be back?" I murmur against her mouth. Before she can answer, I drop kisses down her jaw, angling her neck open so I can feel her pulse against my lips.

"I told Mar to call me if there's an issue. But the DJ is good, so there shouldn't be an issue."

I tilt her face back to mine, kissing her bruisingly. My hands drop to her hips, and though her dress is tight to her body, I creep it upward, curling my fingers in the fabric and gently tugging.

The light in here is dim, just what's filtering in from outside, but when I pull back to look at her, her lipstick isn't even smudged.

"What the fuck is on your lips?"

She blinks quickly, and then reaches up as if I've told her she has a mustache.

"No, I mean..." I sigh. "Is that some designer shit? Is that why it doesn't get messed up when I'm kissing you?"

"It's Hazel Renee," she says simply. As if that answers it.

"I don't give a fuck who it is. I want you to look debauched when I'm debauching you."

I'm irrationally angry about this, but she stares at me like I just turned into a puppy with a bow tie. She kisses me again, and I aim to mess up her hair if I can't ruin her lipstick.

I push her into the wall, one hand tugging at her hair, the other slipping her dress higher up her hips.

"Show me one of the tattoos," she whispers.

"I'd rather do this," I say, running my fingers over the front of her underwear.

She whines but grabs my collar. "I want to see them. Show me one."

"And if I don't want to?"

"Well," she says with a wry smile, "only one of us has orgasmed? So I'd say it was a polite gesture from the guilty party…"

My cheeks burn, and I drop my head on her shoulder. She laughs, her fingers running through my hair.

"Fine." I step back from her and tug my shirt upward. The only light is from the glittering patio lamps, but she still glues her eyes on my right side as soon as my ribs are visible.

"Cry violet," she says softly. I'm surprised she remembered. "Extinct."

Her eyes flutter up to mine as she reaches forward, asking permission. I nod. Her fingers are warm as they dance over my stomach. She catches the purple petals, circling around the yellow center. "When do I get to see another one?"

I wet my lips. "You'll have to take me to dinner first."

She laughs, and I'm shocked I'm doing this well. I take her hand and lead her to the loveseat that I'm positive several newly married couples have put to good use. I tug her down to sit next to me, and before she can get comfortable, I turn her jaw and kiss her again. Reaching across my body, I slip my fingers over her thighs, pushing her dress up again. Just before I move her underwear to the side, I pull back to look in her eyes. She nods and grabs my neck, pulling me toward her.

The lace moves aside easily. And I think I groan at the feeling of her folds against my fingertips. I can't be sure. My head gets a little lost. She's wet and hot, and I slip through her like butter. She pants against my mouth as I drag my fingers over her, finding her clit with much more finesse than I'm accustomed to.

She hums, our mouths so close to each other that I feel like I'm swallowing her sounds.

"Tell me where another one is." Her voice is reedy and high.

"I'll show you all of them if you come with my fingers inside of you."

Her head drops on the back of the loveseat, and she sighs as I press more firmly. I'm watching her chest rise and fall, and I wish her dress wasn't so tight, or else I could just move aside the fabric and watch her tits pebble and darken.

"Tell me? One more?" she whines.

"You like my tattoos?" I say, leaning in to run my teeth over her jaw.

"Yes. Yes."

I slip one finger down to her entrance, circling it gently, and she moans, grabbing my shoulder.

"Why, Ama?"

Breath puffs out of her lips, almost a laugh. "I love the way you say my name."

"How do I say it?"

"Like Emma. Like you're too fucking lazy to say Ama."

I push my finger inside of her tight, wet heat, and she chokes off, scratching my neck.

"Why do you want to know about my tattoos?" I ask, dipping in and out of her, watching her throat work and her eyes squeeze closed.

"Oh god, Elliot. I'm gonna come."

"Tell me why you want to know." I twist my hand until I can circle her clit with my thumb. She gasps, and I can feel her muscles fluttering around me.

"B-because I want to know you. I want to know what you like, what you hate—even if it's me." I start pressing a second finger inside slowly. "Fuck fuck fuck—I want to love what you love, even if it's extinct."

She's saying the most insane things—things that only get whispered to you in dreams. The kinds of things you'd kill other men for. I press my mouth against her jaw, sucking at her skin, hoping there are bruises on her when they cut the cake.

She drags me to her lips, and I pump my fingers into her quickly, swirling her clit. She comes quicker than any woman I've ever had the pleasure to pleasure, and while that number isn't high, it's still astonishing to watch her back bow and her hand slap over her mouth.

I think if she never talks to me again, I could probably survive off the feeling of her fluttering around my fingers, the choked gasp behind her hand, the impossible grip of her fingers on my collar.

To my credit, I keep moving in and around her until she finally takes a shuddering breath and grabs my wrist. I pull out of her gently, and wait for her to catch her breath.

She looks at me with glassy eyes, and I think even though her lipstick is still perfect, she looks perfectly debauched.

"Show me," she pants. "I came on your fingers. Show me."

I bark a laugh, and she smiles. "There's one on my back and two on my legs."

She bites back something that sounds like a groan, and before

I can question it, she's swinging her leg over mine, straddling my lap. My cock is straining against my zipper as is, but her legs on either side of mine may drive me mad.

She starts unbuttoning my shirt while kissing me, and mutters against my mouth, "Back, this time."

I help her with the final buttons, and quickly it's down my shoulders. She stretches up to her knees to curve over my back, and I feel her fingers running over my left shoulder.

"What is it?"

"Kadupul."

"Tell me about it?"

From this position, her chest is pressed right against my jaw, so I take the opportunity to drag my mouth over the skin above her neckline. I feel her shiver.

"It's from Sri Lanka, and it's the most expensive flower in the world, because it's literally priceless. Never been bought."

"What else?" she asks. I feel her hands running down my stomach. When she tugs at my belt, I try not to choke.

"It only blooms at night, and dies before the sun comes up."

She hums and starts nipping at my neck. My zipper is pulled down.

"You had to wear these fucking jeans again." She laughs against my skin. I help her tug them open and down my hips.

My hands are on her waist, so I don't even know what she's intending until she pulls me out of my underwear. I feel the lace against my cock, and my head drops back.

"Ama. Are you sure?"

"I have an IUD," she says, as if that answers it. Her lashes flutter at me. "How long do you think you can talk about flowers while I bounce on your cock?"

I feel the tip of me push against her heat. My eyes glaze over. "Not very long, actually. I think I'll probably get...easily distracted."

She shifts her hips, and I watch her tongue flick out across her perfect mouth. She leans forward to kiss me as her body takes me in. I pant against her mouth, and she sucks at my lower lip. I'm only a bit in when she curses.

"What's wrong?" I grip her hips.

"Fucking *god*, Elliot," she whimpers. "I forgot how big you are."

I have to stare at the ceiling and count to ten to not lose it right then. She pumps herself on me, taking more each time. I try to keep still, but then I hear a zipper and the flutter of fabric. Her dress slides off her shoulders.

Now it's my turn to curse. I grab her rib cage, tugging one bra cup down and quickly pulling her nipple between my lips. She gasps, and her hips start moving. I'm not fully inside, but I don't care because she's rutting against me like she's going to come again.

I drag my fingers over her other breast, tweaking and pulling. The moan that falls out of her mouth is sinful, and maybe loud enough for the other side of the door. I don't think either of us cares.

She's got her face buried against my temple, and I can hear her breath ragged and shallow in my ear. She's muttering little affirmations of *yes* and *please* and *Elliot*.

I switch to sucking on her other breast and let my hands dig under her dress. The lace of her underwear is rubbing against my cock, and I push it even further aside so I can circle her clit.

"Oh fuck!"

My lips release her breast to shush her, but her body is riding me, panting and moaning. I press hard on her clit, swirling different patterns, and I hear her gasp, her hips locking up. I'm so fucking close, but I have to hold it together so I can feel her come on my cock.

Her hands scrabble at my back, and when I realize her fingers are pressing into my kadupul tattoo, I groan. My hips jerk upward.

She yells, and at first I wonder if I hurt her, but then I realize I'm fully inside, her thighs are against mine. Her breath is hot on my ear as she whines out curse words. And then her walls are fluttering again.

She's coming again, just because I filled her up.

My forehead presses against her shoulder, and my hips can't stop moving. I'm flying in a tailspin as she clenches over and over, her fingers digging scars into the ink. My hips jerk up into her, and with every pump she hiccups a beautiful half moan.

I look up at her face just before I come inside of her, and I see her perfect mouth in an *o*, her eyes closed, and her jaw dropped.

"Amaryllis."

Her lashes flutter open, and she's staring into me as I release, hot and bright. Everything is starlight for millennia.

I'm panting, dropping back against the couch. As my heartbeat hammers and finally starts to slow, I look at her. Her dress is shoved down and rucked up. Her lips are still perfectly glossed, but there's a raggedness about her eyes and hair that makes me proud.

I reach up and fill my hand with her breast, memorizing the weight of it. She shudders, and I lean forward to kiss her again—just as she dismounts from me.

She tugs her panties back into place, rearranges her dress,

and zips it back up. I'm sitting with my dick out and my chest panting.

"I have to go check in out there," she says with a quick smile. I nod, thinking I'll probably just sleep here until she says it's time to go home with her. "This was great. Are you good?"

I blink at her, realizing there is no going home with her. "Yeah. Yes. I'll see myself out."

"I'll see you next weekend." Maybe I'm imagining the tightness of her smile.

I nod and memorize her, in case this didn't go as well as I thought.

When she slips out the door, I'm trying to remember her exact words: *I want to know you. I want to know what you like, what you hate.*

I button and zip my pants. I check to make sure there's no trace of us.

I want to love what you love, even if it's extinct.

I focus on the words rather than the hasty exit, the way she didn't let me kiss her afterward. I go to my truck until it's time to break down the reception, turning the engine on and blasting something asinine just to blow her words out of my head.

17

Ama

Mom stays for three weeks this time. She asks about my dating life only once a day, which is a new record for her. And she asks about Elliot only twice.

At the end of three weeks, she's found a nice rental a few blocks over from me, and a week after that, she's found a nice fiancé a few years older than me.

"He's not her fiancé yet, but I'm sure it will only take her a few months," I clarify to Mar over drinks. I signal for another martini. We just finished a *very* rough wedding—minister in a car accident, hungover bridesmaid, and a broken reception hall A/C—and are in need of alcohol.

Mar scrutinizes me over the top of her mezcal margarita. "Is this the youngest she's gone for? Twenty-nine?" When I nod, she says, "Is that weird for you? Like...do you need therapy now?"

"If I didn't need therapy before, I'd probably need it now, yes."

Mar thinks it over. "Have you asked her why she does this?"

"Why she can't just be alone? Or why she can't just date a person without involving Kay Jewelers?"

"Both, I guess. I'm sure it's the same answer." Her phone dings, and she digs it out of her pocket. "Okay, Michael is free. Do you want to meet him?"

Michael is Mar's new guy. I jerk my head enthusiastically. "Tell him to come here. I'll beat it after half an hour or so."

"You don't have to. We can move to that booth."

I shake my head. "No offense, but that sounds terrible. I definitely don't want to be a third wheel on a Saturday night."

Mar makes a face and texts Michael where we are. "So," she says as she pockets her phone. "Are you meeting people? Do you need to get laid?"

They are two very different questions, and I parse through my brain's reactions to both of them. "No, and yes, but not yes please."

She stares into her drink and swirls the ice. "How long has it been?"

"Okay, one," I say, taking my new martini from the bartender, "I'm terribly busy, and yes, that's a valid excuse. And two, you know that I've been with guys since Elliot, so don't act like I haven't."

"Two people. Both more than a year ago. Both of them you claim to have butchered." I wince and she rolls her eyes. "Not like, their bodies, but the date."

I nod, gulping half my drink. The first was a hookup and nothing more. I couldn't come. And not for lack of trying. And the second—we had to stop in the middle because I was crying. I told him through tears that I didn't know why and it was fine, he could keep going. But to his credit, apparently it was a turn-off.

"Yep, I butchered them into a thousand pieces."

"Have you thought about...I dunno, dating?" She smiles brightly at me, like a toothpaste ad.

"You know I don't do that," I say quietly.

Mar snorts. "Allow me to condescend briefly, but Ama, you're twenty-six. You don't know what you don't do." When I frown into my glass, she says, "You *did* do that once."

"And look where it got me," I murmur.

I think back to the Gordon wedding. How I truly thought I could keep it casual. How it wasn't until after he'd rocked my socks off on a couch in a back room that I realized I wanted to go home with him. How I'd said things I couldn't take back.

And in the afterglow, he'd looked at me like no one else had ever in my life. Like he agreed. Like my words meant something to him, instead of just pleasurable mumbling. It made me question if it *was* just mumbling, or if I'd meant it.

It would have been simple if I could have just called it a great hookup and moved on. But it was wedding season by then. And I was seeing him *every* weekend, and *every* weekend my resolve dwindled from "Don't do it again" to "Casual could work" to "Define casual."

I'm determined to never let that happen again.

Mar is watching me, so I say, "I'll let you know when I'm ready to see someone. I can't even think about guys right now with all the weddings I have. Which reminds me, I need you on January thirteenth."

She pulls out her calendar. "Where's the wedding?"

"The Four Seasons."

"The hotel? Or Total Landscaping?"

I snort. "Don't pretend I didn't double-check ten times."

"Is this a new one?" she asks, plugging the date into her phone. When I nod, she says, "Are you okay taking on more work?"

I wave my hand. "I'm fine." But my leg bounces on my bar stool. I couldn't say no to Ginny and Dustin. They're so freaking cute. He was going to propose to her at the Disneyland castle, but got nervous and did it over a turkey leg in Adventureland by accident.

Michael arrives. When Mar jumps up to greet him, I see he's at least 6'4" with dark brown skin and many, many muscles—and oddly familiar?

"Ama!" he says.

I'm speechless as Mar looks between us.

"Mar, you're dating...one of my ex-stepbrothers," I say.

Michael laughs. Mar's mouth opens, and I see her doing the incest math in her head, trying to figure out if this is weird.

"Um, Mar is also one of my ex-stepsiblings," I clarify for Michael. He thinks it's funny. Mar isn't there yet. "He's not related to either of us," I tell Mar. "Chill."

She wearily orders another drink, and we all catch up for a few hours. I feel like a proud matchmaker even though I did absolutely no work here.

When they head out, I say I'm going to stay for one more drink. I look around, checking out the one a.m. clientele at our favorite trendy bar. Some guys are my type, but none are interesting to me. The only one I'm considering going to talk to has long black hair and full lips, and when I realize what—or who—I see in him, I close my tab and go home alone.

Hazel is in town the next week. She's done filming, but she's called back every so often for pick-ups and postproduction magic, so while she's here we're going to knock out a few things. We're four months out, so we're really cutting it close on ordering invitations, but thankfully I have a few calligraphers who love me. I need to make sure Hazel's friend the designer is on track too. I haven't had my hand in the wedding dress/suit business aside from glancing at designs, but so far the bridal party is almost settled.

We meet at Weatherstone again, and Hazel is ripping a maple bar into bite-sized pieces as she says, "Okay, so two things. First, the bachelorette party."

"Yep," I say, opening my iPad notes. "Is there anything Chelsea needs help with?"

Chelsea is Hazel's best friend, and the reason Jackie and she met in the first place. She's going to be the MOH on Hazel's side.

"We want you to come," Jackie bursts out. "Please, please, please."

I paint on a smile. "You two are so sweet." I swallow. I have practice with this, but it's hard when it's Jackie and Hazel Renee.

"There's a spot for you on the plane, all expenses paid," Hazel says. "And I happen to know that you don't have a wedding that weekend." She winks at me over her coffee cup.

I grin down at my hands. They're going to Vegas for three nights. The whole party is flying out of Sacramento so Hazel's friends can see the city.

"You're right. I don't have a wedding—yet." I look between both of them, my throat dry. "I just have a policy against it. I used to get invited to bridal showers and bachelorettes a lot, and it ended up making things too messy." I think of Whitney taking me off weddings, brides texting me all day and all night, couples running ideas by me after we'd already nailed down themes and colors. Mess.

"Oh, come on," Hazel moans around her donut. "You're already breaking all the rules with us anyway. I mean, you're making a reception hall *from scratch*. Let's be messy together." She laughs, and it sounds warm and inviting. Like happy memories.

"I'll think about it," I say, sipping my cold brew with regret.

I know I won't be going. I'll find some reason. It's not professional, and it raises the question: are you working for them, or are you their friend? It's not an easy answer.

"What's the second thing?" I ask, changing the subject as fast as I can.

Jackie gestures to Hazel, and Hazel finishes chewing. "So I got approached by *Fabulous Dream Weddings*."

"The show on TLC?" I ask. That show is almost as big as *Say Yes to the Dress* and *Bridezillas*. Whitney was almost on it once with one of her weddings, before scheduling issues arose.

"Yep. They want to send a crew out and film the whole thing! It would be a lot, I know, but I have to say, I think it would be amazing to get some exposure on you, on Elliot. On everyone in Sacramento working so hard on this."

Hazel's eyes sparkle at me, and I think quickly.

"Wow. I think the biggest thing is, what will they have control of?"

Hazel shakes her head with a frown. "Nothing."

"Right, but those shows only work if something is going wrong, right? So will they have us stage things or try to create drama where there isn't any?"

"That's a good point, Hay," Jackie whispers to her.

Hazel hums in understanding. "Let me chat with my agent and see if she can negotiate something. She's really pushing for it. And Jackie and I think it's a great idea!"

She places her hand on Jackie's, and I see the moment Jackie fails to immediately smile in agreement before catching herself.

Hmm.

I think it over. It would be good coverage, for sure. My biggest hesitation is that there are some behind-the-scenes things going on that I'd rather not have a camera crew for. The expense and effort to clean up the space next door is extreme. I'm already running into roadblocks that I'm not sharing with these two, so to explain it on camera sounds like a nightmare.

"I'd like to talk to a producer before I agree to it," I say. Jackie nods, but I can see Hazel stumble a bit before nodding too. I think she's a bit surprised that I would object in the first place. Sorry, Hay. You hired *me* to be in control of this wedding.

I take them to meet a few of my calligraphy artists over the next few days, and we do a walk-through at the ballet studio one more time with my full renderings, showing where all the rental equipment and floral design will be. (Thankfully, the bats have been relocated.)

After talking with Hazel and her agent to get more information about what the film crew would need, I get on a call with Bea, the episode producer for *Fabulous Dream Weddings*, and talk it out with her. I want to make it clear that the week of the wedding is mine.

"I guess my biggest concern is the staging needed. I watch the show enough to know that storylines have to be crafted in order to make for good entertainment," I say to Bea on Sunday night after a long wedding day with a rogue ringbearer—a pet German shepherd who ate the ring.

"Of course," Bea says. Even as her voice soothes me, I can tell she's doing ten different things while taking my call. "I think what we're most interested in is the 'dream' aspect you've created here. From what Hazel and Jackie have said, it sounds like you have whipped up something truly special."

She's seducing me, and it's working. "I appreciate that. I think what I need from you going into this is transparency, and also to know that the wedding takes precedence. There are four events I'm coordinating for that week alone, so I want to know that if I tell you 'No crew' or 'We can't refilm that,' that it would be respected."

"I hear you. I think we can make that happen."

When we hang up, I know I'm biting off more than I can chew, but I can't help myself. This would be huge. Even if TheKnot.com and *People* don't come through with a highlighted article, this is still amazing exposure. I email Hazel and Jackie to let them know *Fabulous Dream Weddings* is on. I sign a contract and everything.

I hire Mar to officially be my second-in-command. I'll be making less on this wedding because of it, but it will be worth it to have someone watching the film crews when I can't. Of all my other ex-stepsiblings, Jake the drama nerd is the one who has actually tried to stay in touch. Our parents split up six weeks ago, but he's emailed me twice since then to see if I need any assistants. I start hiring him weekly to train him for Hazel and Jackie's. Sarah, who's worked with me before, albeit reluctantly, almost turns me down before she finds out I'm paying more than last time.

Things are moving smoothly. The film crew arrives for establishing shots. With some hesitation, I agree to let them into the reception space so they can get a sense of the "before" in our before and after. I practice for my first "talking head" ten times with Mar, trying to get a sense of what I want to say about Jackie and Hazel.

When Bea's crew sits me down in the Rose Garden, the only place I stutter is when they ask me how the couple found me.

"Jackie's boss—the senator—the senator found me. Sorry, maybe we shouldn't say she's a senator? Did Jackie disclose that she works for the government? Sorry."

I fumble my way through.

Eventually they decide to stick with asking Jackie that question.

The bakery is happy to stage a cake tasting to pretend as if they haven't already chosen their cake—a bourbon caramel and cardamom crumb brown butter cake, topped with almond Swiss meringue buttercream. (Yes, I did taste it, and yes, I did expire.) I go with them and reenact the entire experience, waiting for Jackie and Hazel to re-create the moment they disagreed about coconut or no coconut. Hazel turns to me just as she did three months ago and asks, "Ama, what do you think?"

I pretend to think about it and answer, "Coconut can be a turn-off for guests, but it's *your* cake."

We wrap filming, and I head to drinks with Mar. We drink a bit too much, because it's all going well.

Better than I could have hoped.

The first thing I think of is that it's odd that my phone is on at all since I put on Do Not Disturb from midnight to seven a.m.

The second thing I'm aware of is that Mar stayed the night and didn't make it to the second bedroom. Her hair is in my mouth.

But the third thing—

"Hello, this is Ama," I try to say, as if I'm the kind of person who is definitely awake by—I check the clock—7:02.

"Hey."

The third thing is that hearing Elliot Bloom's voice first thing in the morning is still my most favorite thing in the whole wide world.

I jolt up in bed.

"What's wrong?"

Mar moans and rolls over next to me.

"I woke you?" he asks.

"What's wrong?"

"I thought you went to the gym at six thirty."

I sigh. "That was . . . three years ago, Elliot. I don't even have that membership anymore."

"I wouldn't have called if I thought you were asleep—"

"Why are you calling?" I snap. Have I mentioned I'm not a morning person?

"The hurricane in the Caribbean last week," he says. I narrow my eyes and try pinching my arm to make sure this isn't a dream. "Have you heard about it?"

"Um, kinda?" I kick off the covers, and Mar asks who I'm talking to. I shush her. There's a noticeable pause. Then:

"It will likely cause a supply shortage of most anthuriums."

Finally all the pieces click together. I run a hand over my face. "How bad is it?"

"Unsalvageable."

Mar sits up, holding her head. "Do you have eggs?" she says, voice thick and raspy from the alcohol.

"Stay here," I whisper to her, then move out into the kitchen. "So, what does that mean?" I ask him. "Are you saying it'll cost more money?"

He pauses again before replying sharply, "How much money do you think you have in the budget to undo a hurricane, Ama?"

I huff. "So *no* anthuriums. At all."

"The only ones available are the pink and whites, the ones for Jackie's bouquet. But Hazel would have to compromise."

I rub my temple. I don't like that option. Hazel and Jackie's personal styles are so different. I just know she wouldn't be happy with her flowers.

I start opening cupboards so I can make coffee. "I think we need to redesign," I say to him.

Mar calls from down the hall, "Are you making coffee?"

I ignore her and listen to Elliot breathing. "Fine. Call me to schedule an appointment when you're really awake."

He hangs up. I squint at the phone, trying to figure out why *he's* the mad one. Clearly he called me at seven a.m. expecting this.

Mar stumbles out in yesterday's clothing. "Why... must you be so loud?"

I throw a K-Cup at her head.

The interesting thing about having a film crew invade your wedding prep is that they love bad news. So much so, that now we are headed to Blooming to make Elliot tell Hazel and Jackie the bad news in person.

I wish I took pleasure in torturing Elliot, because this is going to be delicious. As one of my vendors, he got the email about the film crew, and he already signed his waivers and returned them to the production team. But I don't think he expected to actually be on camera. I told Bea that the florist meet was probably not going to be re-created and offered her other vendors instead. But now...

Now someone is coming at Elliot with a powder brush, claiming he's "shiny."

"Get the fuck away from me," he says, as politely as he possibly can.

I sigh, swaying on my feet a little. No time for donuts this morning. No time for coffee, no time for breakfast. We're in panic mode, in a way. The cameras are elevating it a bit, but a full floral redesign at the three-and-a-half-month mark isn't good. Especially when the floral design is as important as this was.

Bea checks in with me. "Hazel and Jackie are in the parking lot. My crew is holding them until we're set. You didn't give them any heads-up, right?"

"Nope," I say. "I hope it's dramatic enough for you." I smile weakly and brace my hand on my stomach.

"I'm sure it will be. What's the matter with you?"

I look up and there's two of her. When they solidify, I wave my hand. "I just didn't have breakfast." I pointed Mar toward the eggs and stove, but I hurried to get ready and come here.

"Here." She slips a bar out of her fanny pack. I see the word *chocolate* and I give her a thumbs-up.

I'm starting to wonder if daily donuts have ruined my blood sugar. Maybe I've been hyperglycemic this whole time, but I wouldn't know because I've had one thousand grams of sugar every morning for the past ten years. (I do not know how many grams of sugar there actually are in donuts, nor do I care.)

My fingers shake, and I lean on the counter for a second to ground myself. Bea is announcing something to the crew, and I'm barely listening as I rip the wrapper open with my teeth.

A hand appears in front of my eyes, and suddenly, with a strong slap, the bar is on the ground. "What are you doing?"

I blink, my pounding pulse making up for low blood sugar momentarily. Elliot is standing in front of me, furious.

"Eating breakfast?" I try.

He bends to pick up the bar, and then shoves it in front of my eyes. "Chocolate and peanut butter bar," he says.

Heat floods my neck and jaw. "Oh. Right." I can't meet his eyes as he slams the bar in the trash can.

"What is wrong with you? Didn't sleep?" There's a bite in his words, like it's an insult or something.

"I haven't eaten. I'm—I'm sorry." I feel shame and mortification bubbling in me. I'm not even sure if my EpiPen is in my small bag here or my tote in the car.

Bea's voice is close to me. "We good?" she says. "We'll send the girls in?"

"No." Elliot's voice is harsh. "I need two minutes." He steps away from me and to the front door. He yells at a random crew member, "And sit her down in that chair!"

I hear the bell above the door. Just before it closes fully, I think Jackie says, "Elliot! Where are you going?"

As someone sits me in a chair and offers me a water bottle, I look past the dahlias in the window and see Elliot crossing traffic, heading for Rite Aid.

I can't look anyone in the eye. I'm ashamed that being hungover might be contributing to all this, but it's also ten a.m. and I am an adult woman who didn't feed herself.

The speed with which Elliot returns has me concerned that he didn't pay for his items, because I know how he feels about self-checkout. He drops a banana, a box of breakfast bars with no nuts, and a bottle of yellow Gatorade on the counter next to me. And I know what you're thinking: he is clearly angry with me if he has bought yellow Gatorade and expects me to say thank you. But alas, yellow Gatorade is my favorite. And I hate that he saved me from eating peanut butter *and* remembered my favorite Gatorade, all in one day.

I start with half the banana, then move on to a bar, washing it down with half the Gatorade. When I'm finally conscious again (albeit quite bloated), I nod to Bea, allowing her to stop stalling.

There are two cameramen, one guy with a boom mic, and Bea crammed in here with me and Elliot. The guys take their positions, and Bea's assistant, who's outside with Hazel and Jackie, gives them the signal to come in.

I stand and smile, hiding my Rite Aid haul behind the counter and hoping I'm not as pale and sweaty as I feel.

Jackie and Hazel come in and say hi to Elliot, hug me, and Jackie whispers, "Are you okay?" I nod into her shoulder.

I know Elliot isn't going to do well with the cameras here, so I take lead. "We have some bad news to chat about." The guy with the boom mic steps closer to me, hanging the fuzzy cloud over my head. "Elliot has informed me that the anthuriums that we want and the amount of them we need are not possible."

The camera on Jackie and Hazel picks up their perfect reaction to the news. Jackie sucks in a silent breath, eyes jumping to her fiancée. Hazel's mouth turns down, her weight shifting to the side. It will make for great television.

"Okay," Hazel says slowly. "Okay so...so we do less? Or..."

I gesture to Elliot, and he frowns at me. The boom mic swings over to him, and he visibly glares at it before speaking.

"We could move forward with the pink and white anthuriums. Those are the ones that were going to primarily be Jackie's flower. But the burgundy ones? The green leafy ones? They're both out."

Hazel is fully in her element when she lets out a dramatic sigh and rubs her forehead. Jackie threads their fingers together and rubs Hazel's side, looking around for a life raft. I clear my throat.

"It's absolutely possible to redesign based on the pink and

white anthuriums. But I don't think it will be anything near what you want."

I see Bea nod her head from behind the cameraman focused on me, and I feel like a true reality TV star.

"I think we need a redesign," I continue. "I think we refocus on what we now know, and try to reshape how we feel about the floral arrangement."

Hazel lifts her head, and there's a childlike disappointment there. Like her Christmas has been canceled. She gestures for me to continue.

"Clearly we have already decided on the dance floor. I think it's stunning, and it will be a real centerpiece for the reception. I think we're good to move forward there."

Jackie jerks her head in agreement, and Hazel bites her lip and nods.

I'm a bit thrown, actually. I haven't said no to Hazel Renee yet. And even though I've done my best to treat her like any other client so far, it feels like this is quickly becoming too personal for me. Her disappointment and disdain for this meeting is showing, and I'm under a microscope to make it better.

"Elliot, can we move into the showroom and start talking through some ideas?"

He leads the way, and one of the cameramen quickly follows. There are cords and equipment everywhere, so it takes a moment to get set up in the back. We have to reenter and pretend it was all one shot.

Before we're even ready to roll again, Elliot is pulling down vases and moving around the room. Bea quickly sends a camera to follow him, which he visibly hates.

Bea gives us the go-ahead to continue, and I take lead.

"So, what we wanted when we agreed on the floral design before was to properly serve both of you. Jackie is classic and elegant. Hazel is modern luxe with a lot of character. We settled on a rare flower in different shades to tie you both together, but maybe that's not how we'll land this time. We can open our minds."

Jackie is hanging on my every word, and Hazel is—quite honestly—acting like a brat. I'm praying this is for the cameras' benefit.

Elliot already has several varieties from the Stem Bar to play with, and just as I should have assumed, one cameraman is trained on only him. He's fascinating, he's handsome, and he's actively doing something.

He looks up, pulling some pampas grass through his fingertips like feathers. "I'm going to start from a clean slate—mentally, creatively," he says. "It's a fall wedding. Fall weddings are wheaty and muted. In terms of classic design"—he gestures at Jackie—"there's blush pink and pampas grass."

He pulls together a muted pink flower with the pampas grass, creating a beautiful bouquet that speaks to Jackie's style. I can even see it in her eyes that she would be perfectly happy with her flowers that way.

"What I also think of for fall is burgundies. Wine. Warm cozy colors," he says. He pulls together the pampas grass with dark red dahlias. He adds a lemon leaf and ties it off with a fraying rope instead of a ribbon.

It's close to Hazel, but it's not quite there. He knows it. I'm opening my mouth to ease the tension when Hazel puts up her hands.

"I'm sorry. Can we stop rolling?" She looks at Bea with a firm expression. One of the cameramen tilts his camera to the floor. "I had no idea I was coming in here for an ambush, so I'm just a little shaken."

My brows draw together. An ambush?

Bea steps forward. "Of course. You know, when working with reality TV, a lot of stuff isn't staged. It's real emotions coming forward. I'd love to continue on while we're feeling raw, but I understand if not."

"Hazel. Jackie," I say. "We don't have to make any decisions today or in front of cameras. We can do a reenactment like we did at the bakery." I can see that Bea would like to persuade us to do it live, but I cut her off. "Elliot, while the cameras are off, do you have anything to add?"

He scratches his chin. "What's happening is uncommon. It's rare that I have this kind of problem with supply, but it's an international shortage. What I can promise you is that this wedding will be beautiful. There's already a killer design in place, and now it's just trying to complement that."

I show my agreement. Hazel is taking deep Zen breaths.

Hesitantly, Jackie says, "I would be more than happy with something like this." She puts both of their sample bouquets together, showing off how good they look.

"But I won't be," Hazel says bluntly.

I see Jackie's jaw snap shut, and Bea's fingers itch to film this.

"There's an arrangement I've been wanting to try for some time now," Elliot says slowly, "but I haven't found the right reason to play with it."

He opens his phone and I see his thumbs flip to Instagram. "I don't have any of the materials here at the shop," he continues, "because they're rare." His eyes flicker to me, and I get it. He's seducing her into this. Rare. The right reason. They're buzzwords Hazel will latch onto.

He hands Hazel his phone, and I see the tension leave her brows as she swipes.

"Queen protea is the centerpiece. They're elegant but impactful. And best of all, there won't be any supply issues. We could even fill the dance floor with them with the budget we'll save from not importing the anthuriums."

Hazel shows Jackie the pictures, and I can see that Jackie is trying. It's not quite her style. I look at the images of the eight-inch cup-like blooms that look more like shrubs than flowers, and I know Jackie sees the spiky leaves and the teeth-like centers.

"Would you do separate bouquets for them again?" I prompt Elliot.

He nods and takes his phone back, pulling up an arrangement that makes Jackie sigh in relief. It's a bouquet of blush pink roses clustered around a white queen protea with eucalyptus leaves scattered throughout.

"I like this, babe," she whispers to Hazel.

Hazel looks up at me, then to Bea and the cameras. "Okay. We can roll. Can we take that again, Elliot?" she says, like a true starlet.

18

Elliot

I haven't talked to Ama about anything but business for two weeks. At last Saturday's wedding at the Willow Ballroom, we were both swamped with work. She had the most decadent design I've ever seen, and it really paid off. But that meant that there was no time for any conversation outside of "Looks great. Move that over two inches."

Now, at the Ng wedding, I've only been contracted for centerpieces, so I don't even see her until she shows up at the reception venue with her Bluetooth in her ear and a fiery face of concentration.

I still don't know how I feel about all this. Have I been blown off? Was it a one-time thing? If so, I'm not going to be the one who approaches her, even though I *do* want to see her again. I want to take her on a date and chat about something other than flowers and weddings. I've been waking up hard every morning since the Gordon wedding, dreaming about being with her again.

But I don't know how to make it happen other than

just…hanging around. I've asked out exactly four women in my life, and statistically, I'm not great at this.

So I set up the tables, take my dolly, and head back to the parking lot. As I'm starting my truck, a knuckle raps on the driver's side window. Ama's bright face is on the other side of the glass. I roll the window down with a push of a button.

"Hey."

"Hi," she says sweetly. "Leaving already?"

"I need to get back to the shop."

She hums and hops up on the step so she can lean her arms in through the window. "How's your week been?"

It hits me that I'm probably not cool enough for whatever this is. Whatever she thinks she's doing, whether it's biweekly hookups or casual dating—I think it's beyond my capabilities. But still I answer her, "Good," with a dry throat. "Yours?"

"Busy. I need this wedding to be over with. They set a low budget and then continually asked me to exceed it." She blows out a breath and runs a hand through her hair. My eyes snag on it. "What time does the shop close?"

"Six. I'll be back here at ten for the vases."

She nods. "Do you want to come back a little earlier?" Her hand reaches out, to adjust my collar maybe, but then she's just playing with the top button. "You can help me set up sparklers," she says in a silky voice, as if *sparklers* means something else entirely.

"Is it really setting up sparklers? Because you know how I feel about you needing an assistant—"

"I mean, come back and I'll fuck you in your truck."

My jaw snaps closed and I bounce my head as if weighing my options. "I was thinking maybe I could fuck *you* in my truck."

Her lips press together to hold back a smile. "I'll consider it."

She drags my collar forward and kisses me. Before I can tangle my fingers in her hair, she pulls away, winks at me, and disappears.

I'm back in the parking lot at 6:02. Before I can contemplate going in to find her, I see a figure leaving the reception. "YMCA" is playing.

As the music changes to "We Are Family," she jumps through my passenger door and slips her underwear down her thighs, and I tell her to get on her hands and knees on the bench seat.

When I got this truck in high school, I always hoped I'd get to have sex in it. Maybe after a football game, where I was inevitably the star quarterback despite never having a natural talent for the sport.

It's a bit more complicated than I imagined, but I still get the hang of it with one knee on the bench. Her hands are braced on the window, the headrest. The truck is muggy and smells like her, and I stare down at her hips as I slam them back against me. My knee is slipping and my hands are sweating on her skin.

"Will you..." she pants, her face against the seat, "call me Amaryllis again?"

I groan, almost losing it there, but manage to whisper her name once before I come.

She puts herself back together much like before. Panties up and a kiss to my lips. I roll the windows down and collect myself as she walks back into the reception.

Two weeks later, she's ruining my floral design at the Singh wedding, rearranging flowers and pulling the spider mums out altogether. When I scream at her in a cleaning closet, she screams back until her mouth is on mine. She drops to her knees that day, and I forget about spider mums. In fact, her ideas were better. They always are.

At the next vendor meeting we have at my shop, she behaves normally. It drives me up the wall. She's all business, and all I can think about is how badly I want to put my mouth on her until she screams. She leaves with the clients, and I don't see her for another week.

I feel like maybe I'm getting over her. Like maybe I'll be fine if we just work together from now on. And then the next time I see her is a venue meet for a couple getting married at the parents' house. She's standing next to me in the backyard, showing me where the wedding arch will be, and I blurt out, "Do you want to get dinner with me this week?"

Her lashes flutter so prettily that I barely hear her soft "Yeah. That sounds great."

I stare at her face, her cheeks popping with pink and her bottom lip caught between her teeth.

"So, what's the chair arrangement?" I prompt her. She smiles and continues explaining her design.

That Thursday, I take her to a little Italian place a few blocks from the shop. She eats more than any girl I've ever dated, and when she belches at the table, I end up laughing so hard the waiter has to check on us.

When she hears I went to college out of state for three years, she makes me tell her everything. "What were you studying?"

"Architecture," I say, the word almost bitter in my mouth.

Her eyes brighten. "That explains a lot." When I frown at her, she says, "The things you're building. The wedding arches, hoops, chandeliers."

"I don't really think I'm using my architecture schooling for displaying baby's breath and peonies," I mumble, poking at my carbonara.

"Really?" She tilts her head at me. "I see it. Did you get your license too?"

"No, I would have, but I left in my final year and just...never went back." I look away from her.

"Did you want to? Go back?" she asks, as if reading my mind. "I mean, I don't know anything about the program, but would it be easy to go back if you just had the time?"

I shrug, trying to brush off the fact that she just nailed it. "It doesn't really matter, 'cause I *don't* have the time. I have the shop and..." I trail off, biting my cheek.

"Did you leave when your dad got sick?" she asks softly. I nod. "What was it?"

"Lung cancer. Never smoked a day in his life." My lips tug in a rueful grin. "Anyway, the shop meant everything to him. I was always going to have the shop. No siblings to take it, no one else. He wanted me to get my degree, but it was always unsaid that I'd have Blooming one day. That day just came sooner than expected. Mom called me and said there was a mass in his lungs and he was never going to tell me himself. So I came home." My eyes flick up to her. "But I do like the shop. It took a while, but flowers are...Well, flowers are better than people." I quote Dad to her with a laugh.

Her eyes sparkle. "Your dad said that to me."

My heart skips. My ribs squeeze.

"He was so nice to me once," she says, eyes a bit misty. I swallow and look away, and she says, "I mean, he was always so nice. Like truly special." She snorts and picks up her wineglass. "Nothing like *you*."

I nod in agreement, and she continues.

"But I was having a really hard wedding under Whitney one time, and he...He made me smile." She does it now. "I don't know if this is weird, but he gave me a handkerchief. I still have it. Would you want it back? I think it's his initials on it."

I remember the crack of her fist against a nose. The pathetic way she held her hand to her chest afterward. Her laugh ricocheting, like music.

I shake my head. "He had hundreds of those. It's fine. I like that you have one."

She sits back in her chair and crosses her legs under the table. "I think you could go back, if you wanted. They have a bunch of online options for degrees. It's up to you, but...you just said it yourself—your dad wanted you to get your degree. And who knows? Maybe it would give you a leg up in some way, when you inevitably open a showroom." She winks at me.

"Maybe." I hate to admit it, but I like the way she can spell out my future so easily. "You didn't go to college?"

"I started with Whitney a few weeks after high school. I guess I could have gotten a hospitality management degree, but I'd have had to go out of town for one. And I was already working under the master."

She has a sparkle in her eye as she talks about Whitney, and I try not to frown. "I always wondered what your title was under her," I say.

"A couple different things. But by the time you were working with your dad, I was director of design."

"And why did you leave?"

"You mean, why did Whitney 'let' me leave?" She echoes my words from earlier this year, reaching for her glass with a teasing tilt to her brow. I roll my eyes. "I was assisting with weddings with budgets in the hundreds of thousands, but I knew I wanted to be working with lower budgets. Lower budgets almost open up more opportunities—does that make sense?"

"Yeah, it does," I answer honestly.

"Whitney was starting to actively turn away anyone who wasn't working with fifty grand or more, regardless of what they could pay her, so I thought, 'I could be taking those. I could be making something really special out of that budget.'"

"So it had nothing to do with your pay? Or how she treated you?"

She blinks at me, and a stunned silence crosses the table. I regret saying it immediately.

"How she—how she treated me? What do you mean?"

"I'm sorry, I shouldn't have..." I trail off, but she's still waiting. "It was clear to every single one of the vendors who was the real brains behind the Whitney Harrison Weddings operation. My father would talk about it all the time—how much Whitney's style was growing, what a change there had been since she hired some fresh blood. Mark at Roscow Rentals used to talk to me about it; Minnie at Freeport Bakery noticed it."

I can see her chest rising quicker and quicker, but her lips are pressed tightly together.

"I mean, Ama, a month after you left, Whitney asked me to replicate the order for the Teele wedding. Down to the bud. *Your* design, copy-pasted onto another wedding."

She clears her throat. "I didn't know that." She sips her wine and averts her eyes. "I mean, to be fair, anything I designed while I was there belonged to Whitney. That was in my contract. So it was within her rights."

My jaw snaps shut to keep from saying anything about that. I can feel my molars grind.

"How much of a salary increase did you get when you were promoted to director of design?"

"I don't remember—"

"She has to outsource her designers now without you. Tamara Birch, who works with her a lot now? Whitney adds in her costs to the total budget. Tamara gets one hundred an hour for her wedding design."

She's staring at me, calculating. I can see she's close to it—close to realizing what bullshit she'd been fed for years.

"But I was paid a salary," she says. "Even if Tamara Birch was doing five hours of work every week of the year, I'd still have been paid more than her. And I had consistency throughout the off-season, so..." She sits up abruptly and flags the waiter for the check. "Let's drop this, okay? I think you have—interesting points, but honestly, I'd like to be in a good enough mood to fuck your brains out tonight."

And who could argue with that? I drain my wine, and when the check comes, I'm already handing him my credit card before she can pretend to reach for it. She grins at me.

"How did you know all that about Tamara Birch," she says with a sly smile.

I sigh, rolling my eyes to the ceiling. "It was two dates."

She laughs. "Do you have a thing for wedding designers?"

I sign the bill and mutter, "Maybe they have a thing for me."

She doesn't deny it.

We walk back to our cars at the shop, and she presses me up against her Camry, kissing me. She opens the passenger door for me to get inside and runs around to the driver's side. She turns the ignition for the A/C, and then mounts me, which I'm learning is her favorite thing to do.

"I'd bring you over," she mumbles against my neck as her hand reaches into my jeans, "but my mom is living with me this week."

"Oh." Her fingers wrap around me, and I find myself still talking about her mother. "Is everything okay?"

"Yeah, she's just getting a divorce." Her teeth run over my jaw, and my cock jumps in her hand.

"She—The wedding I just did the chandelier for? I'm sorry."

Ama's grinding on my thigh, so I guess the conversation doesn't really faze her. "It's okay. It happens."

My hands slide under her dress and press to her center. She moans as my fingers dips into her.

Over her shoulder, my eyes catch on her dashboard.

"What's—what's up with your car?" I ask, breathless.

She seems to know exactly what I'm talking about when she says, "I just gotta get it to the shop."

Her thumb swirls over the head of my cock, but I can't even enjoy it because there are *seven* lights on.

"You...Are you sure you can drive this thing?"

"I have been for like two months."

"Two months!" I pull her back from my neck. "Ama, you can't drive a car when it's like this."

"It's fine! It needs a nail taken out of a tire and an oil change. I'm sure it's fine."

I'm seeing airbag lights, maintenance lights, and something that I've never seen flash in any car that I've owned. "Ama."

"Relax, and keep calling me Emma."

Her mouth covers mine and her tongue does wicked things, but I push her back even as she starts to squeeze my cock again.

"I can't. We could die in this car, just by sitting here." I nudge her to dismount.

"No, wait—"

"Pop the hood. I'll take a look."

"Elliot Bloom, if you sit still and forget about this, I promise to suck your soul out through your dick."

Her eyes are fierce, and her breath is coming quickly.

"I...Ama, I can't. I can't!"

I shove her to the side and open the door. I tuck myself back in my pants and gesture for her to pop the hood. We spend twenty minutes glaring at each other through the windshield before I tell her I'm calling a tow truck and driving her home.

Needless to say, she does not suck my soul out through my dick that night.

19

Ama

Film crews make things ten times more complicated. It seems a stupid thing to only just now realize, but it's true.

Because Hazel and Jackie are hiring a wedding garment designer from out of town, the film crew is going to miss their opportunity to do a montage of trying on gowns at a bridal shop. So Bea asked if we can stage it, because that's apparently a very important thing to have in the episode.

I give Bea the names of the best shops in Sacramento, and we call them together to get this setup. I have to arrange a last-minute appointment to try on dresses that won't even be purchased, and Bea has to clear the film crew by them. A store called Spring Maiden in Carmichael agrees to the shoot, as long as their store name is mentioned and the shop is shown favorably.

I let Bea handle Jackie and Hazel, giving them a script to loosely follow, and I just try to pretend it's a normal vendor meet.

Spring Maiden is a lovely shop that I've been to only a few times, but thankfully the owner still remembers me from when

I worked with Whitney. I arrive early to make sure we have the privacy we requested and to meet the assistants helping us today. The owner greets me and pulls me to the side.

"So we were able to close the shop to the public so the film crew isn't stepping on anyone's toes. But there was one appointment already on the books when you called, so they're on the other side of the shop. I've let them know what's going on."

"Great," I say. "That shouldn't be a problem."

The cameras get Hazel and Jackie walking in and the owner greeting them. Our assistant for the morning takes us to our private room with mirrors and a pedestal. Jackie and Hazel each talk through with the assistant what they're looking for in a dress. Bea has decided that Hazel's decision to wear a suit should be a "journey" she goes on through the scene, so Hazel is trying on dresses that "just aren't right."

Bea flags me over to the door, and I follow her out.

"Can we get an interview with you about dress shopping?" she asks.

"Sure."

"Let me give Hazel and Jackie a break, and then I'll have a cameraman set you up in this sweet little corner." She points to a matte wall with the shop's name painted cleanly onto it.

I'm waiting for the crew to get set and checking my emails when I hear, "Ama, I wondered if it was you." I look up and Whitney Harrison is stepping out of the private room on the other side of the lobby.

"Whitney, hi!" I jump up to give her a hug before I can remember that I'm still suspicious of her. She clutches me tight, and I wonder again if maybe the vendor thing was a huge mix-up. "I should have guessed you were with the other party."

"I hope you don't mind that we couldn't be rescheduled," Whitney says, pushing a lock of hair away from her face. "My bride has had this appointment for over a month."

"Oh, no, not at all." I wave my hand. "I don't care about privacy. I think it's just for the film crew to have fewer people around."

"That's right," she says. "How is the filming going? Does it interfere much?"

"Not so far." I laugh. "It's just a bit of staging with the vendors. The girls actually already have their attire," I say quietly, "but the production crew wanted a wedding dress shopping scene."

"Oh, good!" she says, placing her hand on my elbow. "To be honest, Ama, I was really worried to hear that the Hazel Renee wedding still didn't have bridal dresses. It's three months away!"

Whitney laughs, like we're sharing a joke. I smile back.

"No, we're all on schedule," I say, shortly.

Just then, Hazel comes into the lobby, looking like she needs a break. She paints on a smile and walks over to us when I say, "All good?"

"Yes. Just stressful." She turns her attention on Whitney and extends her hand. "Hi, I'm Hazel."

"Hazel Renee, of course. Your wedding is going to be all anyone is talking about." Whitney grasps her hand firmly.

"This is Whitney Harrison," I say. "She's a fabulous wedding planner."

"Oh! I've heard a lot about you from Ama. And from my fiancée, when we were searching for planners." If she remembers Jackie's hesitations about Whitney, she doesn't show it.

"Well, obviously you hired exactly the right fit," Whitney says, dropping a hand on my shoulder. "Ama worked under me for years, so I can confidently say she's remarkable."

"Oh, we know!" Hazel laughs. "We're really happy with her." She sends a pleased smile my way, and a shadow of a wink crosses over her face.

"She's one of a kind, for sure," Whitney says. I try to parse out any sarcasm or ill will in her words, and I can't find any. "Where's the reception? I know it's the Rose Garden for the ceremony."

"We have a found space in Midtown," I say, treading lightly. It's kind of massive, what I'm doing with the old ballet studio. I've already got contractors telling me it can't be done—that is, until I show them the budget.

"Ama's going to make magic out of thin air," Hazel says, bumping my arm.

"That's very ambitious," says Whitney. I can hear some of that old let's-talk-shit-about-this-later attitude I remember from my years at WHW.

Hazel continues, and I get the feeling that she's bragging for my sake. "I'm just so impressed by her. I'm going to try to convince my engaged girlfriends to consider her for their own weddings." She turns to me casually. "You'll meet them at the bachelorette."

I . . . can't feel anything for a few moments. My cheeks are so hot I think my face may have melted off. I turn from Hazel's grin to Whitney in slow motion.

"The bachelorette," Whitney repeats, eyes sliding to me. "Well, it's nice Ama can carve out some time for that. Getting friendly with the clients was always her forte."

I look to my shoes. What a fucking mess. I haven't agreed to the bachelorette yet, but Hazel has been insistent. She doesn't know what a minefield she's triggered.

Bea interrupts us. "Hazel, can we go again? And Ama, I'll have Nick come right out for your interview."

Hazel follows Bea inside, and I feel like a dog, staring down the end of a newspaper.

"Well, some things never change," Whitney whispers.

"I'm not going on the bachelorette," I say quickly. "They invited me, but I know it's not professional—"

"But they *invited you*, Ama." She levels her gaze at me, lifting one perfect brow. "You've overstepped far enough for that to be okay."

My throat feels stuck, lodged shut. "I'm sorry."

She laughs, a tinkling sound she would reserve for grooms who thought they were comedians.

"Ama, you don't work for me anymore. You can run your own business however you like." She squeezes my arm, and I feel a manicured nail catch my skin. "I just hope you don't get burned."

I nod, my mouth unable to work. My eyes are pricking, and I want to run into the parking lot and scream.

"Call me if you need anything," she says, walking backward. "It's a *huge* undertaking."

She disappears back into her private room. When Nick comes out with the camera and sets the lighting, I feel hollow. I don't remember my answers to their questions.

When I tell Hazel and Jackie that I can't come to the bachelorette weekend, I see their disappointment, but I stand firm.

20

Elliot

She didn't talk to me for a week after our date. And when she saw me on the weekend for the Wilmot wedding, she kept it businesslike, unfortunately.

I posted a picture yesterday of the beginnings of a rose wall. It's only four feet by eight feet, and there's really no room for lettering, but I at least added a *B* for Blooming. She hasn't liked the picture yet.

It feels like there's this game we're playing, and I have no clue who's winning, but it can't possibly be me. It's already August. The end of wedding season is coming soon, and I'll be seeing less and less of her until it picks up again. That is, if she decides to continue contracting me.

We have a location meet on Friday, and my plan is to ask her on a second date. If she says no, then at least I'll know for sure where we stand.

I'm in the back room trying to clean up the worktable from the mess of roses I've made. The phone rings at the front, and I hate that I'm hoping it's her.

"Hello."

"Elliot. Whitney Harrison. How are you?" Her saccharine-sweet voice pierces my ears, and I tap the volume button on the phone to try to dampen it.

"Good. Hi, Whitney."

"Listen, one of my social media assistants just showed me your rose wall. My god, it's beautiful! I didn't even know you were working with custom installations!"

"Yeah, thanks. It's pretty new. Just something I'm trying."

"Well, it's *wonderful*," she says, and I can hear her typing. "I'm looking for a piece like that myself. I was going to talk to Briar Rose Designs about it, but I'd love to work with you. You know how well your dad and I got on."

She says it like they were in diapers together, when in reality, my dad tolerated her at best. She was the top wedding business in town, so the only thing to do was work with her. Dad gave her a discount to entice her to keep coming back.

"Sure," I say. "Do you want to come in and take a look? I only have that one piece done right now."

"Yes, let's set up for next week? I'll email you, and if you can quote me for a wall ten feet across? And itemize the add-ons, will you? By letter, by rose colors—the good stuff."

I bite my tongue from telling her I have a four-foot-wide piece that has a *B* and that's it. If she does want one, I'll figure it out, I guess.

"Sure." Her fingernails clacking in the background make me think of how they used to dig into Ama's arm, and I say, "And just so you're aware, this installation business is considered independent from Blooming. They'll be invoiced separately and the normal discounts won't apply."

She stops typing, and I smile.

"Of course. Understandable, Elliot. I'll email you!"

She hangs up before either of us has a chance to say goodbye.

I might have lost business, but at least I don't have to give Whitney that bullshit discount on things I'm making by hand.

The door swings open, and as I grunt a hello, I see Ama on my welcome mat. I clear my throat and lean forward on the counter.

"You here about the rose wall?" I ask.

She opens her mouth and pauses. "Did you post a rose wall?"

With little ceremony, she drops off her purse near the register and walks straight into the back room. I clench my jaw at the intrusion, but then I hear her gasp.

"Oh, wow. This is great!"

I follow her back and lean in the doorway. "I just wanted to try it."

"Are you going to make the rest of Blooming? The other letters?"

I shrug. "I could, but to be honest, this was a lot. Time and money." She barely seems to hear me, just reaches out to run her fingers over the petals.

There's a clawing in my chest, and I feel like a toddler about to start screaming about absolutely nothing.

"What brings you by?" My voice is gruff, and she turns at the sound of it.

"Um…" She presses a hip against my worktable. "Are you seeing other people?"

The question knocks me off my feet. "Am *I* seeing other people?"

"Yeah."

"'Other people' implies that I'm seeing an existing someone. And I haven't *seen* you in two weeks," I mumble. I know I sound immature, but I can't help it.

Her lips twitch. "Well, I'm here now. *Seeing* you. Being *seen*."

She steps forward, and before I can remember that tantrum I wanted to have, her arms wind over my shoulders, and she presses up to her toes. Her lips are warm and full, and her chest pushes against me. My hands slide to her hips, and even though I know we should talk, I lose myself for a moment in her mouth, her body.

"So," she whispers against my lips. "*Are* you seeing other people?"

I blink down at her. "Am *I* seeing other people?"

"That's what you said before."

"Because I still can't believe it's a question."

She swallows and looks at my collar. "Because...it's a stupid thing to ask when we weren't exclusive? Or...?" Her lashes flutter when she looks up at me.

I feel like a lot hinges on my answer. Like suddenly what I have to say about this strange relationship we have is going to affect the future of it. I bite the inside of my cheek, searching for the right words.

"I don't even know what this is," I say honestly. "We see each other once a week maybe, and we fuck, I've taken you to dinner, but I'm just..." I swallow. "I feel like I'm just waiting for you to tell me the rules. I'll keep playing even if you never do, but—but no, I don't sleep with other people when I'm...doing whatever this is."

The unclear intensity in her gaze makes me squirm. I feel like I need to keep talking in her silence, but I know it's her turn.

"The 'rules,' huh?" She smiles ruefully at my shoulder. Eventually she takes a deep breath and meets my gaze. "My mom gets married a lot. Like, *a lot* a lot. The wedding you did in April was her fourteenth."

I feel like my eyes shouldn't bug out of my head, so I force them not to. "Okay."

"She's never not had a man in her life, from the moment I was born," she continues. "And she makes it down the aisle every time. Fourteen fiancés, fourteen weddings. I asked her once when I was a kid if she ever got scared about saying *I do* like the movies show, but she said never. She said, 'Love is like the wind. It will come and go. Weddings are just a party.'"

She grins at the memory. I'm still reeling a bit, but I'm listening.

"You know, it's not really the fourteen weddings that are important. I guess I'm talking about the divorces. Fourteen times now, she's called it quits with someone who meant a lot to her. Who she loved. And I really believe that she did love some of them," she says. "It's not like my mom was fine after every divorce, ready for the next guy. She was in pain *a lot*. Days where I didn't think she'd ever eat or get out of bed. She always told me that marriage was worth it, but I don't think it is."

She catches herself, like coming out of a trance of memories, and looks up at me. "So I guess what I'm saying is, I don't see the point of commitments that end. I don't date," she says. "Not long-term anyway. I do...what we're doing now. A little bit here, a little bit there. But I don't do commitments." She laughs lightly. "I'm well aware where that stems from, of course, but I've seen too many men make promises to my mom—to me—that got broken when things got hard. There was this one stepdad, Warner, who I grew really attached to. My mom was with him for five years. I was ten when they broke up, but he promised me we'd still see each other." She shakes her head. "I asked my mom about him all the time, but I never saw him again."

She pauses, pursing her lips together in thought. My throat is tight, and my hands are still on her hips, but they feel cold. It sounds like she's letting me down easy, and maybe I should pull my hands away, but then she places hers on my forearms.

"I know it's weird that I'm a wedding planner who doesn't believe marriage works, but that's exactly it. Weddings are just a party to me. Marriages are things that end. And I don't think love should lead to a commitment when the emotion is so fluid and fickle for everybody."

"Not for everybody," I whisper. She blinks up at me, and I take my chance, hoping she'll give me a try. Because I'm pretty sure I'd never lose my grasp on her if given the opportunity. "Not everyone is fickle about it."

She bites back a grin. "Is that so?" Her arms wind up around my neck.

I nod solemnly. "I don't let go of things so easily." I feel my pulse in my throat, but I force myself to speak around it. I can tell this is the all-or-nothing moment, and I need her to know I'm all in. "If you want to move forward with whatever this is between us, you don't have to worry about me backing out. You may think everything ends one day, but you haven't had 'everything' with me."

I watch her take a slow, deep breath, her gaze casting over my face. I'm hanging on the edge of a cliff, waiting for her. Always waiting for her.

Finally, a teasing smile tugs at her lips. "So the rules of the game?" Her fingers run from my ear down to my collar and my heart thumps. "I came here today because I missed you, and the sudden realization that I may not be the only person you're seeing... actually made me mad." She laughs. "And that *never* happens. So, Rule #1—We're not seeing other people. Rule #2— I want to see you more than once a week." She pauses and looks at me intently. The smile melts from her face. "But I don't want to call it a relationship. Rule #3."

I feel something wilt inside me, but I focus on what I hope is the unsaid *yet* at the end of the sentence. It sounds like she wants exclusivity and more time together without labeling it. I can do that. Aside from Mom, there's no one in my life I could introduce her to as "my girlfriend" anyway.

"No labels?" I add helpfully.

She grins. "Labels have expiration dates."

What I'm hearing is that she doesn't want this thing between us to end. That excites me. The idea that she wants to look into the future and still see *me* is intoxicating. It whispers promises into my chest that she's making clear she won't voice aloud.

"And the last rule of the game?" She steps into me, and her grin turns mischievous. "Your tattoos. I have an all-consuming need to see all six of them."

I hum. "My pants would have to come off for that."

"What a shame." She pops my top button, and I grab her hands.

"I'm going to flip the sign and lock the door. Give me just a second."

She calls after me, "Don't want to play it fast and loose, Mr. Bloom?"

I throw up the BACK IN 15 sign and lock the dead bolt. With a flick of my fingers, I push the phone off the hook as I return to the back room.

She's sitting at the head of my worktable, kicking her legs innocently. I haven't had a chance to clean it up yet from the rose wall and a few other projects, so she's sitting next to potting dirt and running stray petals through her fingertips. She taps the edge of the table near her knee. "Did you do this?"

I look down and see my initials carved into the corner of the table, where I'd sat doing homework when I was a kid. "Yeah."

"You're a rebel. Defacing property?"

"Mm-hmm." I come closer, slipping easily into the space between her knees. She's wearing a dress, like she always does, and I push it up her thighs as I press my mouth to hers. Still holding the rose petal, her hands cover my cheeks and jaw. She tries to force me to kiss her differently—harder, faster—but I rub my thumbs over her thighs and keep it slow.

Her hands continue their path down my buttons, and soon she's pushing my shirt off my shoulders and shoving up my undershirt. Once it's off, she runs her palms over the violet on my ribs. My breath is coming quickly by the time she kisses over my jaw, down my neck, and travels past my chest to my ribs. The first swipe of her tongue over the purple petals makes my stomach tighten. She kisses it, and sweet little moans pop out of her throat.

I pull her face back to mine and let my tongue sweep through her mouth. My arm snakes around her waist, dragging her closer to the edge of the table. She helps me tug her dress from under her and toss it off and into a corner. My hands want to be everywhere at once.

"You know this is the first time we've gotten this undressed?" She laughs.

"I'm well aware," I mutter, staring at the lace over her breasts, the small slip of it between her legs. I attach my lips to her neck and track my hands over her skin. Her hands are in my hair, and her knees tighten around my hips when I suck on her throat. My fingers tug down the lace over one breast, and air whines out of her lungs as my thumb passes over her nipple.

She's tugging at the button on my jeans, but I pull her away. "Wait."

She huffs. "I can't."

I kiss her firmly, and then push her to lie back. She tears her bra off with greedy fingers and easily opens her legs to me. There are rose petals scattered everywhere, potting dirt unswept, but she stretches her muscles and invites me to press my mouth to her skin.

I lean over her, kissing just below her breast and trailing down. Her fingers slide into my hair and push me lower. I'm sucking at the skin between her belly button and her underwear when she sits up on one elbow and says, "Please, Elliot. Please, faster."

I look up at her, the planes of her naked body between us. "I've been wanting to do this for a few months, so if you could be patient, that'd be great."

She groans and drops back to the table, her hands scrabbling at her face and neck.

I switch to kissing the inside of her thigh, and she reaches up, behind her head, and I watch her fingers tangle in the rosebuds on the table. They crumble in her fingertips, flower petals bursting.

I push her panties to the side and taste her, my tongue slipping slowly over her center.

She chokes out a moan, and her knees come up to bracket my ears. I push them open again, holding them down to the table, and when I flick my tongue over her clit, her hips jerk. She mutters incoherent things as my mouth gets to know her. She tastes perfect. My lips latch over her, and I suck.

A long groan pushes out of her throat, and her hands tug at my hair again. I can smell the earth and roses under her fingernails. It mingles with her scent into something I could bottle. Her thighs start shaking under my hands, and I push them upward, opening her. She's cussing and yelling at me and talking to herself. I glance up at her, and she's watching me. There's soil and rose petals stuck to her skin. One pink petal is placed perfectly next to her nipple, and I groan at the sight.

My lips and tongue suck at her clit, and her hips jerk against my face, begging me for more.

My hand leaves her thigh, and I slip one finger against her entrance. The sounds she makes are feral as I push inside of her. She comes instantly, fluttering around my finger, hands holding my face against her. She squeals, and I'll never forget the sound, the smell.

I keep sucking as her hips relax. Tiny tremors seize her every so often, and she can't catch her breath.

"Elliot," she says, her voice almost gone. "Please."

I slip from her and unzip my jeans. She sits up in a flash, scooting closer to the edge of the table and dragging my mouth to her. She kisses me like she's searching for the taste of her. I pull myself out of my boxer briefs, and she stops me.

"Off," she rasps. "Take them off."

She wants to see the tattoos.

I toe off my shoes and push my jeans to the floor. Her eyes pass my cock and land on the red flower on my right thigh. "What is it?" she pants.

"St. Helena mountain bush. It went extinct only twenty years ago."

Her fingers wrap around my cock, pumping me. She whispers against my lips, "Where's the final one?"

I take her hand off me so I can turn, showing her the side of my calf. "*Valerianella affinis.*"

She licks her lips, and before she can ask me questions about it, I drag her mouth back to mine. I pull her knees around my waist and line my cock up to enter her. I push in slowly, and she still tightens like she's suddenly on the edge again. With shallow thrusts, I move inside of her. Her breasts press against my chest, and I can feel the dirt and roses between us, mixing into the sweat.

"Fuck," she moans against me.

I tug her knee up, and push in further.

"Oh fuck!"

We're panting into each other's mouths as I bottom out inside of her over and over. My hand falls to her breast, and it fills my palm.

"Vietnamese orchid, Benjamin Franklin tree, kadupul," she says against my jaw. "Cry violet, St. Helena...and *Valer— Valerianella—*"

"*Affinis*. Yes." I kiss her cheek. My hips have started to jerk. I let my fingers start to rub her clit.

"Vietnamese. Franklin"—she pauses to moan, and I can see her eyes rolling back—"cry violet and kadupul. St. Helena, *Valerianella affinis—*"

"And amaryllis," I hum into her ear.

She tightens. I feel her stop breathing. She chokes, drawing a ragged breath. There's no room inside of her, but I fuck her like I belong there.

"Amaryllis. Ama." I pant. "Ama."

Her fingernails are scratching patterns into my back. She's barely making any sound, and then she's gasping for breath. She yelps in small uneven patterns, and her walls flutter over and over.

I wrap my arm around her waist, melding her to me. There's nowhere for me to go, but I grind against her, murmuring her name into her neck until I come. The pleasure blinds me. I think

I bite down on her skin. My hips are still jerking against her, searching for more.

When I can breathe again, I pull back to look at her. She's wrung out entirely. Her eyes are heavy, and her chest rises and falls. Her tits are covered in flower petals and soil, her nipples tight and begging for more attention.

She pants against my face, and her hands drag over my hair, my cheeks.

"You're fucking incredible," she wheezes, and I feel my chest inflate at the praise.

I'm opening my mouth to say something back to her when a harsh knock sounds at the front door.

I glare over my shoulder in the general direction of the front. "I put a sign up. I guess it should have said, 'Getting Laid, Back in an Hour.'"

She laughs through her thin breathing and pulls my face back. Her mouth moves sensuously over mine. If she hadn't just said that she's not a relationship person, I would probably tell her I love her right now, as our sweat dries with dirt and roses.

Because I think I do. I've never wanted someone like this— their body, their conversation, their mind—

My phone rings from my jeans pocket. I frown down at our rumpled clothes on the ground. When I locate it, my phone screen flashes MOM at me.

I wince and answer it. "Mom?" Ama's brows jump to her hairline.

"Where are you? Why is the shop closed?"

Human language evaporates from my brain. "I—I...what?" I gesture to Ama to get dressed and grab my underwear.

"The shop is closed," she says slowly. "What's wrong?"

"Right. I'm not feeling well. So, yeah. I closed the shop." My jeans sound too loud as I fumble my legs into them.

"Your truck is here," she says, voice flat.

"I'm at Rite Aid. Getting medicine."

"Sweetheart"—her voice changes from suspicious to motherly in an instant—"what kind of medicine? I have a whole pharmacy in my purse."

"No, it's fine." I leave my undershirt on the floor and grab my button-up. Ama is only in her bra and underwear. "I'm just going to go home."

"Let me drive you. I'll meet you in your parking lot."

My head doesn't work anymore when I say, "No. No, that's okay. It's a head cold or something. And I'm—" I cram one boot back on. "I'm already back. Coming in the back door."

Ama looks at me like I'm a nutcase, and I probably am because Mom says, "I didn't even see you cross the street. You honestly didn't see me at the front door?"

I can't get my heel in my other boot, so I just limp out of the back room, pointing to Ama to slip out the back door to the parking lot.

"Here I am," I say loudly. Mom hears me through the phone and from inside the shop and turns around, hanging up.

I unbolt the door and open it, and Mom looks me over like she knows I've been fucking someone on Dad's old worktable. Her hand comes to my forehead immediately, pressing her fingertips all over my neck and cheeks.

"You look terrible."

"Right. I know."

"And you're covered in dirt."

"Flowers," I say, as if it explains it away.

I may just pass out and add to this whole sickness scheme.

She pushes past me into the shop, and I'm hoping I just heard the back door shut.

"Elliot, you need a second clerk. When you get sick like this, you can't just shut down the store."

"You're right. Yep. What brings you by?"

I almost applaud myself for changing the subject until I see Ama's purse on the counter. I sidestep around my mother and block her view with my back as I drop it behind the register.

"Well, I have some news, but I think we could wait until you're feeling better."

My mother is not one to wait for "news." She interrupted one of my birthday parties once to announce that her bill had been signed. I watch her push her black hair over one ear and smile at me.

"What's the news? You can tell me," I say.

Just then, the shop door yanks open, Dad's bell rings, and Ama steps in with a wide smile. Blood drains from my face.

"Elliot, just the man I wanted to see!" she says, in a false chipper tone. "Oh, sorry." She pretends to spot my mother. "I didn't see you had a client. I'll wait over here!"

As she turns to look at the orchids along the far wall, I see there's dirt smeared over her neck, and a rose petal stuck in her hair.

And so does my mother.

So that's how I'll shuffle off this mortal coil.

My mother turns to me slowly, brows raised. When I can think of absolutely nothing to say, she prompts, "Elliot, introduce me to your friend."

I clear my throat, but it still rasps. "Ama, this is my mother."

Ama spins around, looking innocently surprised. "Oh, Senator

Gilbert! It's an honor to meet you." They shake hands, and all I can think is that there's probably dirt under her nails too.

"Ama is a wedding planner," I say. "She used to work under Whitney Harrison. We work together a lot. She knew Dad."

It's like diarrhea.

My mother smiles at her. "That's lovely. What kind of weddings do you do, if you don't mind me asking?"

To her credit, Ama falls easily into business, telling my mother exactly what her style is and what she brings to her clients. Mom asks about a specific wedding she went to last year and guesses correctly that it was Ama's design.

They're getting along like gasoline and a box of matches, and I'm over here sweating.

"Well, I just wanted to stop by and ask Elliot if I left my purse here yesterday," Ama says confidently.

"You did." I grab it from behind the counter.

"Silly me!" Ama takes it from me. "It was wonderful to meet you, Senator. Elliot, I'll see you this weekend—for the Bigg-Mosby wedding," she rushes to add.

When she's gone through the front door, I busy myself clicking things on the computer.

"She's very sweet," Mom says. "Pretty."

"Is she? Sure. Maybe. Short."

"Elliot, she took her car keys out of that purse on her way out the door. That's not something she'd forget yesterday."

I press my lips together and bite down on my tongue.

"So," Mom starts slowly, "I guess you don't *have* to mention girlfriends to me, but—"

"She's not my girlfriend," I hurry out, remembering how Ama didn't want that. "But...I do feel strongly about her."

A smile spreads over Mom's face. "Well, then I'm glad I met her. Could I maybe meet her again sometime?"

I nod, mortification flushing my cheeks. "Sure. What's your news?"

Mom pivots like she does when she debates: new topic, new energy, new smile. She moves closer to the counter and clears her throat.

"Stefan proposed. Last night."

I'm surprised to hear it, even though I knew this was coming. "That's great. Congratulations, Mom," I say with a real smile.

Stefan is great. Last month, he asked me for my blessing, and I was happy to give it. They've been together for two years. Their first date was two nights before my dad died, and I really appreciated Stefan sticking around for all of it.

"You can be uncomfortable, if you'd like," Mom says.

I roll my eyes. That's how she was growing up too. *You can throw a tantrum, if you'd like. You can fail biology, if it makes you happy.*

"I'm not uncomfortable. I do like him."

"Good," she says. Then softly, "No one should have to wait for happiness a second longer than they have to." She smiles and pivots again. "Will Blooming do our wedding?"

"Of course." I pull up the calendar. "Do you have any details yet?"

"I'd like to get it done before the end of the year," she says matter-of-factly. *Get it done.* "Maybe December?"

"It's quick, but it's fine for me," I say.

"Should I hire Ama?"

My gaze jumps to her to see if she's serious. "I wish you wouldn't."

She laughs. "Why? Wouldn't it be great for her business?"

"She literally just told you what she does. Weddings for politicians at the Sutter Club wasn't one of them."

"Her style sounds lovely." She plucks imaginary lint off her blouse. "And she worked under that pretentious bitch, so I'm sure she knows the Sutter Club already."

Mom never liked that Whitney talked Dad into that discount. That, and before Ama, Whitney had absolutely no taste in her designs and used to steamroll Dad into really tacky arrangements instead of taking his advice.

I sigh. "If you think it's a good idea, then I'm sure Ama would appreciate the opportunity."

There's a sparkle in my mother's eyes when she grins at me and says, "I'd love her number."

21

Ama

AUGUST

At the T-minus two-month mark, we move into the ballet studio and start gutting it. Clearing the last of the permits stretched us thin on time, but we're finally in. When I'm not meeting with clients or vendors, I'm at Weatherstone, overcaffeinating.

I grew up pretty well off, but I've never been able to throw money at a problem like this. It's intoxicating. Mold on one of the walls? Boom, money. Contractor complaining about time frames? Zap, approve the hire of a new worker. City fines for noise complaints and parking permits? Send me the bill, Jeeves.

Everything is going through Hazel and Jackie, of course, but when I gave them the estimate for what it would take to turn this space into a reception hall in two months, I included a twenty percent cushion for these kinds of issues. I'm still on budget thanks to that.

I'm on my way today to finalize the transportation for the guests from the Rose Garden to the reception. We're contracting the company that does hayrides in the autumn and giving their carts a makeover. When I told Jackie that I figured out how to give her a horse-drawn carriage, she burst into tears, but now it's my job to make sure they look less like French Revolution body carts and more like Cinderella carriages.

And that means Elliot.

It's the first time I'm seeing him in a month, and that's not really that long, but it feels like an eternity after the exposure I've had for the past six months. I've been emailing him my ideas, instead of what I used to do—pop into the shop for a quickie and a brainstorm—but I can't get a read on his workload without looking at his face or hearing him sigh over the phone.

In the times we've been at Blooming, I haven't seen an assistant, so I don't know if he has enough help to get all of this done. His cousin Ben usually helps on wedding days, but he's not a florist; he's a grunt worker. And this wedding is a *huge* order. One of the most floral-centric designs I've ever worked with. Maybe it's because I was stumbling around the desert for so long, but he's like a refreshing yellow Gatorade I can't get enough of. Maybe I've overdone it on floral for this, but I just couldn't help myself, knowing that Elliot was back. Adding this last layer may be too much for him, but he hasn't complained.

Yet.

I pull up to the warehouse that the hayride carts are stored in, and I'm not surprised to find Elliot's truck already parked next to the film crew. It will be another ten minutes until Hazel and Jackie arrive, historically, so maybe this is my opportunity to ask Elliot if I'm throwing too much at him.

I can see Bea inside briefing Vince, the hayride company owner and the man we're renting from. I say hi to the crew, who I've gotten to know pretty well by now, and prepare myself to speak to Elliot again. He's chatting with the sound guy. It's hard to tell if they're getting along or if Elliot's just tolerating him—that's just how his face is.

"Morning," I greet them. "Can I talk to Elliot for a second?"

The sound guy dismisses himself, and Elliot looks at a place past my ear.

"Two months out!" I say. "I just wanted to make sure I'm not throwing too much at you."

His eyes slide over to me, but his frown remains in place. "What's that mean?"

"I—I just mean, this is a huge wedding. And I keep asking for more. Do you foresee any problems?"

I could probably count all of his eyelashes in the time it takes him to say, "There won't be any problems."

I force a grin at him. "And if there are, you'll tell me?"

"There won't be any problems."

He walks past me to grab his supplies out of his truck, and I pretend everything is peachy as I greet Bea.

When Jackie and Hazel arrive, I can see on their faces that they anticipated a carriage, not a wagon.

"Here's the plan," I tell them once the cameras are rolling. "We replace these hay bales with cushioned benches." I climb up into the cart and start pointing around. "Elliot's going to attach three arches to hover on top, wound with roses—which will connect back to the Rose Garden. Along the outside he'll attach boxwood." I turn and sit comfortably on the hay bale. "It's a ten-block ride in a horse-drawn carriage covered in flowers. I think it's charming and unexpected."

Hazel is nodding, but Jackie is wincing what she thinks is a smile.

"Elliot," I say, "anything to add?"

He looks directly at Jackie and says, "This will not look like a hayride on your wedding day. I guarantee it."

That calms her, just as I knew it would.

One camera follows me over to talk with Vince, and the other stays on Jackie and Hazel to "talk through their fears," as Bea calls it. Elliot comes with me to discuss how he'll be attaching the arches and to sign waivers, and everything's going great until Vince says, "Don't load 'em up with more than ten, and you should be good."

I look up from my paperwork. My brows jump. "I thought it was fifteen."

"Ten adults is best." Vince scratches his beard. "Fifteen is usual when you're loading up seventy-pound kids."

"You just shorted my headcount by a third with this news. Why wasn't this mentioned in our emails?"

I feel the camera step closer to me, and suddenly the second camera is covering Vince.

He shrugs. "I didn't know what you'd be using 'em for. Fifteen adults... well, that would tire out the horses."

I do the math of how long guests would be waiting at the Rose Garden for the first set of carriages to return from the reception hall to reload.

"I'm renting twelve carriages and horses to cover my guest count, but you're now telling me I need six more. How many more can I have?"

"Well, it's October. It's the hayride season—pumpkin patches and all that," he says, trailing off as if that explains it.

"How many more can I have?" I repeat.

"I need to run my business with the other eight horses. It's a Saturday in the dry part of fall, so I'm going to be full with hayrides that day."

All I hear is eight more. Out of the corner of my eye, I see Elliot open his phone quickly.

"So what will it cost to have an additional six," I demand.

"I can't give my horses away—"

"Who said I'm not paying for them?" I scoff. "You're dealing me a huge blow here. I don't remember any mention of weight limitations anywhere in our correspondence."

"My business is seasonal, sweetheart," he says, and my fingers curl. "I only get eight weeks a year to run these wagons and horses, and you want to kill my stock on a Saturday of all days—"

"Have you sold tickets yet?" Elliot's deep voice cuts through our conversation. He's still typing quickly on his phone.

"Some, I'm sure—"

"Great, if you check your email, you'll see a reservation for fifty guests under Elliot Bloom for Saturday, October seventh." He snaps his eyes up to Vince and waves his phone. "All paid for. We're gonna need those horses and carriages at the Rose Garden that day."

I'm blinking quickly, staring at him with an open mouth. Vince is doing the same. Something burns deep in my chest, an ache that feels so good. The cameras and Bea are just as captivated.

Vince throws up his hands and says, "Fine. Fine." He retreats back to his office to get the paperwork updated.

"Great save, you guys," Bea says, genuinely impressed. "I love drama I don't have to stage."

"Invoice us," I say to Elliot quietly, and he just nods.

I check in with Jackie and Hazel. They were eavesdropping.

"That was hot," Hazel says. "You two should bang."

I flush scarlet, and Jackie says, "That's what I've been telling you!"

I center my thoughts. Jackie has pried into my love life, and now Hazel has, too. They're treating me like one of their friends instead of someone they hired. Although I don't always agree with Whitney's procedures, this is one instance where I wish I had more space from the client.

I check over my shoulder to make sure Elliot isn't in earshot. "Glad you were entertained, but not gonna happen."

I'm about to change the subject *drastically* when Jackie says, "Because you have a boyfriend? Come on, you yourself said you don't do long-term."

My mouth opens and closes. "I have a what?"

Hazel looks bashful. "I already tried digging for info with Elliot. I'm nosy, I'm sorry." She laughs, but I feel like I'll never laugh again. "He said you had someone in bed when he called you once."

My mind whites out. I feel like a computer that has crashed.

"Is there...when did—"

"Are you still with him?" Jackie pushes, with mischievous eyes. "If it's not serious, I really think Elliot would be down to clown. You're so fucking hot, and he's always looking at you—"

"I'm sorry." I brace my hands against the air that's suffocating me. "Elliot said I had a guy in bed? What the fuck did that mean? Why was it—his business, or..."

Hazel shrugs. "He said he called you early one morning and heard you talking to someone." She winces. "I'm so sorry, this feels really personal now and suddenly like something I shouldn't be teasing you about."

I want to scream. Mar. Mar staying over after drinking and asking for breakfast. She doesn't have a super deep voice or anything, but it's the only person I've woken up with in two years.

My face tugs until it's smiling wide. "I'm just confused because I haven't been sleeping with anyone. Um…" I swallow, choking. "So, Elliot said I had a boyfriend?"

"Well, a guy. Not a boyfriend. I think he knows you don't do boyfriends."

It feels like everything inside my stomach switches places with everything inside my chest. It's sickening and dizzying.

"He said that?"

Hazel jumps to correct. "Not in a slut-shame-y way. God, no." She cringes at Jackie. "Wow, this is all coming out wrong, and I'm just trying to get two hot people laid—"

"He's worked with you a bunch!" Jackie says. "Maybe he's just observed it! I agree with Hazel. When she told me, it didn't sound like he meant it to be disparaging. Maybe like…a clarification that the dude in bed wasn't your boyfriend, or…"

I bark out a laugh and squeeze their arms with fingers that have lost all sensation. "It's fine. I didn't take offense. I'm still just confused where this guy in my bed came from." I chuckle, mirthlessly. "But yeah, don't worry about hooking us up. We know we're not compatible."

I look over my shoulder at him getting into his truck. He starts the engine and reverses without a glance at us.

"He's a relationship guy," I say, then add softly, "from what I've observed."

22

Elliot

Ama's cat is a menace.

We locked Lady Cat-ryn out of the bedroom, and still I woke up to a paw swiping at my face. The cat can *open doors.*

I'm appalled by this revelation, but Ama just nods sleepily and nudges the cat off the bed.

"Do you even like cats?"

"Mm-hmm," she says as she curls up against my side. "They're my favorite."

Ama's out in an instant, but I'm just staring at this cat who is sitting between me and the door, flicking her tail at me.

Contrary to what I believed of her, Ama does own a fridge and a stove, and she does eat other things aside from sugary crap in the morning. But by nine she's tugging on my sleeve to get dressed so we can hit J Street Donuts on the way to the shop.

We haven't had another conversation about what this is exactly. All I know is that if I want it to keep going, I should probably not label things. I'm still waiting for that moment when she gets tired of me being around or scared of this noncommittal committed relationship. But when I gave her two drawers and six hangers last month, she was ecstatic. And she shows no signs of being tired of my presence. For the past three weeks, she's been spending ninety percent of her time at Blooming, working in a corner on her emails or designs and running out to get lunch for us about midday.

"You don't have to stick around if you have work to do," I tell her one day in October as I'm watching the clock tick toward five.

She looks up at me from where she's been typing furiously at her laptop. "No! I love working here. I feel inspired, you know?"

I stare at the fertilizer and spare pots and vases on either side of her. "Okay..."

"I could set up a desk and run my business back here forever." She gestures to the mess and rotting baseboards, and I try to see what she's seeing.

"As long as I'm not keeping you." I head back to the front counter to write up an invoice. "You could, you know," I call back to her. "Set up a desk. It's not much but...if you don't mind the smell of fertilizer...and promise not to eat donuts—"

"Are you serious?"

She snuck up on me, now leaning in the doorway to the back room, a smile playing around her lips.

I shrug. "Yeah. I like having you around. Keeps the day interesting."

Her eyes are glittering. "What if I were to take meetings back there? Not now, while it looks like this, obviously," she says. "But...what if you were to move further into installations...and I were to start offering custom installation packages through you?"

My brows draw together. "It's kind of what we're already doing, right?"

"But officially. If—*if*—you ever decide to build a showroom back there, then I'd be meeting with clients *in the middle of it*." She's starting to speak quickly, ideas flowing, hands casting spells. "It wouldn't be a partnership in business terms, but it could be— could be, I don't know. Something new. Something that's only really done in San Francisco and LA. If they want Ama Torres, they're getting Elliot Bloom. If they want Blooming, they're pushed toward Ama Torres." She takes a breath. "Okay, that sounds…a little more opportunistic than I meant it to be, but—"

"It's like having a Starbucks in the middle of your department store," I say, seeing where she's going.

"Exactly! It's like, 'Oh, now that I'm here, ya know what? I *do* want a Unicorn Frappuccino,' or 'I really only wanted a latte, but the shoe department is right there.'" Her eyes are bright, and I nod in agreement. I feel cautious though. Like maybe I'd be getting the better deal.

"I dunno," she says, running a hand through her hair. "Maybe it's elitist or exclusionary? Like, you might lose a lot of business from wedding planners and event coordinators who think you work exclusively with me."

"Well, and the flip side," I say. "You wouldn't get to work with other florists or custom fabricators—"

"I don't want to work with anybody else," she cuts me off. "I want the best."

I swallow thickly. I want to tell her that I'm only at my best when I'm working with her. But I think she knows it. I think she sees the whole picture here.

"It's something to consider after my mom's wedding," I say. She beams at me. "You know, legally—for business reasons, you might have to pay me rent in something other than sex."

"Donuts?"

I glare at her. "No."

For the rest of the day, I fill an order, and she finishes up calling vendors before heading off to meet my mother. When I agreed to Ama doing my mother's wedding, there were some things I didn't think about. Namely, my mother and Ama meeting for coffee or vendor meetings once a week. There's no reason for me to be there with them, seeing as Ama thinks we were quite sly about her coming in for her purse. She has no idea my mom knows we're fucking. But every Thursday, my mother and my not-girlfriend sit at a café downtown to plan a wedding, and I stare at the wall of the shop, bouncing my knee for that entire hour.

Mom wants the wedding before the end of the year, and she has the budget to do it fast. Ama suggested a classy New Year's Eve wedding, which my mom loved. Ama's been hustling every day, trying to make it happen. She'll show up at my place at eleven some nights, either bursting with ideas or slipping her jeans off. Sometimes both. When I get the text *on my way* now, I don't know whether to brew a cup of Keurig and clear the coffee table or get hard.

Ama likes working on the floor around my coffee table—she also likes fucking on my coffee table, so you see the dilemma I'm in?—mainly because she doesn't have a coffee table. Mine's an IKEA thing that I've had since college and doesn't match any of my furniture. One night after she's dissected what we'll need to do with the centerpieces—and after she's writhed under me on my scratchy rug—I say, "I need a new coffee table."

"Oh, can I have this one?!"

There's a kid-at-Christmas joy in her eyes, like I'm giving away a Barbie Dream House. "You want it? This one?"

"Yeah, it'll make me think of you. All of you." She lifts her brows suggestively and kisses me so deeply that we end up fucking on said coffee table for the second time that week.

The next day, we're coffee table shopping, and the day after that, we're moving my old one into her house.

I lie in bed with her that night, my fingers playing with her hair. It's November already. We've been doing this not-a-relationship thing for three months, and six weeks ago was the last time I slept alone.

I keep waiting for the day she decides we're done. I poke and prod at her rules of the game. I suggest we take a trip to Napa before wedding season starts next year. She loves that plan. I ask if she wants me at Mar's birthday party, which she's planning. "Of course I do!" she says. Her mother gets engaged, and she talks like I'm not just doing the flowers. She talks like I'm going to be her wedding date. Like she'll introduce me to people there.

And the biggest dent in her rules—she keeps making plans for our combined studio space, wrapping herself around me, intertwining our lives for the future. Like she doesn't see an ending.

After my mother's wedding next month, I'm going to ask her if we can redefine the rules. She may not believe in relationships, but that's what we're in. She may not care to introduce me as her boyfriend, but I'd like to bring her to dinner with my mother and Stefan sometime. She may not need to define *long-term*, but to me, forever sounds nice.

If she doesn't want to adjust her rules, I'll be fine with it, I guess. But I need her to know I already think of us as long-term. I already see the business signs and the trips out of town and the slow dances in white dresses—even if she doesn't want to name it.

She's tapping away at her phone absentmindedly next to me in bed. I turn to her.

"What do you like most about weddings?"

"The proposal," she answers quickly.

I look at her. "The part you have nothing to do with?"

Blinking rapidly, she looks at me. "Oh, wow. Yeah, I guess so." She puts her phone down and twists on her side to face me. "Did you mean, like, flowers or food or DJs?"

I shrug. "No. Just what makes weddings the thing you want to do?"

"I like individualizing the wedding to the couple most. I love when I feel like I've truly nailed them. And for me, the proposal story is the thing that tells me exactly what to give them."

My thumb swipes her bangs away from her eyes. "Why's that?"

She thinks on it. "You really learn who a person is when they're afraid, you know? And anyone who says they're not afraid to propose is lying. I think the proposee has a moment too. Just terrified. 'Is yes the right decision? Is this really how he's proposing? I can't believe he waited ten years; isn't that a bad sign? Did I pressure him into doing this?'"

The questions spiral out of her, like steam from a kettle.

"I also think *how* the proposal is done is really telling. Specifically about the groom—or proposer."

I don't even need clarification on that. It makes sense.

"When they tell me about the proposal," she says, "I get such a glimpse into them as a couple. It's invaluable. One time, a couple refused to tell me! They said they'd prefer to keep it private, and I swear to god, that was the worst wedding I've ever done. It was under Whitney."

She laughs and picks up her phone again.

I feel my heart pounding, and I can't figure out why until the words spill out: "How would you like it?"

She turns. "Being proposed to?"

I nod, and it feels like I'm flying too close. Like maybe we could have held on to this moment forever if only I didn't have to ask—but I *have* to ask. There's a part of my heart that's been planted for three months too long, unable to break the surface and stretch toward the light.

"What kind of fireworks do you want? A surprise or not? Intimate or crowds?" I say. "What do you imagine?"

Her eyes are soft, and I wonder if that fear that she's talking about is there. The *Is this right?*

"I don't," she says. "I don't imagine. I don't want one."

I think I hear her. I think I understand. I think that there's no complication, no oversimplification. *I don't want a proposal.*

Especially when she leans forward and kisses me, tossing her phone away and running her hands over the kadupul tattoo. Her lips follow, curving over to kiss my inked shoulder blade. She's done this dozens of times now, almost as if she has to say good night to each of them. She presses soft lips against my thigh and my calf, her tongue traces the cry violet at my ribs. She sucks at the two on my arms, and then she finally moves down the bed to where I'm hard again. Her mouth moves over me, and I'm lost to it all. Her tongue savors me, and my hands slide into her hair.

But I think I've heard her.

She doesn't want a proposal. No spectacle.

I file it away for the day she finally tells me we can talk about forever.

23

Ama

OCTOBER

The week of a wedding is usually huge, but this is gigantic. I feel like David battling Goliath at times as I fend off one attack after another. Between Hazel's agent updating her list the week before and the ballet studio remodel finishing, I'm up to my ears. I'm basically paying Mar to live at Weatherstone so she can be the point of contact on minor details the workers need. She appreciates the distraction nowadays after breaking up with Michael. It was her decision, but she's still really upset about it. Thankfully, I have plenty of practice being supportive in these types of situations.

The good and the bad of this week is that Elliot is at the site for a couple of hours every day, so with Mar there to coordinate, I don't get to or have to see him. While the reception hall is built, I'm with Jackie and Hazel doing last-minute work and final approvals. If this were a normal wedding, things would be going swimmingly, but I had to add a construction project to it.

I don't even bother Elliot for final looks and approvals. I run it by Jackie, but we both agree: he is to be trusted. He can't install the dance floor until Wednesday for fear of the flowers wilting by Saturday, but he's there with the crew every day, monitoring the other installations and double-checking all the measurements. Mar reports back that he's been getting along with the workers, observing and discussing changes. His architecture license ends up being a godsend.

When the inspector comes on Thursday afternoon to review our new floor built around the dance floor, Elliot is there to answer all of his questions. That's the only time I see him that week. I can hardly take the time to appreciate it because the inspector is trying to find anything he can to shut us down, but I'm ready for him. I've got all my permits, my numbers, and my approvals. I've done nothing else for a month but live and breathe Jackie and Hazel's wedding.

I got through my September weddings—including one that got cold feet at the half-hour mark—and am both dreading and dreaming of the small break I'll have after next week. In the past six weeks, I've had eight or nine couples calling and emailing me about interviews, all people who've heard about the show filming or who follow Hazel and are so excited for the wedding. I've had to postpone every meeting until next week. I hope I live to see it.

Yesterday, I sent Jackie and Hazel to be pampered—waxing at Dirty Bird and mani-pedis at Nature Love, my favorites. Today, they had the brunch at Jackie's parents' house. Elliot basically dropped off the flowers with a grunt, mumbled that Ben would be back to break down, and left. I wished I could have gone with him. After, I'm a bit pressed for time to get the rehearsal dinner set up before we head to the Rose Garden for rehearsal.

We arrive at the Firehouse at noon, which is the earliest they'd allow us in, and sweep in like a tornado. I wanted Mar with me for an extra set of hands, but there are final touches being done at the ballet studio, so she's still stuck over there. I give Jake an extra seventy-five bucks to come unload cars with me.

The Firehouse staff, bless them, hasn't prepared for us at all. So I'm dragging the tables into place, getting plenty of help from the busboys because I'm in tight jeans and heels. Behind an armful of napkins that need to be steamed, Jake mumbles, "The florist and the film crew are here."

I grab the top half of napkins, revealing his face. "Enunciate, Jake. You're an actor."

"Oh, sorry. The florist—"

"No, I heard you. Check with George to see if you can switch to help bring in flowers, and then lead the film crew in the right direction."

"Who's George?" he asks.

"He's the rentals guy. Big, ginger hair."

He scampers off like a rabbit, and I start dragging chairs over. I have a box of name cards and macarons for each place setting, but I need the plates set up first. While I'm talking to the head of the kitchen staff, two gigantic vases march swiftly past me in a pair of strong arms. Jake follows them with a sheepish shrug and says, "He wouldn't let me help."

I'm too distracted by the absolute majesty of the queen protea arrangements in Elliot's grasp. He places them gently into their spots—the two corners of our section of the restaurant. When he turns to head back to the parking lot, he pushes his hair out of his face with one hand, and I see the dark circles and bloodshot eyes.

It knocks me back for a moment. Because I know that means he hasn't been sleeping. Which means I definitely gave him too much.

"Ama, did you hear me?"

I spin and find Bea in front of me. "Sorry, no! God, those flowers are beautiful, aren't they?"

"It's great," she agrees with a grin. "I'm just going to have the crew get some B-roll of the place being set up. I was thinking a time-lapse thing? Set up one camera in the corner in a wide shot and just record tape for the next six hours. And then, as the table is set, I was thinking we could do a final interview with you, since I know you won't be available tomorrow."

"Sure, of course. Thank you for that." I clear my throat and lean into her. "And uh, the kid over there? That's my stepbrother, Jake. He's an actor. If you happen to find a use for him in the B-roll, I'd really appreciate as much screen time as he can get."

Bea winks. "Noted."

Jake is relegated to straightening the table settings as Elliot and his cousin Ben bring in the centerpieces. He's still making trips to and from when Bea sits me at the table next to the model place setting I've done up for Jake to go through and copy.

Once the camera and sound guys are situated, Bea says, "I know we did an intro already, but let's do another. The lighting and setting here are a lot better than before. So give us your name and info, how long you've been doing this, and so on."

Cameras roll, and I push my hair over my ear.

"My name is Ama Torres, and I'm Hazel and Jackie's wedding planner. I've been in the wedding industry for over eight years, and this is my fourth year running my own business as a wedding planner."

"Good," Bea encourages. "And what drew you to weddings?"

"I've always been in love with weddings," I say. "As far back as I can remember."

Elliot passes behind the camera again, and I try to keep my attention on Bea and the bright lights.

"Is there a specific wedding you remember growing up? Were you the flower girl for an aunt or anything personal?"

"My mother's weddings." I remember to rephrase for the interview and say, "I specifically remember falling in love with weddings during my mother's."

Bea says, "Is that how Jake came to be your stepbrother?"

I see Jake pirouette to face us at his name.

"No, that was a more recent relationship." I should probably walk this back, but the light on the camera is distracting, as are Elliot's footsteps as he stomps around the table. "My mother has been married several times, so I've gotten to experience a lot of weddings growing up."

I can see Bea tilt her head, and I've come to realize that it's not a good thing—for me.

"How many times has your mother been married?"

I hear Jake snort before he says, "A lot."

All of our heads snap to him, and he looks shocked at himself. "Sorry," he tries, "I—"

"Go pack up my car, Jake," I say icily.

He gapes at me before recovering and dashing out the door in shame.

But Bea's eyes are still on me. "How many times?"

"She's um…My mother has been married sixteen times." I laugh, like I always do when I say it. "You could say she loves weddings as much as me!"

"So, that's why you became a wedding planner?"

"Yes, you could say that." My smile feels waxy and fake. Bea gestures for me to rephrase. "I guess that's why I became a wedding planner."

Bea's eyes almost look wolf-like, yellow between the forest trees, prowling. I can feel myself start to sweat.

"How was that for you? Growing up like that? Do you think it's had any effect on your personal life?"

My mouth opens. My throat squeaks. I smile widely, and my eyes spring with nervous tears.

"Are you actually going to use any of this?" a gruff voice snaps from somewhere beyond the light of the camera. "Isn't your show a half hour?"

My eyes focus, and Elliot is standing behind Bea with his arms crossed.

"Er, yes," Bea recovers. "But the Hazel Renee wedding will be a two-parter. I think it's great exposure for Ama to get as much airtime as possible. Let the viewers get to know her—"

"Great. Ask about her favorite color. Her ridiculous Gatorade preferences. Ask her about donuts!" His voice rises. "Don't dig into her personal life. Are you serious?"

I feel like I can't breathe.

"No one's going to come to Sacramento and hire her because her mother's been divorced fifteen, sixteen times. They're going to hire her because of this," he says, pointing at the table setting and the centerpieces. "They're going to want her because of tomorrow, so why don't you save your film for the things that actually matter."

Finally the camera guy points the camera away and the light is off me.

When I clear my eyes, Elliot is stomping away, off to get his next few vases.

"Excuse me. I need a moment." I jump to my feet and run the opposite direction, toward the small hallway that leads to the restaurant offices. Bea calls out an apology, but I'm not listening. I'm taking gulping breaths, pressing my knuckles into my eyes to push back the tears.

I don't even know what's making me cry harder—the embarrassment about my mother or Elliot being the one to stop it. I lean against a wall, curling over with my hands on my knees, trying to breathe.

He had no reason to step in. Elliot, the person who has experienced this firsthand. He knows exactly what kind of effect it had on my personal life. He didn't have to do that at all.

I don't know how long I stay in the hallway. I know that when I cry, I swell up like a pufferfish, Hazel Renee makeup or not. What I really need is ice on my eyes and lips before I can show my face to the world again, but since that's not happening, I just take time.

There's a window at the end of the hall, and I go to open it for some fresh air. I pull my hand back when I see one of the cameramen—the one who was filming my interview—smoking by a car, and Elliot standing by him.

I hide against the wall, peeking out to watch. The cameraman looks around, as if not to be caught, and then presses a button on his equipment. A memory card pops out, and he extends it to Elliot like he's making a drug deal. Elliot puts it in his pocket and moves to his truck, grabbing the final vases to bring upstairs.

24

Elliot

New Year's Eve

The night before my mother's wedding, Ama is up all night.

I know this, because she keeps *me* up all night.

At two a.m., she turns to me and shakes me awake. "Hey. Hey."

I rub my face. "What's wrong?"

"I'm gonna take a bath."

I stare at her blearily. "Okay."

"You don't have a tub," she says.

"Okay."

"So, do you want to come with me to my place or stay here?"

I suck in a deep breath and suppress a yawn. "I guess...I can come with you."

She beams and says, "Good."

Then she rolls toward me, presses her body against mine, and kisses me so deeply that I'm suddenly *very* awake. My hand threads into her hair, holding her head in place, and I kiss her back. I indulge in the feeling of her body pressed against my side, the way her hips start to press into me. She whispers against my mouth, "Will you take a bath with me?"

"Will I fit in your tub?" I chuckle.

She reaches down, cups her hand over my groin, and says playfully, "Oh, I'll make you fit."

Then she tumbles out of bed and starts dressing and getting what she'll need for tomorrow. I'm hard as a rock, still trying to get my jeans on by the time she's ready at the door.

She talks a mile a minute in the truck on the way to her place, walking through the plans for tomorrow and the potential sticky areas. When we reach her house, she's so focused on the wedding that I start to lose hope that I'll be having sex *or* sleeping anytime soon.

But she walks into her house, greets the cat, and starts stripping, all while finishing the list of things to do in the morning. When her jeans are kicked off, she looks at me and says, "Are you gonna take a bath?"

"Uh...sure." I follow her to the bathroom and strip while she starts the water and complains about the caterer.

"If he rushes my courses again, then that's the last time I'm using him," she says, reaching for bath salts. "Do you think he respects me? I don't think he respects me."

I nod. I agree. I listen. But I've accepted the fact that I just drove fifteen miles at two thirty in the morning to squeeze into this bathtub and listen to Ama wheel-spin. It's fine. I may fall asleep, slip under, and drown. But it's fine.

She's lighting candles, turning off lights, and setting music to play on her phone. But she's also getting worked up about seating arrangements.

"If I hear from the governor's assistant one more time about where he's sitting, I'm going to lose my fucking mind."

She points at the tub and I stumble to it, slipping into the warm water, the perfect temperature for dozing off. I lean my head back on the tiles and listen as she rants about one of Mom's high school friends who didn't RSVP.

She steps into the tub and sits between my legs, bringing the water dangerously close to the top. She's still talking a mile a minute when she leans back against my chest and takes one of my hands, bringing it between her thighs.

"Do you—do you want to take a breath?" I stutter out.

"A breath? What do you mean?"

"You can just relax. Let your mind drift." I let my fingers dance over her core to let her get the message.

She turns over her shoulder to me and says, "This is me relaxing."

I bite back a smile and say, "Go on."

The venue coordinator is the next topic for discussion. She leans her head back on my shoulder and vents until she's gasping, moaning about time frames and condescending emails.

"If she thinks—if she thinks she can steamroll me—then—then—"

When Ama comes on my fingers with a soft groan, it's the quietest she's been for the last half hour. I think momentarily that she's fallen asleep, but then she tilts her face to mine and kisses me.

"Thank you. You always know what I need," she says.

I push her hair away from her face and ask, "What else do you need? What's your to-do list?"

She breaks down her worries, her regrets. I don't comment. I just allow her brain to organize. When she grows quiet, I reach forward and unplug the drain. I wrap her in a towel and carry her to her bedroom. I make sure the alarm is set and the coffee is prepared. When I pull back the covers to slip in next to her, she rolls toward me and says sleepily, "What if I'm forgetting something?"

"You're not."

"What if something goes terribly wrong?"

I pull her closer to me, and she lets herself curl into my side. "It won't. And if it does, you'll fix it. You're amazing like that." I kiss her hair. "AmazingAma."

She snorts a laugh, and I almost say it. I almost say *I love you.*

But I don't know that she wants me to. I think we could be together for forty years with twenty kids, and she still wouldn't want to hear it. So I hold her until her breathing evens out, and whisper it soundlessly, like a prayer.

My mother's second wedding is beautiful. And every chance she gets, my mother tells her guests that she owes it all to her wedding planner and her son. The Sutter Club—a members-only event venue for the Sacramento elite—is a common wedding venue, but not like this. This is exceptionally done, and I just know that my mother's friends will be recommending Laura Gilbert's wedding planner for years to come.

Ama is stressed until the first dance. When "At Last" plays, I see a visible tension drain from her. She looks at me for what feels like the first time since the bathtub this morning.

Earlier today, Ben and I set up the floral in the ceremony room and the reception room, and then I had to go get showered and dressed, so really, I *haven't* seen her. All through cocktail hour and dinner, I've had to sit through my mother's friends asking if I'm seeing anyone and then immediately pulling out their contacts to set me up with someone. And the entire time, I've wanted to scream to the entire room that I'm perfectly happy with the perfect person—and she's right over there. I'm sure I'll have to put up with a few calls about blind dates in the next month, but I'll manage.

As the first dance ends, Ama checks in with the DJ and hands the reception to him. I excuse myself from the table I've hardly paid any attention to and follow her to the kitchen.

"Amazing," I tell her, pressing a kiss to her cheek.

She beams at me. "You think? It went well, right?"

"Perfectly. I don't know if you've ever done a better job."

She laughs, a sound like bubbling joy, and says she'll be right back.

As the reception moves into bittersweet ballads and jazzy up-tempos, I wait for her near the kitchen. When she comes back, "The Way You Look Tonight" is playing, and I turn to her.

"Would you consider it too unprofessional if I asked the wedding planner to dance?"

She bites back a smile and agrees without a second thought.

I take her hand and lead her to the dance floor. I expect her to insist we stay in the shadows, like we have for half a year now, but she lets me put a hand on her waist and hold her palm in my other. She lets me take her into the center, a passing glance away from my mother. And she smiles at me the whole time. I have to focus on the soft look in her eyes and the warmth of her waist to keep myself from saying *I love you*. I can tell it's going to get harder and harder as time goes on.

"What are you thinking?" she asks.

"Just... how happy I am."

She snorts, like I've taken her by surprise. "I'm happy too." She seems to think a minute, and then starts fiddling with her clipped bag—which is clearly a fanny pack, no matter which way she cuts it. "I have a surprise for you."

"Okay."

She pulls out an envelope, hands it to me, and then places her arms around my neck so we can still dance while I open it. There's a piece of paper inside. An email exchange.

> Dear Ama Torres,
> Thank you for reaching out. Yes, we do have a Franklinia that we're nurturing. It's not part of the exhibit, but since your friend is such a fan, I would consider allowing him to visit the flower (with supervision) at any point in the future.
> Let me know if you ever make it over here, and I'll happily give you a tour.
> Frank Hitchkins,
> Arnold Arboretum Manager
> Harvard University

I blink down at the words, reading them over and over. When I look up at her, she's smiling nervously.

"Wanna get away?" she says, laughing. "I was thinking in the fall, when its leaves are red. Harvard's one of the only arboretums that has the Franklin tree, and I..." She swallows and places one hand on my right forearm, where the tattoo is. "I want you to see it."

There's a bubbling inside me. It's so strong and addictive. I had a good childhood, so it's not like I've never received an excellent present before. But it's the surprise from someone who knows you on a level no one else will—someone who's opened up your chest and fit themselves inside.

I look down at the email again. *The Franklinia.* And she knows it's my favorite even though I never told her.

I glance at my mother, just a few couples away. She's beaming at Stefan, in a different way than she looks at anything in her life. It's something I've seen in the mirror a few times over the past six months.

The brewing in my chest rises. My eyes prick and my throat tightens to keep the words inside of me. But I look at her *at her*—and I see that she doesn't need me to say thank you. Because she knows how well her arrow landed.

She smiles softly at me, and says, "I think...I think I may be falling in love with you."

My heart thumps. I can't believe she said it first. I can't believe I have permission to say it.

Her eyes flick up to mine hesitantly, as if she ever needed to doubt I'd say it back.

There's a flower in my chest, just now starting to meet sunlight, finally blossoming. I can hear my mother laugh at something Stefan says to her, but I can't take my eyes off Ama. I hear my mother's happiness in her laughter—I've seen it. *No one should have to wait for happiness a second longer than they have to.*

Mom's right. If you know it's forever, why wait?

Ama's eyes are bright and brown and lovely as I say, "Marry me."

Those eyes blink once.

My skin buzzes and my chest aches, but I'm not afraid.

She smiles. Breath pushes out of her in a laugh. "What? No."

I can't hear it at first with the blood rushing in my ears. But I see her smile fade, and her brows draw together. And the bubbling in my throat turns to bile.

I place my hand on her waist. "Ama—"

"Why would you—" She shakes her head. I see her chest rise and fall rapidly. "I told you I didn't want to." Her eyes are accusatory. I feel chastised.

"You...you said you didn't *believe* in marriage, but that was before—"

"What? Before *you*?" She's squinting at me like I'm nothing.

"Yes," I fight back. "Yes, before me. Before you gave it a chance."

"I was *never* going to give marriage a chance, Elliot. That was never in the cards," she hisses.

She lifts a hand off my shoulder to rub her brow, and looks around us, as if realizing for the first time we're in the middle of a wedding.

I want to leave. I want to get out of here and drive my truck into a brick wall, but I know if I leave, I'll never see her again. I just know it.

"What's the next step then, Ama?"

She breathes roughly. "What?"

"When you have feelings for someone like you do about me, what do you envision is the next logical step?" I say, trying to keep the sickness in my chest from turning on her. "We continue as we have for the next seventy years? Maybe you move in, but that's— that's the end?"

Her nostrils flare at me. "I don't know! I *told* you I don't do relationships—"

"And yet here we are." She stares at me, like I've disappointed her somehow. "I mean, Ama"—a hollow laugh bursts out of me—"you want to merge our businesses, but you don't want to date me?"

"That's *business*, not a *marriage proposal*, Elliot—"

"You want to go to Napa next month, and Boston next fall, but you 'don't want a long-term relationship'?"

Her eyes are wide, mouth open. I see her try to speak. She looks terrified of something.

"I don't know," she squeaks out. "I don't know, Elliot. Everything was going so good. Just as it was. But you *knew* I didn't want to get married, and you did this anyway?"

I know she's right. I know she said it, and I thought it would change. But there's so much happening in my chest, so much regret, so much I'm losing at this exact moment, that I can't stop myself trying to turn it back on her.

"And why is that? Because of your mom? Because fourteen times now she's made bad decisions, and you think that's just life?" She glares at me, but I can't stop talking. "Do you really think it's hereditary, Ama? That if we get married—hell, if you say the word *relationship*—you'll open up some kind of door to your own fourteen marriages?"

"No, it's because marriages *end*! Relationships *end*!"

I shake my head and correct her, "*Can* end. *May* end. And because you don't want *us* to *end*, you don't even want a beginning?" Softly, I ask, "Ama, if we're not in a relationship by now—what are we?"

She bites her lip, and a tear breaks past her eyelashes. "I don't know...I don't know what I'm doing. This was a mistake."

I feel her step back, and I follow her, tightening my grip on her waist. The physical sensation of her pulling away from me triggers the realization that she's doing it internally as well.

"Ama, wait."

Her lips press together, and her eyes are shining with tears. I feel her body trembling and I realize how badly I just fucked this.

"I love you," I tell her. "I've loved you. I can't imagine losing this, but I only wanted more—for a *second*. That's all it was," I say, as if I hadn't been wanting more for six months. Longer. I squeeze her waist. "I jumped the gun. I never thought I'd hear you say 'I love you,' and then you did. It made me think I could have everything, but I moved too fast, okay? Let's forget this."

"You can't unsay it," she whispers.

"Watch me. It's unsaid, okay?"

"I'll always know what you want, and what I can't give you," she says, and a tear tumbles down her cheek.

"That's bullshit. I want you to give up your damn cat, and you won't do it, so we already have these problems—"

"Don't try to joke about this," she hisses.

There's a flash of light next to us, and we both turn to see the wedding photographer, taking the picture of the couple behind us. As he turns to us, she puts her hands on my shoulders and looks past my ear. There's a flash.

I'm staring at her, memorizing her. My palm sweeps over her hip, pulling her closer to me by the small of her back. She allows it.

"It never happened," I say in her ear. "You'll never hear about it again."

She's quiet. And then she shakes her head softly. "I should have never gotten involved with you."

It hits me like a bullet between the eyes. I clench my teeth to keep from screaming at her.

"We're coworkers in this industry," she continues, whispering into my collar. "It's completely unprofessional. I always do this."

I scoff, and it's meaner than I'd like. "You always get involved in half-year relationships with your vendors?"

She shifts back, and I let her. She looks defeated. "I confuse business and fun. I make a mess."

Fire scratches at my throat. "Is that Whitney talking?"

"She's right. I'll never—I'll never survive in this industry if I can't be professional."

"Great. So we're breaking up because you want to be a better wedding planner."

Her eyes turn to ice. "We're breaking up because you proposed. And because I never should have fucked you in the first place. This whole thing is a mistake."

This time when she steps back, she slips out of my arms. I try to make my fingers reach for her, but they don't.

"I have to check on the kitchen cleanup," she mutters. When she turns on her heel, she snakes into the crowd and disappears.

I'm left with an email in one hand and the memory of her warmth in the other.

I stuff the paper in my pocket and walk the opposite direction.

25

Ama

THE WEDDING

I wake up crying on Saturday. One of those dreams that you can't quite grasp, but you're devastated when it's over. I put cold patches under my eyes to keep the swelling down and start my day at six.

Mar texts me at seven and says:

> Don't forget grandpa's basin, whatever that means

"Fuck." I stare at the phone.

I told her to text me that today. And I'm glad I did.

The antique basin that will hold craft beers at the reception. Does it go with the theme? No. Will it make Kim Nguyen happy? We can only hope.

That will have to be at noon when I head from the Rose Garden to the reception hall to oversee final touches. It'll take me twenty minutes out of my way, but as usual, I'm low on help today. Jake and Sarah stay at the Rose Garden. Mar stays at the ballet studio. And I bounce to the brides when needed.

I get a text from Bea at eight a.m., asking if there's anything she can film today before the crew heads to the Airbnb for the brides getting ready. I send her to the Rose Garden. There will be plenty of disasters to catch there. There always are.

Our permit at the Rose Garden doesn't allow us in until eleven for our two p.m. ceremony, but I get there at ten thirty and stare at the park. Taking deep breaths, I tell myself that everything is going to go perfectly. The weather is amazing, brisk and sunny. Hazel and Jackie are on schedule in the Airbnb. And as George and his crew from Michelangelo's Rentals pull up in the truck with the chairs and stanchions, even the setup is going according to plan.

Jake arrives at quarter till, apologizing for his misstep yesterday by being one hundred percent focused today, which is all I could ask for.

When the box truck containing all the floral pulls up, sans wedding arch and sans Elliot, that's the first time something goes wrong. I ask his cousin Ben where he is, but all he says is "He just told me to get over here and ask you where everything goes."

My pulse spikes, but I let Ben and Jake start the floral setup.

I give Elliot until twenty after before I text him.

All good?

He writes back.

give me 10min

I start chewing on the inside of my cheek. Elliot's never late. I think of the dark circles from yesterday and how easily he snapped at the camera crew. He used to tell me all the time that I needed an assistant, but now it's him who needs the extra help.

Fifteen minutes later, his black truck rolls up to the loading zone, a floral arch standing proudly in the back like a chariot rider. Jake runs up to help him unload it, but Elliot just tells him to get back. He gingerly unties the cables and lifts it down to the ground. I meet him at the altar markings I've made in the grass as he carries the arch over him, moving slowly.

"It's beautiful," I say. It's not a lie, but I'm also not looking at it closely. I'm too busy trying to gauge his stress level.

"It's temperamental," he says.

"Troubles?"

"It snapped in half about an hour ago."

My heart stops. I look up to the top, and only now can I see a crack. "What do you need?"

"Nothing. It'll be fine. Before I head to the reception, I'll run back to the shop for spackle and paint, and if there's time, I'll solder a rod to hold it up."

I nod, as if I can see the perfect image he's painting instead of the horror show where Jackie and Hazel say *I do* as their arch snaps in half and stakes the minister in the heart.

I check my watch. "I have to go. I'm running errands, so if you need anything—"

"Go."

I spin and dash to my car. It's after eleven thirty, and I need to check to make sure the horses and wagons are set to arrive, pop in on the brides, and call Mar for any errands she needs.

When I'm finally on my way to Jackie's grandmother's house

to pick up the basin, I'm thirty minutes behind schedule, and I barely got to check on the Airbnb. The only saving grace is that Mar says things are going perfectly at the ballet studio.

I pull up to the address Kim Nguyen sent me in the email I barely glanced at. Her mother isn't going to be home, so I'm looking for this basin at the back of the driveway. When I walk up and turn the corner, I stop dead in my tracks.

I don't find a basin. I find a bathtub.

My mouth opens and closes. I can't form words, and even if I could, who would I be complaining to?

I whip out my phone and read over Kim's email, searching for the word *bathtub*. I curse when I see she did call it an antique tub. I'm racking my brain trying to figure out why I'd thought this was a basin that could fit in the back seat of my car. Maybe something was off about the way Kim first described it to me? Hadn't she held her hands out to the side, indicating how large it was?

Now, looking at this antique clawfoot tub, I can see that, one, it won't rest on the table we've put near the bar and, two, *it's a fucking bathtub*.

I clap my hands together. "Okay. Okay."

At least whoever placed it in the driveway for me kept it on the furniture dolly they'd used to get it here. The difficult part would be getting it into the back seat of my Camry.

I glance at Kim's email again.

You'll need 4 to 6 men to lift it!

I close my eyes, suck in air through my nose, and summon the energy of four to six men.

First, I run back to my car and back it up the driveway. There's no way I'm going to let all these neighbors see me do something so colossally stupid. I line the back seat up to the tub and push my front seats forward. It could work. The clawed feet may pose an issue, but I think the tub will fit in my back seat. If I could flip it, that would be best, but I don't think I can—despite my bravado.

I roll the tub on the dolly to my back seat and take a fortifying breath.

In those seconds, I imagine pulling up to the reception hall and paying the catering staff fifty bucks each to come out to the loading zone. I imagine Mar and me reworking the bar section to fit this tub, perhaps elevating it so people aren't bending over to grab their bottles.

But I also imagine just leaving this tub right here and going back to the important things. And the look on the face of Kim Nguyen, who has been an angel of an MOB in comparison to Hazel's team—Kim Nguyen, who asked for this one thing from me—Kim Nguyen, who told me not to come without four to six strong men…

I kick off my heels, bend, and lift from my knees.

At first, nothing happens. No progress made. And then two things happen quickly.

The front of the tub lifts up, almost high enough to get one clawfoot onto the floor of my car. I'm elated. And then the dolly, which had tilted under the weight, *allowing* said tub lifting, slips out from under the tub and zooms under my car.

The tub comes down. And my bare foot is under it.

It's a crunch like I haven't felt since I fell off my bike in sixth grade. Lightning shoots up my leg. I yelp and fall on my ass next to my car. With the adrenaline of a mother lifting an SUV off her child, my good foot presses against the side of the tub until it rolls off my foot. I scuttle backward like a crab and take shaky breaths until my mind can work again.

My right foot is pink and swelling already. I can't move my toes without screaming out. I bite down on my lip as the tears fall down my cheeks.

The tub... is still in perfect condition, except it's on its side in the driveway instead of inside my car.

But me? I can't walk. I can't get to my feet. My phone is in the car. I have my Bluetooth in my ear, but I can't call from it, only answer. And the wedding starts in ninety minutes. I can't catch my breath, and I realize I'm hyperventilating.

My face crumples. I choke back a sob, and my hand covers my mouth, trying not to alert the neighbors until I'm sure I want to.

I lie back on the driveway and stare at the sky, watching clouds move slowly, imagining myself among them.

Forcing myself to breathe, I try to consider my options. I could yell for help. The neighbors would call an ambulance, and I'd still have a broken foot and a tub in the driveway. If I went in the ambulance, I would miss the wedding.

Or, I get to my phone and figure the rest out.

I turn on my side and try to get to my hands and knees. Pain lances through my foot anyway, even when I'm not putting pressure on it. I try for a few feet before I have to stop, sucking in air like I've run miles.

I fall over on my back again, elevating my foot on the side of the tub. My chest is shaking as I realize what's happening. The wedding starts in ninety minutes, and I'm not at one hundred percent. I'm not even at fifty percent. The wedding of my career.

The budget of my dreams. The film crew, the eyes from Los Angeles, the opportunity of a lifetime for Elliot.

Tears are streaming down my temples into my hair. I'll give myself one more minute, and then I'll try getting to my feet.

A melody starts in my left ear, and I sob when I realize someone is calling me. I tap the side of my Bluetooth. "Yes, who is it?"

"I need spackle," Elliot says, voice coming quickly. I swallow a cry. "I'm all out. Can you grab some or are you already back at the garden?"

"I'm—I don't... Elliot, I need help."

There's silence on the other end. And I start to shake at the thought that I lost the call. Then he says, "Where are you? What's happened?"

"I'm—I'm at Jackie's grandmother's house, and I hurt myself. I can't... I can't walk, I can't drive."

"Text me the address."

"I don't have my phone. I'm on my Bluetooth. But it's on Titan Court, in Tahoe Park." I hear his truck starting, and I panic. "Wait. Go to the Rose Garden and send Jake—"

"No, I'm coming to get you."

"Elliot, the wedding."

"It won't happen without either of us, so I guess we're running late."

A sob bubbles out of me. "Call—call Mar. Tell her to get over to the Airbnb. And we need like three other strong guys. Is your truck bed full?"

"What?"

"I was picking up something, and it's too heavy. Who can come over here to load it?"

"Jesus, Ama."

I gasp a cry, hearing his vowels betray him like they used to as he pronounces it "Emma."

Then he says, "How heavy and how important?"

"It's a bathtub. Like a full fucking bathtub. And probably not important at all, but it has to be perfect, Elliot. I'm so close. This is for Jackie, and you know how much of this wedding has been commandeered by Hazel's agent and Hazel's reality show." My voice cracks, and I heave in air. "This wedding is so out of control. It barely feels like *her* wedding."

He's quiet for a second and then says, "Fine."

The line goes dead, and I'm alone again. I sit up and maneuver myself against the side of the car until I'm standing on one leg. My foot is throbbing, and I hear the crunch replayed over and over.

It feels like years go by before my Bluetooth rings again. I tap it. "Elliot?"

"It's Mar. What happened?"

"I think I broke my foot. I can't walk."

She curses. "That's... that's fine. Who needs to walk? We'll pop you on some crutches and call it a day. Maybe Elliot can put some floral design on those bad babies and you're good to go."

"Are you on your way to the Airbnb?"

"Yeah," Mar says. "What do you want me to say?"

"Nothing. Absolutely nothing. Make something up about an issue at the venue that made us switch places if they press, but whatever you do, don't draw the attention of the film crew."

She sighs, and I can just imagine her rubbing her forehead. "Yeah, okay."

"And Mar?" I ask. "Doesn't Michael live in Tahoe Park?"

"Michael, my ex? Your ex-stepbrother?"

"He does, right?"

"Ama, whatever this is, don't do this."

"Hey, I've been working with my ex for six months. You said it would be 'professional'—"

"Don't you dare," she hisses.

"Please, just see if he can come to Titan Court in the next ten minutes."

"This is low, even for you."

I smile. "Promise him a blow job."

She hangs up on me. I spot my phone in the front seat, and I'm just about to stretch for it when a black truck pulls up. Three people jump out—Elliot and my only two assistants for the day—Jake and Sarah.

"No, no," I say. "We need one of them back at the Rose Garden."

Sarah pops her gum. "I'm set up. I asked the cello-ist to call us if anything weird happens."

I squeeze my eyes closed at this shit show as Jake corrects her pronunciation.

Elliot makes a beeline for me, rounding the bathtub without a second look at it. He crouches down in front of me, and I press my lips together to keep them from trembling. His fingers reach for my ankle, and just the slightest pressure on the top of my foot makes me hiss.

"Can you stand on it?" Jake asks.

I shake my head. "Thank you for coming," I say to my ex-stepsiblings. "There's another guy on his way, hopefully. We just need to get the bathtub into Elliot's truck. There's a dolly under my car somewhere."

Jake starts to work on locating the dolly as Sarah takes a picture of my foot. I turn to Elliot. "I'm fine. We can load up the truck, and then I can probably drive with my left—"

"I'm taking you to the hospital," he states.

"No. There's a wedding. We still have to get spackle, right?"

"Jake will take my truck. I'll take you to the hospital. That's the end of this discussion."

"Elliot." I level my eyes at him. "That is not an option."

Just then, a voice calls, "Uh, hey? Is Ama here?"

I look over the top of the car, and there's Michael. Just as toned as I remembered.

I stand on one foot and wave him down. "Thank you for coming! We just need your help lifting something heavy, and then we won't bother you again!"

"Sit down," Elliot says, putting his hand on my shoulder. I slap it off and smile brightly at Michael, even though I probably look like someone whose career is being stabbed to death before her very eyes.

Jake has the dolly, and he's looking doubtfully at the height of the truck bed and the weight of the bathtub.

I lean on the car and start to hop over. "I'll help you guide it in—"

Gravity upends me, and suddenly I'm in the air. Warm arms have swept me off my feet—literally—and Elliot is bridal carrying me around my car and to the passenger side.

"Save your strength," I say, for lack of any intelligent thought. "I hear the tub's heavy."

He tugs the door open with a scowl and gently sets me inside. When he shuts the door on me, I take a deep breath and thank god I at least have my phone again.

I see twenty texts from Bea, Jackie, Hazel, and Mar. I dial Jackie first, sending the call to my Bluetooth and watching through the windshield as Elliot and a small army of my ex-stepsiblings back the truck into the driveway and prepare to lift the tub.

When Jackie picks up with "Ama! Is everything okay? Mar said there's an issue at the ballet studio," I'm wincing, watching Michael and Elliot get under the tub while Jake heaves it upward from the truck bed. Sarah braces the dolly with a bored expression.

"Hi, yeah. Hey! Everything's okay! I'm on my way back, but is there anything you need?"

"No," Jackie says, dragging the word out so I know she's lying. "I just...God, it sounds stupid, but I could really use your calming presence right now."

The men are grunting. Elliot yells for Michael to jump out and help Jake, and I gasp as Elliot is left under the tub.

"Ama?"

I close my eyes. "Jackie, you're totally right. I should be there. I want nothing more than for you to feel calm and pleased right now. Give me ten minutes, and then I will be your cannabis gummy for today, okay?"

Jackie laughs and says, "As a state employee—ahem—I, of course, have no idea what you're talking about, but I appreciate the sentiment."

I hang up with her, and when I open my eyes, the tub is in the back of Elliot's truck, and the men have not died. I open the door and thank them profusely.

Michael is sweating and glaring at the tub. "They better be getting married *in* that tub."

I smile weakly. "It's going to hold artisanal craft beers at the reception." He turns his glare on me. "Of which you will all be getting a six-pack, in thanks for your six-packs. And that reminds me..." I gesture for Elliot to come closer. "The tub needs to go on the rooftop. Up the stairs."

He frowns at me, then turns to Michael. "Michael, right?" He shakes his hand. "Ama just told me she'll give you a hundred bucks if you can come help us unload this thing."

I open my mouth, and then close it with a tight smile. "Yep."

Michael agrees, and Elliot talks quickly with Jake, handing him the keys to his truck. Michael walks over to my side of the car and kneels down.

"It landed on you?" he asks. I nod and remember he was in med school. "Can you put any weight on it?"

"No."

He hisses and shakes his head. "You gotta get that in a cast real quick," he says, just as Elliot comes within earshot.

"We are," Elliot says. He claps Michael's shoulder. "Thanks for your help."

"Thank you so much," I add. "If there's anything I can ever do for y—"

And then Elliot slams the door on me again. I scowl at him as he waves at Jake and Sarah to go. I call Mar.

"How's it going?" I say as she picks up.

"I mean, it's going well?" she says. "Like, for a wedding without a wedding planner, I think it's top-notch, really."

"Okay, well, I'm on my way back. Michael came through, so maybe consider getting back together with him, yeah?" She groans, and I add, "Also, he's coming to the ballet studio with Jake and Sarah right now. Thanks, bye!"

"Ama, *what*—" I end the call.

Elliot pulls open the driver's door, slips inside, and reaches his hand out for the keys. I pull them close to my chest.

"We're going to the garden," I say.

"We're not. We're going to the hospital."

"Elliot."

"Ama, give me your keys!" His voice booms in my small car, jarring me. I hand them over. He slides back the seat for his long legs, and turns on the ignition. The dashboard lights up with all my warning lights. "Are you fucking kidding me with this car?!"

"It's drivable! It's fine!"

He shakes his head and pulls out of the driveway. To my dismay, he turns left—away from the Rose Garden. My foot throbs, and I start running through the timeline in my head. I feel my ribs contracting, realizing I can't do this. I can't make this happen if we go to the hospital. But I know he won't turn around.

My head feels light. The only thing centering me is the pain in my foot. How can the ceremony possibly go on without me? I am the only one who can run it, because I am the only one who knows all the details. I don't even know if Jake has a fully updated schedule—

"The wedding is going to be fine," Elliot's voice floats to me, tethering me. "But you need to be fine first."

I turn my head to disagree with him. But he's already staring at me. His eyes are dark and focused, and I fall into them.

"You are more important than the wedding, Ama."

He's wrong, but it still fills my chest with butterflies and my head with lovely thoughts.

I watch the blur of the city as the hospital comes closer, listening to him breathing in the silence.

26

Elliot

New Year's Eve

I walk through the hallways of the Sutter Club in a daze. There are a lot of corners and doors and plenty of places to lose yourself, but I walk in circles trying to figure out what just happened.

I proposed.

I proposed, and she broke up with me.

She broke up with me, but made me question whether we were really even together.

And I regret it with every ounce of myself. I couldn't have been content hearing her say she loves me? I had to take it one hundred steps further?

I try calling her twenty times. I text her. I know if I just keep wandering the Sutter Club, I'll find her. We're in the middle of one of her weddings. She can't be too far away.

When I pass the dance floor again, searching for her head along the perimeter, my mother sees me. I give her a wave and keep moving. I'm in another alcove when Mom finally catches up to me.

"What's wrong?" she says immediately.

I feel like a child again. I'm miserable, and she's an angel in white who will make everything better again. I don't know what to say to her because *I proposed to her* sounds ludicrous now. It sounds absolutely mad.

"I saw you dancing with Ama," she offers, stepping forward. "You make a fine couple—"

"We're not." I leave off the obvious "anymore." Mom has been surprisingly good about not pushing for details and not giving her opinions.

But I can see it on her face—the same pity she had when I'd come home from fifth grade, bruised and beaten. Back then, she would rally into Senator Gilbert, looking for places to shed light on injustice, calling the school, calling parents.

Now it's just pity. There's no higher power to which she can file a complaint. No bill she can pass.

"That's fine," she says after a moment. "You work together, after all."

It slices through me. As if everyone could see why it was a bad idea except for me.

The DJ calls for my mother to come throw the bouquet, and I wave her off with a smile. But as soon as she's gone, I lean on the wall next to a closet, and I let myself cry.

My chest shakes with it, as if it won't ever be full again. Just this morning I'd held her as she slept, and I knew everything was perfect. I'd squeezed myself into her life, but it was working. I fucked it up.

I can't breathe with the ache, and my throat is tight with unvoiced screams. I take one of Dad's old hankies from my pocket and clean my wet face. I stare at his embroidered initials and wish he was here to tell me what to do.

When I can breathe again, I step off the wall and go find more wine. All night I hope I run into her, but she never comes back. I text her over and over and clean up the wedding by myself, as if it was in the plan all along, lying for her when the vendors ask after her.

27

Ama

THE WEDDING

Elliot drives to the ER. He ignores every single word I say in the car, even when I resort to begging. By the time he's lifting me into a wheelchair, I'm back on the phone, checking in with Vince about why Jake says the horses aren't there yet.

"Vince. Vince," I cut him off. "Are you telling me that you didn't leave with enough time to prepare for traffic? Is that what you're telling me?"

Elliot wheels me up to the check-in as I listen to Vince's excuses. He's writing down my name and information as I pull out my health insurance card.

"Vince, just pretend for one second that we're paying customers. Let's *pretend* that we not only rented your horses, but we also bought out your hayrides for today. Let's *imagine* a world where that exists, and get your fucking ass to the park."

I hang up on him and smile up at the nurse behind the desk. "Hi! What's the wait time like today?"

She lifts a brow at me. "Honey, this isn't an Applebee's."

"Right. I just mean, if I need an X-ray, how long am I going to be here? Ballpark?"

Frowning at me, she points to the waiting room, which looks suspiciously full.

Elliot wheels me over and places me next to a chair that he drops into. "You need to chill for a second."

"The wedding starts in an hour." I can hear the terror in my voice. "This is not chill."

"Tell me the list. What do you need to do?"

His voice is calm, and his eyes are on me. I sink into them for a moment, and I remember his mother's wedding—how he let me keep him up all night, how I forced him to listen to my lists, how he got me off just how I needed it. My throat bobs at the memory, and heat flushes my cheeks.

"Prioritizing," I say, thinking. "The wedding arch is possibly broken. The florist needs to arrive at the venue and fix it." I keep from nagging him and just stick to facts. "I need to confirm that the officiant has arrived. I need last looks at the Rose Garden. I need—" Yet another thing suddenly occurs to me and I press my eyes closed. "I need to lay out the programs on the chairs."

"Continue," he says, stopping me from spiraling out.

"I need to be with Jackie and Hazel. Jackie is freaking out. I can hear it in her voice. I haven't even spoken to Hazel since last night. I need to make sure the film crew isn't taking up valuable time and pushing them off schedule." I suck in a breath. My eyes snap to him. "Whitney. I can call Whitney and see if she can spare someone today."

"No." His voice is cold, but his eyes are ice. "No, she isn't getting your big day. Over my dead body, Ama."

It jars me. My foot throbs and my heartbeat stutters as he glares at me.

"Continue," he says firmly. I swallow.

"I need to know that Vince and the horses are set. I need to check the reception hall. I haven't even been there today. I need to get more ice, now that I know the basin is a bathtub. I need to elevate the tub somehow…"

"Elevate?" he asks, and I realize he's not just getting me to calm down. He's listening.

"The 'basin' would have laid on the table next to the bar. Now that it's a tub on the ground, people are bending over, maybe not even seeing it. It needs to be displayed better or…I don't know."

He nods. I take a breath and continue.

"I need to do final checks on catering. I need to double-check George and Mar. I told them how to do the table settings, but I need to see it."

He doesn't tell me I should trust them. He doesn't tell me what should come off the list. "That's all preshow. What are you responsible for at go time?"

The realization that I may not make it to go time is seeping into my veins. I take a shaky breath, and Elliot reaches out, placing a hand on my knee. I look down at it. It calms me for two seconds before I see my knees and dress—scratched and stained from the driveway.

"I need to change my clothes."

"We've moved on," he says. "We're on to go time."

"Jake leads Hazel down the side street to the back of the garden. Mar stands with the bridesmaids in the Airbnb. I cue the musicians. I cue Mar on each bridesmaid. Then I cue both Jake and Mar for the brides to leave from opposite directions and arrive at the center. I cue the music throughout. I cue Jackie and Hazel's carriage to arrive, and shortly after, the line of carriages come. I stay until the last guest is loaded, and then Sarah waits for George to break down the ceremony while Jake and I go to the reception—"

"Alright. We'll start with that," he says, standing. "You are calling Jake about the officiant"—he counts off on his fingers—"calling Mar about the schedule of the wedding party, calling Vince again. I'm going to the Rose Garden now to fix the arch. I'm going to put Ben on bathtub—ice and elevation." He pauses. "Which is comical, considering your condition."

I snort, and something flickers across his face.

"When you're done with your calls," he continues, "you will call me, and cue the wedding from here."

My stomach twists at the impossibility of this. "Can't I just come with you?"

"Not until you've been seen by a doctor."

I'm numb. I feel like everything I've been working toward for seven months—for more than that—is all falling apart.

Elliot reaches forward, and I think he's going to cup my jaw, but instead his fingers carefully remove the Bluetooth from my ear.

"What are you doing?" I ask.

"If I'm going to be the wedding planner today, I need the wedding planner Bluetooth."

There's something very heroic about it all. He gives me one final glance and marches toward the sliding glass doors. I feel my heart lifting—like maybe we can do this. Like maybe it'll be like old times where we created magic together.

Suddenly, Elliot pivots and walks back to me. I'm petrified something's happened—

"How do..." He stares down at the Bluetooth sheepishly. "How do I use this thing?"

28

Ama

THE WEDDING

The officiant is there. The first guests—assholes—have arrived twenty minutes early. Mar says the brides are on schedule, but Jackie keeps crying through her makeup. I'm two seconds away from calling her when Vince calls me back.

"We're here," he grumbles.

"Great. Can I speak to the driver of the bridal carriage, please?"

I get across to the driver the approximate time I'll need him arriving and how I'll cue him.

Bea keeps calling and I keep ignoring. She leaves one voicemail, and I glance at the text of it.

> I'm just offering my support. I know you probably think we're—we're trying to film a good story, but if you need an extra hand, it will be off the record. I really care about this wedding.

I chew on my lip, trying to decide what to do with that.

As I'm staring at my phone, I get a notification from Instagram. Hazel Renee is going live. I click on it and see her gorgeous face.

"So today's my wedding day," she squeals. "I can't show you our wedding clothes, but just know that we are straight fire today. I'm really excited, and I know Jackie is too. Everything's..." She looks around the empty room she's in. I recognize it as the upstairs of the Airbnb. "Everything's really good, but no one can find our wedding planner." She laughs.

My stomach drops. My lips part.

"It's so weird. But I guess she's busy, or whatever."

I can't breathe. My tongue is dry. I can't believe she just... told her millions of followers that I'm MIA on the day of her wedding. The followers who she has been promoting me to for months now.

I close Instagram and stare at the wall. My phone rings, and I'm hoping it's Elliot.

Whitney Harrison calling...

I feel like a child when I hit the green button quickly. "Hi."

"Ama? I just saw something strange on Instagram—"

"Yeah. I saw it too. I'm... I'm at the hospital."

"Oh, Ama. Ama, this is your big day! That can't happen!"

I swallow thickly. She's saying everything I've been thinking. "I'm—I'm on my way over to the venue. Just as soon as I get an X-ray."

"Ama," she says quietly, as if moving into a different room. "If it's just a broken bone, then I don't see what the fuss is about. Get a sling, get a crutch, whatever. Why are you at the hospital for an X-ray?"

"I—I know. I'm—"

"Do you need me at the Rose Garden? I can go there right now and take care of this."

I blink. My throat is tight. "Don't you have like, four weddings today?"

"Mm, I have one, later this evening. Remember when I showed you my calendar? Nothing today."

My eyes press closed as tears leak out of them. I want to scream. I want to ask her why she sabotaged me. But I also want to ask her to go to the Rose Garden. Because Jackie and Hazel need a wedding planner.

There's a beep, and I look at my phone. Elliot is calling. I remember the look on his face when I suggested Whitney, how adamant he's always been about the ways she used me. I tell myself I don't need her. I have him.

"Whitney, I have to go. Thanks for the offer, but we have it under control."

I end her call, and take Elliot's.

"I'm here," he says. "I'm going to fix the arch, then you tell me what to do about programs."

"Okay."

I listen to him moving around, the slam of his truck door, the sounds of the park. The...squawking?

"Ama, we've got geese."

"Damn it. Put Jake on it."

It's only five minutes later when Elliot announces that the wedding arch is fixed. I have an eye on my watch the whole time. We're cutting it too close. I tell him how to lay down the wedding programs—"At an *angle*, Elliot"—and he grumbles his agreement, but I have a sneaking suspicion that those programs are being laid down however Elliot can do it quickest.

I hear someone call his name through the phone and say, "Where's Ama? What's going on?" It's Bea.

"Everything is fine. She's dealing with something, but we have it under control," Elliot responds crisply.

"Okay. Can we get a crew over to her? Whatever is going on, we can help or at least include it in the program—"

"Nope."

"Alright," Bea says, "I know my contract isn't with you, it's with Ama, but we need to be filming the ups and the downs of this day."

"I don't really give a fuck what you film," Elliot says. "My first priority is to this wedding. Then my second is the *flowers* for this wedding."

"Alright, Mr. Bloom—"

"You wanna know where you and your cameras fall on the list? Wayyy down, lady. Maybe twentieth. Twenty-first if there's a flower girl in this wedding."

I snort, listening to him. "You lack finesse, Mr. Bloom," I say.

I hear him huffing, and I assume he's walking quickly away from Bea. "I'm headed to the Airbnb now."

"Okay, confirm with Mar that she feels good about the reception hall."

"Will do."

It's strange listening to him do normal things, having him in my ear while he's walking or grumbling about traffic. It's intimate, and it's something I miss in a way, even though I never fully had it.

"Ama, we got cops."

I blink at the man sitting across from me, holding a bloody towel to his elbow. "Um, okay. Let's see what's up."

"Officer," Elliot says, "I'm Elliot Bloom. I'm temporarily in charge of this event. Can I help you?"

"Mr. Bloom," says a gruff voice. "You have permits for this street closure?"

I gasp and clutch my fanny pack—where the permits are safely tucked. "Fuck."

"We do," Elliot says smoothly. "I can get those for you in a moment. Can I ask if there's a problem, or if you're just checking on us?"

"We had notice of H Street being closed, but not McKinley Boulevard. Could be a miscommunication, but I'd like to see the permits."

"Of course. I'm on the phone with the event coordinator now. I'll clarify. Ama?"

My head is dropped in my hands when I mumble, "They're with me. In my pack."

"Officer, our coordinator does have them. She'll be over shortly," he lies. "I'm just headed to our rental here—"

"Sorry, Mr. Bloom. I need to see that permit or else I'll need you to clear off of McKinley."

"What about a picture of the permit?"

The officer must say no, because then Elliot says, "Ama, hold please."

The line goes dead. I pull the phone back to see if he hung up on me, but the call is still going. Did he mute himself? Is he doing a back alley deal with the cops of Sacramento? Does he not want me to hear his mafia connections?

In the silence, a nurse calls my name. I wave my hand and yell out for her. She sees that I'm unable to walk to the counter and comes out to me.

"Hun, we're gonna get you into an exam room."

"Perfect! Thank you. I'm—I'm actually on an important

call. I'm running a wedding from this ER. Can I be on my phone?"

"A wedding?" Her brows jump up. "You got yourself run over by the newlywed car or something?"

"That would be less embarrassing, but essentially." I grin.

She wheels me out of the lobby and down the hall. "You can keep your phone, but when the doctor comes in, I'll ask you to please hang up so she can examine you."

I check my phone and see Elliot still has me on hold. Then suddenly I hear a tinny sound. "Hello? Elliot?"

"Who am I speaking with?" says a female voice.

Before I can stutter a response, I hear a new male voice. "This is Officer Bell of the Sacramento Police Department."

"Officer Bell," the woman says, "good afternoon. This is Senator Laura Gilbert with the state senate."

I clap a hand over my mouth. When the nurse sees my eyes bug out, she mouths, "Bride running?"

I shake my head and listen to Laura, not knowing if she's aware I'm on the line.

"Officer, I hear there's a permit issue. I know you're doing exactly what you need to be doing. I appreciate your work. I just want to know what I can do to help this process."

Officer Bell clears his throat. "Ah, Senator. Well, we need to see the permit for closing off this street. It's not on our records."

"Can we send you a photograph of the permit?"

"Uh, sorry, Senator—"

"I can get the city manager on the line and confirm that it's in the system. Would that work?"

"It's—it's Saturday, ma'am."

"Please call me Senator Gilbert. Would you like me to call the city manager so you can speak directly to him? Or I can call Chief Adams of the Sacramento PD to clarify. I have both of their numbers."

I feel like I can just imagine Officer Bell scratching his stubble. "I . . . No, Senator. There's no problem. I will contact Chief Adams myself and ask him to double-check his records for today."

"That's wonderful, Officer Bell. I'm glad to hear it." Laura hangs up.

The nurse gives me a wave to say the doctor will be in soon. I send her a thumbs-up.

Elliot's voice comes back on the line. "Ama? Still there?"

"You had to call your moooom," I sing-song.

"You forgot your permits," he mimics back. "I'm at the Airbnb. Is it unlocked?"

"Should be."

I hear him knock and then open the door. There's a flurry of activity on his side. People are asking for me, the bouquets, a Valium.

"Where's Hazel?" Elliot asks.

I hear him cutting through the crowd of people and heading upstairs. He knocks on a door.

"Hazel? Ama is on the phone, checking in."

"Oh my god, where is she?" I hear Hazel say. Is that annoyance I hear tinged in her tone?

"She's dealing with an issue and delegating to keep us on schedule."

"What's the issue?"

"Don't tell her," I say to him. I'm seriously mortified that I've already jeopardized this wedding so much by not reading the email from Kim Nguyen, by trying to lift a bathtub myself, by not having enough assistants. This day is about the couple, and

I've made it about me so much already. And I don't want her followers to know this too.

"Last-minute issues. She told me to come to you first because she knows she's been neglecting you."

"I mean," she starts, then pauses. "Yeah, I'm fine. Just wish I knew what was going on."

I coach Elliot to tell her "You're getting married today." He repeats after me. "That's what's going on. And smile at her."

"That's what's going on," he repeats. "And smil—"

"Not her! You smile!"

"And smiling...will be had by all," he finishes lamely.

I hear Hazel say, "O-kay."

"Ama is available by phone if needed," he says, and then I hear the door shut. "Where's Jackie?" he asks someone in the hall.

"Last door!"

Another knock. Another door opens.

"Elliot! What's going on? Is it time for the bouquets already?" There's a hysterical quality to her voice that spikes my blood pressure.

"Wow. Jackie. You look amazing," he says, and I can almost see it myself.

"Thanks. I'm just...God, Elliot. Where the fuck is Ama?!"

"Tell her. Tell her and not Hazel," I say.

He coughs. "Ama injured herself." Jackie gasps. "She's at the hospital getting checked now."

There's a whine and a sniffle, and I close my eyes as I realize Jackie is starting to cry through her makeup again. I'm praying for the Hazel Renee setting spray to work its miracles.

"Hey, hey. She's fine." There are sounds of Elliot getting closer. "Jackie, we've got this under control. You're getting married."

"Mm-hmm," she says, voice tight like a reed. "I just... Today's been really stressful. And Hazel didn't want us to see each other beforehand, even though I asked her if we could please—" She chokes a sob. "I don't want to sound ungrateful for everything you and Ama have created for today, but this doesn't even feel like my wedding anymore."

I pinch the bridge of my nose. "Damn it."

"I can see that," Elliot sympathizes. "That's really hard."

"And she's—she's doing Instagram videos instead of sitting in here holding my hand. And I'm just...I just keep thinking that...What if this isn't right? What if I stop loving her one day?"

"Put me on," I say. "Give her the Bluetooth."

I hear Elliot tap the device, like a sonic boom in my ear. "Jackie," he says softly.

"Elliot, give me to her."

I hear the Bluetooth get tapped again, and I think he's trying to hang up on me, or mute me. But I can still hear Jackie sniffing.

"That's not how it works," he says. "There is no falling out of love for people like you and me."

I hold my breath. My skin buzzes.

"I see how you are with Hazel," he says. "Trust me, I know that when you're in love with a person who's that dedicated to their career, sometimes you don't feel like you come first."

My eyes press closed, and I stay deathly quiet, begging him to continue.

"Sometimes you just count down the days, the hours, until you can be useful again," he says. "And if it ever ends, Jackie?" He lowers his voice. "You're still counting away. The months since. The exact days since. Like a tally of moments you've spent not being important to them. But don't ever think you'll wake up and not be in love with her."

I need air. My lungs won't work, and I can't hear anything aside from Elliot and my heartbeat.

Suddenly, there's a knock on the exam room door and the doctor steps in. I throw my hand up like a man drowning and wave at her to be quiet. She squints at me in confusion, and I point to my phone, mouthing "I'm sorry."

"God," Jackie says. "Elliot, I shouldn't have pushed you to date Ama. I didn't know you were still in love with Kate."

I feel like an antique tub has fallen on my stomach this time. Kate. The girl after. Is it possible he's not talking about me?

He clears his throat. "It's . . . I just wanted you to know that you won't fall out of love," he says. "It's been years, and I can still tell you the number of days since she last needed me. Since I last held her through the night."

I suck in a breath. It is me. I hang up, hearing everything I needed to. I look up to the doctor with wet eyes and say, "Sorry, I'm . . . a wedding planner and I'm here instead of the wedding."

The doctor is an older woman with kind eyes. "Aw. Did you just hear the vows?"

I bite my lip and nod.

29

Ama

THE WEDDING

It's a hairline fracture across my metatarsal, whatever that means. The doctor got me into radiology within twenty minutes because I couldn't stop crying about how I was going to miss the whole thing.

On the way out of radiology, Elliot calls, and I walk him through the cues for the ceremony again. He remembers everything I said in the waiting room, and now it's just trusting him to know how to count measures of music. I cue the wedding with him as the nurses wheel me back to the exam room, and when I say, "Go bride," one of the patients in the hallway looks at me like I belong in the psych ward. Once the wedding has started, Elliot hangs up to focus, and I send him the phone number of the bridal carriage driver to cue.

The doctor sets me up with crutches and a walking boot and gives me an appointment to come back on Monday to get a cast on it. I take the painkillers they give me and order an Uber as I buy a pair of flat shoes in the hospital gift shop to fit my one good foot.

Elliot texts the group chat of me, Mar, Sarah, and Jake to say the bridal carriage is off and the first guest carriage is loading, so I set the Uber destination for the reception. I have to tell my driver about the street closures around the park, to which he says, "That's ridiculous."

"It's a wedding, I think?" I say innocently.

"What genius thought of this?!"

I press my lips shut and stare out my window as he follows the detour signs.

He drives up the side street to drop me at the back entrance, where the caterers entered. He helps me get on my crutches, so I'll forgive him the remarks.

As I'm navigating stepping up to the curb, Bea's van pulls up to the front, about twenty yards away. I take a fortifying breath, knowing I'm likely to end up on TLC in my boot and crutches. The two cameramen and the sound guy jump out, grabbing their equipment and scurrying to be inside when the first guests arrive. I'm just reaching for the back door when Bea jumps out of the driver's seat, and the passenger door opens to reveal Whitney Harrison.

My breath stops. She's dressed in her pale blue Stella McCartney—her favorite for interviews or important weddings. She has an iPad in one hand and a Bluetooth in an ear. She's talking quickly with Bea, nodding and looking over the venue with laser-focused concentration.

She looks like the wedding planner. She looks like Hazel and Jackie's wedding planner.

I told her not to come, and she came anyway.

I'm trying to catch my breath as my thoughts tumble around my head.

Bea catches sight of me first. She smiles in such relief that I don't know what to think. As she runs over to me, Whitney looks out over the street, waiting for the first guests to arrive.

"Ama, god!" Bea reaches out for my elbow to help me up on the sidewalk. "What happened?"

"What's Whitney Harrison doing here?" My voice is hollow. As if her ears were ringing, Whitney turns, sees me, and waves merrily from halfway down the street.

"What's—What do you mean?" Bea says, brows drawing together. "She said you called her to come run the wedding."

"Elliot ran the wedding," I snap.

"Yeah, but—well, Whitney managed Hazel. She walked her around the park with Jake, she took the 'go bride' cue—"

My crutches really get in the way of the angry stride I'm trying to accomplish, but I still make it to throwing distance of Whitney.

"What are you doing here?" I snap.

"Ama, oh my goodness," she says sweetly. "Is it broken, dear?"

"I told you I had it under control. I told you I didn't need you."

Whitney gives me that face—that face that she used to give brides who asked if she had any cheaper packages—as if to say *Bless your heart.*

"Ama. Clearly you *do* need me. There was no wedding planner here!" She chuckles.

"The wedding was called perfectly without you—"

"Of course, and Elliot did well with what little experience he has, but Hazel Renee was clearly not happy with you." She reaches out to squeeze my shoulder, and I jerk it back. "Ama—"

"Why did you overbook your vendors for today?" I say.

She tilts her head. "What are you talking about?"

"I know you scheduled at least three fictional weddings today—*after* I gave you the date. *After* I came to you for advice."

"Ama, you left my company on good terms," she says simply. "I will always support you, but I'm not going to turn down work for you. After we talked, I booked up. I mean, how long did you wait to contact those vendors after we talked? How long was I expected to wait to book?"

Acid in my stomach burns up to my throat. "What happened to those three weddings then? You only have one later today. That's what you told me."

"They canceled." She shrugs. Like it's easy. "Things change. One day, when you start working in as high of a volume as I do, you'll see three weddings cancel, just like *that*." She snaps.

I don't believe her. I have Elliot's voice ringing in my ear from years ago, telling me that she copied my designs, that she underpaid me. I can feel her nails like claws in my arm, hissing *Be a professional* in my ear as my hand throbs and my tears fall, my skin still buzzing with the memory of a stranger's hand on my ass. A clarity washes over me, warm and focused.

"You're right," I say softly. "One day, I'll know what it's like to have four weddings in one day. One day, I'll understand what it's like to book up so quickly that I forget the conversation I had two days ago." I nod, a smile curling my lips. "Because I'm coming, Whitney. I'm on my way up, and nothing you do to sabotage my business is going to stop me. I'm worth ten of you. I've *always* been worth ten of you, and you were right to fear me moving in on your market."

Something shifts behind her cool blue eyes. I step into her, ignoring the pain that lances up my leg, and say, "Now, back the fuck away from my wedding."

Whitney's lips are tight. Her gaze cold. But I'm not afraid of her anymore. I hear the click of horse hooves as the first carriages approach. It's only now that I see one of Bea's cameras pointed at the two of us.

She leans into me, and her teeth click over her consonants. "You think you can speak to me like that? I *made* you. How many clients have I sent your way, just for you to repay me like this? You think you're moving in on my market? *My* market?! I've been working nationally while you've been slutting it up at bachelorette parties and flirting with my vendors just to get the same discounts."

My jaw drops. A laugh bursts from my throat. "I don't know what's funnier—that you think San Francisco and Lake Tahoe qualify as 'nationally,' or that you think you're the only wedding planner who gets industry discounts. Bye, Whitney. I have a reception to run."

Her claws reach out, snatching my arm. "Don't walk away from me, you ungrateful bitch—"

I get to see the moment Whitney realizes we're being filmed. It is—by far—the greatest moment of my life. She goes pale underneath her concealer, and her neck snaps to the cameraman inching closer to us. She's speechless.

I place a condescending hand on her shoulder, like she always did to me. "Whitney, come on. Be a professional."

She seethes, steam practically spouting from her ears. She spins on her heel and marches into the street just as the first horse arrives. Whitney jumps back, screeches, and the horse rears on his hind legs. I gasp, slapping my hand over my mouth. She scurries out of its way in just enough time, but the carriage driver has to soothe the horse.

As soon as the shock has passed and I realize how comical that really was, I turn over my shoulder to Nick, the camera guy. "Did you get that?" I say with a smile. He nods, smirking.

I take a deep breath and paste on a smile to greet the first guests, apologizing for that moment with the horse. Bea is still standing on the sidewalk, grinning from ear to ear.

"So, you probably can't use that footage, huh?" I say. "She won't sign a waiver now."

"She already signed a waiver." Bea's lips twitch. "At the bridal boutique. When she approached me about being interviewed."

I blink at her. "You interviewed her? What did she say?"

Bea steps closer. "She said that you worked under her. She taught you everything you know. And…that you were too inexperienced for a wedding of this magnitude."

Heat flushes my cheeks. My teeth grind together.

"So," Bea continues, "I'm just imagining how great that will be, juxtaposed with what just happened here." She beams at me. "I *love* good drama."

"Well, you're very welcome." I lean on my crutches. "Let's go have a party."

Bea meets with her team, and I hobble to the back door, not wanting my crutches and stained dress to catch too much attention. The catering coordinator greets me like I haven't been missing this whole time. There's a quick exchange of words about my boot and crutches, but soon I'm stepping through the make-shift kitchen and into the fairytale wedding that I created.

Even though everything here was in a design either drawn or rendered by me, it still knocks me off my feet to see this old dance studio that we turned into a wedding reception. Elliot's floral chandeliers are being lit from the sides by soft LEDs, and his columns with vases of queen protea sit in every corner. There was no time for first look with Hazel and Jackie, but the dining area is well preserved for their grand entrance, as the guests are directed up to the roof for cocktail hour. The girls will see all of this for the first time when they arrive.

I mill through it as the guests arrive, checking every place setting, every centerpiece. I shift things slightly, I straighten knives, but really—it's almost perfect.

A guest comes down the stairs and gestures to her friend. "You have *got* to see this!"

And I just know she means the dance floor.

After I confirm that all the guest carriages have arrived and everyone has headed to the roof for cocktail hour, I heave my way over to the bottom of the stairs. I shake my head at the stair lift that we installed to meet ADA standards. I sigh and push the button for the chair to come down to me, chuckling at how things had turned out.

When I'm at the top of the stairs and back on my crutches, I get to see the rooftop for the first time since Thursday.

It's absolutely remarkable. The guests step over Elliot's gorgeous dance floor tentatively, as if afraid to walk on it. Some of them point down to it, nodding to their friends, taking pictures. The cocktail tables are set perfectly, and the boxwood lining the sides of the rooftop brighten everything up. I see the canapés being rotated, and the guests giving orgasm eyes after the first bite. I see the second bar line, just as full as the first, and I pat myself on the back for knowing my Hollywood winos.

And I also see an antique tub holding craft beer, displayed on god knows what, but it's three feet tall and perfect with a tablecloth thrown over it. And next to it, Jackie's mom is placing a proud hand on the side, showing it off to whoever will listen.

"Basin," I huff under my breath. And that's when I finally see Mar.

She's standing in the corner, eyes flitting over everything, like she's cataloging the places she could have missed something. Her gaze lands on me and she jumps. She rushes over to me on her long legs and sweeps me into her arms.

"Ama."

"You did it, babe. You're killing this."

"*You* did it." She pulls back from me. "You did all of this."

At that moment, the wedding announcer takes the mic. "Ladies and gentlemen, please turn your attention to the entrance. The happy couple are almost here."

The crowd titters. I frown at my watch. "Already?"

"Yep," Mar says. "Elliot kept us on time."

As the bridesmaids finally make it upstairs, I get to see the *wow* on their faces as they emerge into the autumn air. Bea and her crew are cataloging every moment. Not five minutes later, I hear Jackie scream from below, and before I can be concerned, Hazel starts laughing.

I wish I could be down there with them to see their reaction to the once bat-infested, abandoned dump I remade for them. But I know Bea is getting it.

"Ama."

I turn and there's Laura Gilbert. My heart jumps.

"Senator. Thank you so much for your help today with the permits."

She waves her hand. "Not at all. And call me Laura."

I absolutely will not.

She continues, "I am so blown away by this. I mean, I adored my wedding, but this is clearly your forte. I'm so glad I pushed Jackie toward hiring you."

"Me too," I say with a smile. "I was honored that you did."

"Well..." She leans in conspiratorially. "I couldn't let that wicked witch have all the fun." I'm about to tell her she'll enjoy what the filmmakers caught, when she says, "And I was happy to see you and Elliot working together again. You go so well together."

My voice is stuck in my throat.

"In business, I mean," she says. When she winks, I think I pass out for a few seconds, then the announcer is tapping the mic again.

"For the first time as a couple, please welcome Hazel Renee and Jackie Nguyen!"

I refocus my attention and let Laura Gilbert slip away through the crowd.

The guests whoop and yell. Jackie and Hazel run upstairs. Jackie is already sobbing, and her friends and family laugh, like this is to be expected. I wonder if she cried throughout the entire ceremony. I'll have to ask someone.

Hazel is speechless on the threshold. I see her take in everything, holding on to her bride, and beaming. She goes off script when she gestures for the announcer to hand her the mic. She drags Jackie up onto the dance floor to stand center.

"I just have to say—I know I'm not supposed to speak yet," Hazel says. The crowd laughs. Jackie sobs. "But our wedding planner wouldn't let us see this for the last two months. You don't wanna know what was here when we last saw the place! So I hope that explains why Jackie can't get ahold of herself."

There's polite laughter, but none of it is louder than Jackie's whimper. Jackie brushes her eyelashes and then gasps. "My grandpa's tub!"

My foot throbs in gratitude.

Hazel continues, "And our wedding planner is really the brains behind this. She created this from nothing. She's been out of commission today, unfortunately—"

Jackie jerks. She's pointing at me. "Ama's here!"

And suddenly I'm crying and waving and hobbling forward. Jackie and Hazel cross the room to me and both hug me. It's a tornado of questions and answers and gratitude and joy, and I'm so swept up in it that I'm surprised I even notice Elliot entering the rooftop from the door, looking for a place to just rest his feet for ten minutes. He looks haggard, never having changed into nicer clothes from this morning, and dirty in the way that he makes look good.

He catches sight of me at the edge of the platform with Hazel and Jackie. His eyes slide to the boot, and he glares. It seems I'm in trouble.

I get the announcer to continue, inviting the guests to get drinks at the bar, find their table numbers on the seating chart, and then head downstairs to their tables. I encourage Jackie and Hazel to take a few more minutes up here and then start moving themselves back downstairs to the head table. I snap for the photography team to catch every moment.

Once everyone is cleared from the rooftop, I take the chairlift down and set up in a corner where I can see the whole room. Mar gladly hands over the walkie-talkie and goes to grab me a chair. I put the earpiece in, press the Talk button, and say, "Ama's on headset."

Jake's voice comes quickly. "Oh, thank god."

"Sarah, how is the Rose Garden? Is George almost done packing up?"

"Who is George?" she asks lazily.

I take a deep breath, reminding myself I can't kill her until the wedding is done. "He is the rental coordinator." When she doesn't respond to that, I say, "Large, red hair, fifties. You are supposed to be waiting for his team to finish packing up the ceremony."

"Oh, yeah. He's almost done," she says.

"Okay," I say. "I need Jake to meet with Vince and the horses to make sure we're all squared away. Jake, you'll need to dismantle the arches. I'll send Mar with you."

Mar groans and then reluctantly nods.

"I can go. Let Mar stay." Elliot's voice. I search for him in the crowd, but I can't find him.

"Perfect, thank you. I could use Mar's feet. You'll let me know if you have an issue breaking down the floral arches?"

"Yep."

I turn to Mar and say off-walkie, "Can you do a round for me and check to make sure we're not slowing down on canapés?" Once she's gone, I say into the walkie, "I'm back in action. You all did amazing work today. I think the brides are crazy happy, and it's all thanks to you."

The next hour goes like all receptions do—in a blur. The food is ready to come out on time, but the guests hover near the downstairs bar, so we hold for fifteen minutes and give the bartenders a spiel to say about dinner starting soon. After the third server stops me to ask how I hurt myself, I ditch the crutches and hobble on my boot. There's a cord situation with the live band, and the bassist is seconds away from running to Guitar Center when someone taps me on the shoulder.

"Do you need a quarter-inch cable?"

I look up, up, up a broad chest to a stern-looking, dark-haired guy in a black leather jacket. His lashes are long, and his jaw is perfectly chiseled. Whoa.

"Yes," I squeak, realizing he's over a foot taller than me. I see the cello case in his hand. "Oh! Are you Xander? Our ceremony cellist?" He nods. "I heard my assistant asked you to keep an eye on things earlier. Thank you so much for that. We had a really important errand, and we would never usually ask."

"Sure."

I wait for him to say more, but it's possible I've found someone who speaks less than Elliot.

"So, you have a cable?"

He kneels down to open his case, and grabs a cord from a side pocket. As I'm texting the bassist to let him know I've got the cord, Xander says, "This is a really nice wedding."

I grin up at him. It looks like giving compliments physically pains him. "Thank you! I'm so glad you could fly in for it. Please enjoy the rest of the night, and I'll get this back to you."

He shakes his head. "I'm headed to the airport now. Just keep it."

Without much more ceremony, he grabs his cello case, squeezes Hazel's shoulder in goodbye, and walks out the door.

Hazel catches sight of me frowning after him and sidles up to me. "I'm sorry if he was short with you. He's always been temperamental, even when we were kids."

"Oh, no," I say. "He just saved the day, actually."

"You'll be seeing more of him. He and I have dozens of friends who are engaged."

I knock her elbow. "Why would your LA and New York friends want a Sacramento wedding?"

"You think you'll be stuck doing only Sacramento? Ama, I have ten New York couples who are already looking at you. I want to introduce you to some of them tonight."

My stomach flutters, and I look down at my dirty dress

and walking boot. "Great. Hey, I'm sorry I wasn't there for you today."

She waves her hand. "It's fine. I actually..." She sighs dramatically. "I did an Instagram Live today that was unfair to you, I think."

"Oh really?" I ask innocently.

"I'd like to fix it though." She takes out her phone and opens Instagram. She takes a selfie with me, and before I know it, Jackie is joining us. They both kiss my cheeks from either side and I'm beaming like a dork.

When I'm tagged two minutes later, Hazel's caption says *This is my wedding planner, Ama Torres. She works in Sacramento, but LA better look out.* When I slide to the next frame, she's got amazing shots of the reception and the horse-drawn carriage ride. The last frame is just a blue background with my name, email, and website in white lettering.

I shake my head and grin. It's not an Instagram Story that will go away. It will always stay up as part of the wedding pictures she posts. I'm still pinching myself that I got this gig, but even more so, that I might be friends with Hazel Renee. *And* Jackie Nguyen. The world didn't end when I allowed myself to get close to them. In fact, it got bigger and better.

Once the cake is cut, I step outside into the alley and breathe. My foot is killing me. I have a sore ass from where I fell this morning, and my body is rebelling because I haven't eaten.

The door opens next to me, and I jerk to see Elliot stepping out. He extends the Bluetooth to me.

"Did you like your first gig as a wedding planner?" I tease.

"Uh, no. I'll stick to flowers." Then he produces a water bottle from the bar and two Advil from his pocket.

I swallow greedily. "Why didn't you say that Whitney showed up?" I ask.

He cocks his head. "She said you called her."

"I didn't."

His eyes harden. "Ah. Well, you mentioned her in the ER, so I assumed..."

"I sent her packing. Bea got it all on film," I say proudly.

His mouth twitches. "That's all the reason I need to watch this stupid show when it airs."

I smile at him. "Thank you for today. And not just today. This wedding...this reception...it's insane. The floral is astounding. I can't believe I made you do all this."

"You didn't make me. I'm...I'm hoping to elevate Blooming, so this is just as...'insane' for me."

I nod. "Good. You're...you're so special, Elliot." Tears prick behind my eyes. "And I can't ever thank you enough for getting this wedding up on its feet today. You've always told me that I need more help, but I really thought I had this one under control."

I choke on my words. The full weight of what happened today hits me.

"It could have been really bad," I say. "I was...I couldn't get to my phone. And I just had to wait for someone to call me or I had to scream for the neighbors, and I just...And then you called."

"Because I broke the arch," he jokes lightly.

"Right." I smile, sniffling. "Maybe it's your turn to get an assistant."

He smiles at me. And it's the first time I've seen it directed toward me since—since he asked me to marry him. My heart hurts with the absence of it. I miss him so much even when I'm near him. I can hear his words to Jackie beating against my skull, and I don't know if he knows that I heard. But I *did* hear.

He's standing there against the brick building with me. I step forward—limping—and rise up on my good toes. He tilts his mouth down to meet mine, and the simple movement cracks my chest in half. I sob against his lips for a moment, threading my hands into his hair. His arms wrap around my back, and I can feel his hands searching for the ends of my hair like they used to, but my hair's cut short now. I press myself against him, and it all fits again. He smells like soil and roses, and I'm so short without heels on that I need to climb him like a monkey. His mouth parts against mine, and I cry more.

I whisper into his skin, "I love you. Elliot, I...I do."

He holds me for a second, and I'm waiting to hear him say it back.

His arms slip from around my ribs, and carefully, he puts me back a step. He won't meet my eye when he says, "I can't. Not...not again. I can't."

Head down, he moves away from me. He disappears around the corner, walking down the alley. I try to follow him. I call his name once. He doesn't turn back.

30

Ama

**TWO YEARS, NINE MONTHS,
ONE WEEK, AND ONE DAY AGO**

New Year's Eve

My feet carry me off the dance floor and away from him. I have the urge to keep running until I'm in a different country, but I find a closet in an abandoned hallway—and that will do just fine.

A call is beeping in my Bluetooth, and I know it's him. I rip it out and stuff it in my pack. Once the door is shut behind me, I lean back, inhaling the scent of bleach and cleaning products.

Marry me.

His voice is still so clear in my mind. I can see his dark eyes when I close my own, staring at me like a painting he wants to look at for the rest of his life.

He ruined it. With two words, he's set it on fire.

Pressing the heels of my hands into my eyes, I focus on taking deep breaths.

Or maybe it was me. Maybe I'm the problem. Maybe there are next steps that are obvious to everyone but me.

What's the next step then, Ama?

What did I expect? I suppose I expected us to outgrow each other soon. Six months is a long time. I suppose I was waiting for it to end, like all things do. But he's right about a lot. I *was* planning for the future. I was okay with tangling him up in my life forever, not expecting an ending.

My throat is tight, and my fingernails scratch at it.

A voice from outside the closet makes me jump. "What's wrong?"

I recognize Laura Gilbert's voice, and I slap my hand to my mouth. Does she know I'm in here? I press my ear to the door.

"I saw you dancing with Ama," Laura continues. "You make a fine couple—"

"We're not."

Elliot. I jerk back from the door. My heart is pounding so loudly that I know they'll hear me soon. I didn't see him follow me off the dance floor, but now here he is.

"That's fine," Laura says. "You work together after all."

It sounds cold. Minimizing. It's exactly what I said to him.

I stare at the door, knowing Elliot is on the other side of it. I press my palm to it, half wishing to swing it open to be with him.

There's nothing for a while. I lean close, waiting to see if they're still there.

A strange hum, a rumble. It's an echo of Elliot's laugh, only hollow. He breathes deeply, and I hear the air catch in his throat.

Sadness rattles out of him. I freeze, listening to something so private, something he hasn't given to me yet, despite the many times I've cried in frustration to him.

He gasps for air, and I allow myself to do the same.

Maybe it doesn't have to be this way. He said nothing had to change—it could be unsaid. But I would always know it in my heart. I would always know that he cried when I told him no. That he found a quiet hallway and wept.

He sniffs, and I hear him compose himself. He clears his throat, and his heavy footfalls move away.

My hand reaches for the doorknob to go after him—

And it drops.

I don't even know what I would say if I went after him. I don't want anything to change, and he does. Wouldn't we be in the same position?

My chest aches, I feel like there's a muscle overworked between my ribs, tugging and refusing to stretch. I wipe my eyes and sneak out of the closet, crossing quickly to the exit and out into the street.

I get to my car, and before I can overthink it, I'm driving home, ditching the wedding, ditching the cleanup. I'll come back when it's over, but for right now, I need to get away from him.

I turn onto my street, and my car slows. Do I really need to get away? I second-guess everything from the last thirty minutes. What would have changed? Yes, things could end; yes, it may be a terrible decision—but is it any different from right now?

If I'm opposed to marriage, does that mean I'm also opposed to being together for as long as we both shall live? Forever with Elliot feels different from any other kind of forever I've thought of. It feels soft and inviting. It feels like warm baths and Sunday mornings and flowers with perfect-shaped petals. But I still don't want to bind us together based on these *feelings*—changeable and erratic feelings.

I could ask him if I could have forever without a white dress and a piece of paper.

My car stops, and just as I'm turning the wheel to flip it around and run back, I see my mother's car parked in front of my house. Curious, I pull forward and park behind her. She waves and gets out of her car as I do the same.

"Mom? What's wrong?"

She smiles, and there's something missing. "Bob and I..." Shaking her head, she knows she doesn't need to say more.

"Why?" I ask, suddenly needing to know. I've never asked in the past, but I'm desperate to hear her tell me what ends a relationship.

She shrugs. "We're going different directions. And it's easier to get ahead of it before it goes too far."

I think of the direction Elliot is going, and the way I want to be parallel to it. The space I wanted to carve out for myself in his life, in his work, in his shop. How all of it is gone now. I nod, pretending to understand. "And what does that mean?"

"Well, Bob wanted to start house hunting outside of California. I didn't," she says. "There's no need for one of us to sacrifice what we want now, when it will all just come apart one day."

Sacrifice. Either we go back how it was and Elliot sacrifices, or we get married and I do.

"When things end," I ask, "is it you who ends them? Or them?"

"Hm...It depends. Today, it was me." She grabs her overnight bag out of the car. "Why do you ask?"

I stand in the middle of the street, my keys still tight in my hand. I ignore her question and say, "Do you think any of them will ever be the one? The final one?"

She tilts her head at me. "Maybe. But I don't think so." Heaving her bag onto her shoulder, she considers for a moment. "There's no perfect someone for everyone. There's just promises and weddings. One can be broken. The other—"

"Is just a party," I finish for her. She smiles at me.

She shuts the car door, and I watch her walk up to my porch. I stare down at my keys.

I could make a promise to Elliot that will only get broken. But why would I put him through that? Why agree to marriage or even just going back to what we had, when I know now that it will end? It will, because he wants something I don't believe in.

The wind pushes through my hair, twisting it around my face. Why begin, when it will end?

I pocket my car keys and follow my mother up to my door. I text my assistants at the Sutter Club that I can't come back.

31

Ama

THE DAY AFTER THE WEDDING

On Sunday morning, there's an email in my inbox from *Sacramento Magazine*, asking to do a feature piece on me and the Hazel Renee wedding. Just under it, TheKnot.com has asked for an exclusive.

It's a lot, to see it all come true. This is exactly what I wanted, only I thought I'd have full mobility and that maybe I'd get to see the wedding in question, but regardless, I'm on my way.

I just never thought I'd be curled up the next morning, wishing I hadn't kissed Elliot Bloom—that my one regret would be Elliot, again.

There's a knock on my door at nine a.m., and I let Mar in with her box of donuts. She's chatty and excitable, reliving all the wonderful things from yesterday.

"Can I hire you on?" I ask, interrupting her. "Photography will always be your main purpose, but can I give you an assistant job?"

Mar shrugs. "You know, I really liked yesterday, but I don't think it's my thing." She smiles at me over her coffee cup. "But Jake, on the other hand..."

"Ugh. No." I close my eyes.

"Yes, Ama. He's obsessed with this whole thing. Think of you when you were young. Didn't you do stupid shit in your first years?"

A white handkerchief flashes in my mind. The sting of bruised knuckles. "I know I did."

"Give him a chance to grow out of his jackrabbit anxiety stage," Mar says. "It'll be good for you to have an eager kid just itching to run to CVS for you."

I nod, chewing my chocolate old-fashioned. "So... What did you promise Michael to get him to come help yesterday?"

"No, no, no." She sets her mug down. "You think I came over here to tell you to hire Jake and complain about my ex? No. I want to know what you and Elliot are up to."

"Nothing," I say. "There's... He was there for me yesterday big-time. But..." I hesitate, but there's no ugly part of me that Mar hasn't seen. "I kissed him and he ran."

Her eyes widen before she can catch herself. She picks her mug up again. "Okay. Okay, that's... Okay." She sips, trying to keep it in. "So that's actually what you did. Essentially."

"No. No, he *proposed* last time."

"And what did that kiss mean if not a proposal, Ama?"

My chest tightens. It reminds me of his mother's wedding, when he asked where I thought we were headed if not marriage.

"Because," Mar continues, "I know you didn't kiss him just to hook up again. And I know you're smart enough to know he's not going to want to just pick back up—"

"Am I?" I drop my head in my hands. "Am I smart enough? I feel very...unsmart."

Mar is silent until I feel I can look at her again. She lets me just chew on my lip and think for a bit until she says, "What do you want? If there were no consequences to your actions, what would you want?"

"To be with him," I say softly. I sniff back the tears that spring.

"For how long?"

I press my lips together. I look up at her.

I pull into the Blooming parking lot at nine thirty. They open at ten on Sundays, but I can't wait for this. I drove over with my left foot on the pedal since my right is in a boot. I haven't showered. I'm not even sure I brushed my teeth.

I crutch my way over to the front door, and after I peer in to see if it's dark, I hobble over to the parking lot. His truck is here. I pound on his side door to the showroom.

When the metal door swings open, I lose my breath at the sight of him. He's in one of my favorite Henleys and the tight jeans that I can barely fit my hand into. He blinks down at me before opening the door wide to let me in. I squeeze past him, my crutches clicking on the floor in the silence.

"What's the occasion?" he says, frowning down at the boot.

Once I've leaned the crutches on the wall, I turn to him. "I made a mistake."

His lips press together. "We can forget about the kiss."

"Not last night. Kissing you was very purposeful," I say. "A few years ago."

His eyes dart between mine before he crosses his arms and waits for me to continue.

"I kissed you because I miss you. Because I still want you." My heart pounds, and I watch him swallow but remain still. "Because I shouldn't have left your mother's wedding, and I shouldn't have given you the gift of the Franklinia and then made you feel like we weren't even close to talking about forever. Because we were. We were forever. I just didn't want a marriage."

He stares down at the workbench—the old weathered one that feels like him in this studio of bright fluorescents and white walls.

"You told me, and I didn't hear it," he says. "It was my fault."

"It wasn't." I step forward on my good leg, and he reaches out quickly to steady me. He wraps his fingers under my elbow, and I place my hand over them. "I wasn't ready. You were my first relationship, and I've grown up knowing that you don't only get one. But...I only want one."

He slips his hand from my skin, and before he can run—before he can say anything—I tuck my bad leg behind me, and I kneel onto my right knee. I look up at him from the floor of the back room where we used to make love, from the place I first fell in love with not only his work but him, and I say, "I only want you. And I'm ready now."

I can't read his face. My eyes are pricking, and he's getting blurry. So I clarify, repeating his words. "Marry me."

32

Elliot

NOW

It's been two years, nine months, one week, and three days since we've been in this back room alone together like this, and all the memories flooded in with her when she crossed the threshold. I stare at her, on one knee, one foot in a walking boot, and her eyes hopeful.

I can still feel the press of her mouth against mine from last night. The way she clung to me. I couldn't sleep last night with the ghost of it hanging on to me.

Marry me.

I clear my throat to keep from choking on the answer, and I step backward. I see her face fall.

"That's not... That's not necessary," I respond. It feels dull and stupid on my lips.

She stays there, on one knee. Waiting for me. It burns a hole in my chest to see her confidence drain like this, but I can't do this. I can't allow her to change everything she wants after just one kiss. That's what we did last time. And look where it got us.

Ama loves big gestures. It's the wedding planner in her. I think of the email about the Franklinia tree—how she just wanted to give me something, and in return I took too much. There's a piece of my chest that's fighting to slot back into place, hearing that she still wants me and hoping. But Ama doesn't want to get married.

She's still on the ground, so I kneel down and grip her elbows to help her stand. But she stops me and keeps me on the ground with her.

"Not necessary," she repeats. "What does that mean?"

Her eyes are wet. I can smell her hair from this close.

"It's not—" I shake my head, gazing at a place beyond her ear. "You don't need to do all this."

I feel her fingers push into my shoulders. Her eyes are wide and almost scared. "I heard you talking to Jackie. You tried to mute, but you didn't."

Fucking Bluetooth. My mind hurries to remember all I said. Things about not ever falling out of love, about needing to feel useful to her, and tallying the days... Waking up in the morning and counting every moment backward. Three years, four months, two weeks, and two days since our first kiss. Three years, two months, and two days since I first slept over. Two years, nine months, one week, and one day since I made a huge mistake.

I look into her eyes, praying she doesn't know what I meant. Suddenly, she looks away from me.

"Right," she says. "It was—it was someone else. Sorry. I'm—I got confused, but we can forget this."

I'm still trying to mentally catch up to her when she starts to push to her feet. I help her up, ready to make sure she understands. "Ama—"

"Can we work together again?" she says quickly. "I—I get now that we won't be together, but the wedding... The work we do is too amazing, Elliot, and I don't think I can lose it again—"

A puff of air bursts out of me. I run a hand through my hair and try not to laugh at her. "You're never done working. You..." I smile and shake my head. "You just proposed to me, and pivoted so quickly to business."

I watch her try to figure out if that's a good thing or a bad thing and can't help the feeling that we're inching closer to it—to the moment. She needs me again. She *wants* me again. And I've never stopped loving her.

I want to say it, but the last time I did, it was for me, not for her.

She looks away, and I watch her fingers run absently over the indents of my initials carved into the worktable. She taps them.

"You know, this table doesn't go with anything now," she says softly. "You should upgrade."

"I couldn't get rid of it." Memories rise—her spread over the table, rose petals sticking to her skin as she tugged my hair to get me closer to her. Three years, two months, and five days ago.

Her eyes meet mine, and I know she's remembering the same. I don't look away, trying to show her that I kept it for the memories of her. That I could never get rid of a piece of her.

"Who were you talking about to Jackie?" she asks, whispering. Her gaze flickers over my face.

I step forward and reach out to brush my fingers over her jaw. She leans into me.

"Someone I met five years, four months, three weeks, and five days ago."

A sob breaks from her chest. She brings her hand up to cover her mouth, but I grab her wrist and pull her closer, dragging her face to mine.

This time when we kiss, it doesn't feel like goodbye, or a mistake, or something to overthink in the morning. It's just...starting.

33

Ama

NOW

This time when we kiss, I focus on the taste of him. The way he threads his fingers through my shorter hair, as if he learned his lesson yesterday about reaching up my back for the tendrils that aren't there anymore. The way his arm wraps around my waist and lifts, trying to keep my weight off my foot for me.

I open my mouth to him, and I feel like a million questions will pour out. He clutches me closer, and then spins us and drops me onto the old worktable. His hands run up my thighs, and he puffs out a laugh. "The one day you've ever worn jeans, and we can't even take them off."

I look down at the massive black boot over the top of my right jeans leg. I smile up at him. "And you? Did you wear these jeans today for any particular reason?" I reach forward and rub my hand over the front of him.

"I didn't expect you," he says.

"Didn't you?" I kiss him, pressing my chest into his and reaching forward for his Henley. I roll it up his stomach and whisper, "Let me see the new one."

My hand travels up toward his left pec, where I'd seen the ink creeping toward his collar. He freezes and stutters out, "I— I don't..."

"I have to see it. Please. What is it?"

I push the sweater up and reveal a Red Pearl. An amaryllis. Its petals bloom out, covering his heart. The stem vines up to his shoulder. I can't breathe.

"Amaryllis?" I ask. "But it's not extinct."

He runs a hand through his hair, and I can tell that I was never supposed to find out about this.

"It's... It was never about extinction. The tattoos..." He blows out his air. "They're ones that I—that I can't have. Ones that can't be used in arrangements, can't be kept in the shop." He looks up to me. "Ones that are likely to disappear before I can love them."

I take a shuddering breath. My fingers trace the edges of the Red Pearl petals. I lower my face and kiss the ink, like I used to. His stomach tightens, like it used to.

"You're a sap, Elliot Bloom," I whisper into his skin.

A laugh bubbles from his chest. "Yeah. Yeah, I am." He pushes my hair out of my eyes. "I'm not going to marry you."

I blink at him and swallow. "Okay."

"I'm gonna date the shit outta you, though."

Biting back my smile, I look up at him through my lashes, just like he "hates." He leans in to kiss me again, dropping his hands on my knees.

There's a lot that goes on when Elliot Bloom kisses. Things he's not even aware of. Things I'll never tell him. He moans in the back of his throat—a lot. It's completely intoxicating. Also, he tugs my body as close as physically possible to him, and it drives me insane. He kisses like someone who didn't kiss a lot, and although we've found a rhythm together by now, it still shocks me when he fumbles or when he loses concentration as I unzip him. Like now.

Elliot looks down at my hands, as if he might stop me, but my favorite thing in the entire world is putting my hand down his jeans. His breath catches, his eyes haze, and he looks like he can't believe I want to touch him. And *I* get to feel him lengthen in my palm, harden and swell.

"Ama," he murmurs, and I kiss him again.

His hands tug at the bottom of my shirt, and once it's off, his mouth latches onto my neck. My skin tingles when I remember the bruises he likes to suck into my skin, the way I'd have to cover them, and the reaction he had to finding the ones I didn't cover.

A sudden thought hits me, and I have to tell him—

"Elliot," I say, pushing him back. "I wasn't with anyone this year. You—you told Jackie I had someone over, but I..." I swallow. "I think you heard Mar on the phone one morning."

I watch his jaw work as his gaze flashes between both of my eyes. "Okay," he says, almost distrusting. "It's okay, though, if you were—"

"I wasn't. I couldn't—I wasn't able to." I glance down at his amaryllis tattoo so I don't have to look at him. "I tried a few times, but it didn't go well, so..." I take a deep breath. "And you were seeing someone? Kate? Was it serious? I mean—god, sorry. You don't have to—"

"No, it wasn't serious."

I look up at him. His eyes are black.

"I haven't been with anyone since you."

I'm on the verge of bursting into tears when he wraps his fingers under my knees and tugs until I'm on my back on the worktable. He's quick to unbutton my jeans, shucking them down my legs. I'm out of breath, completely floored by my own emotions. He rips off my one shoe, pulls my jeans off one leg, and places a hand on my stomach to hold me down as his full lips drop over the lace covering my center.

I gasp, slapping a hand to my mouth. "Ell—"

His fingers tug the lace to the side and then his tongue is on me again. And just like it did years ago, my brain leaves my body. I'm hardly aware of my jeans dangling from one leg. I can't even keep my eyes open as his mouth moves over me, kissing and licking and sucking.

"I miss you," I mutter to the ceiling.

"I'm right here." The vibration of his voice curls my knees to my chest, and he quickly presses my thighs open, spreading me wide for him. I start heaving for air as his tongue dips inside of me—and the moaning starts from his throat.

I've never come as quickly with anyone as I have with him. It's not just the size of him; it's moments like this when he takes his time, driving me crazy until I pop like a cork.

I slap my hands down on the sides of the workbench. "Did you think about this when you worked on this table?"

His answer is quick. "Every time."

My thighs shake. I'm cresting the ridge that he always rockets me toward.

"It was the worst professional decision of my life," he says, "to keep the table."

I laugh, and then his lips close over my clit and I scream. I can hear myself cursing, mumbling nonsense words about love and forever, sucking air back into my body.

He doesn't stop. He pushes two fingers inside of me, and I quake with it. His lips are sucking at me, his fingers pumping into me, and I break apart again, shaking and sobbing. I can't keep my hips still, fucking his mouth and rolling against his face.

When he pulls back and quickly pushes down his jeans, he says, "I'm gonna come. I—I can't—"

"Inside. Inside please."

My thighs are still shaking when he tugs me to the edge of the table, lines himself up, and pushes in. He groans from his chest, and I can't believe how wrong I got his size. I tried toys to match him, and I was wrong. My eyes roll back in my head and I'm coming again. I can't focus on anything but the pleasure ricocheting inside of me, the sound of his hips slapping against my skin.

I hear him yell out, and I know from experience that he's coming. But my knuckles are between my teeth to keep myself grounded, to keep from screaming again.

He grabs my wrist and tears my fingers from my teeth, thrusting once, twice more, and I let loose a cry that would embarrass me if I had a brain anymore.

When we're panting against each other, he leans down, moves the fabric of my bra to the side, and lays kisses on my breasts. Like an afterthought. Like he forgot to, and he needs to make it up to them. My skin hums.

"I love you," I whisper.

His dark eyes flick up to me. "That's the second time you've said that to me."

Heat fills my cheeks as I realize he hasn't said it back. Not since his mother's wedding. "Oh. I can stop if you—"

"I'm just so mad that you thought you could walk in here, propose, and tell me you love me." He smiles, his nose brushing against my cheek.

"Things don't really change, do they?" I say. "I've always done whatever I wanted in this back room."

He brushes my hair over my ear. "That's why I love you."

34

Ama

In the mornings, I wake up in either Elliot's bed or mine, but his arms are around me just the same. I turn in his embrace and run my fingers over his eyebrows until he wakes up. When his lashes flutter open, I say, "Will you marry me?"

He shakes his head. Or mumbles a no. Or turns over and tells me to fuck off.

And I say, "When then?"

"Maybe tomorrow," he always says.

I like to gather up Lady Cat-ryn in my arms on Elliot's grumpy days and drop her from a height over my head onto his stomach.

I used to be able to wander to my laptop somewhere between eight and ten in the morning and start my day whenever. That's not possible anymore. The TLC special aired three months ago. I'm now booked out two years in advance, and a year from now, when Jake has had enough training, I'm starting double-wedding Saturdays. So now, Elliot and I head into Blooming at eight a.m. every morning and get to work.

And it's not just that Hazel and Jackie's wedding was highlighted perfectly on *Fabulous Dream Weddings*, putting me in the spotlight. It's that no matter how hard her lawyers fought, Whitney couldn't get Bea to drop her from the episode. Her outburst was televised to the nation, including calling me a slut and bitch. And if that didn't ruin her reputation, the horse meme did.

Whitney almost getting run over by that horse is now a national treasure. The way she jumped back, screamed, and recovered all in one take has gone viral. I've seen several different captions for it.

When you get your tab at the bar
Me going into 2024 like
When she says she wants to see your porn folder
Horse girls encountering real horses

I got meme'd too. It didn't stick like Whitney's, but *Whitney, come on. Be a professional* made the rounds on Twitter as a clapback for a while. And the day the episode aired, Hazel Renee tweeted "Because I'm coming" and nothing else. It was what I said to Whitney when I told her she should fear me.

Two weeks later, Elliot replaced the *Blooming* rose wall in the showroom with *Because I'm coming* spelled out in white roses against a pink rose background. He didn't say anything about it, just continued on with his day. They're silk flowers, so now, all future couples who meet me for the first time at my office in Blooming get to see my catchphrase.

I cleared a space for myself in the showroom. It's a simple desk with my laptop and my Rolodex, next to a portion of Jackie and Hazel's dance floor hanging on the wall like a window—we dried the flowers so that it would be a permanent reminder of that day. My little office is like a Starbucks in the middle of a department store.

"June fourteenth is a great date," I say to the couple sitting in the chairs in front of me. "I'll be able to add you to the calendar now."

"Wonderful!" the woman says—Beth. She sits back in her chair, as if all her problems are now over. And they might be. "I'm so glad we could nail you down."

"And remember," I say, "if June of next year is too far, you can always go with a different planner who has availability this year—"

"No, no," the groom says. He waves his hand. "She's really adamant about you."

Beth nods vigorously. I smile. "Okay! Sounds good."

"Do you think…" Beth leans in. "Do you think we could do a found space like Hazel Renee's?"

"Absolutely. We can talk budget and wish list at our next meeting, but send me that Pinterest board that I know you've been building, and we'll get started!"

Elliot comes into the showroom then, cleaning his hands with a rag. "I have an installation at the high school dance to get to, but I'll be back in an hour."

I nod and stand from my chair. "Will you pick up on the way back?" I ask, and he rolls his eyes. "Please? You know Jake is in class right now."

"Chocolate old-fashioned and a maple bar?"

I beam at him and press up on my toes to kiss him goodbye. When I turn back to Beth and Robbie, I say, "You are under no obligation to contract Blooming for flowers, by the way. I'll go over all your vendor options at the next meeting."

"That's cool, though," Robbie says offhandedly. "That you guy are like a team. I think I like that."

Beth leans into me. "I saw from Hazel Renee's Twitter that she and her wife set you two up! That is the most amazing story!"

I smile. "It is. Hazel and Jackie were excellent matchmakers." I send Elliot a wink, and he grumbles.

He loads up the truck with the rose wall St. Joseph's ordered for their photo background, and Robbie won't take no for an answer when he offers to help Elliot lift it into the truck bed.

Beth turns to me. "It must be so hard to plan other couples' happily-ever-afters with your own boyfriend. When are you two getting married?"

I smile at her, folding my hands under my chin. "I keep asking him the same thing."

"Ah, noncommittal type?" she pries with a grin.

"Something like that," I say. "So. Tell me about your proposal story. They're my favorite."

As Beth tells me everything I need to know to make her wedding the perfect day, I realize it's a pretty good one. They'll probably last.

I love a good proposal story, but my favorite one I've heard? Well, I'll let you know when he says yes.

DON'T MISS JULIE'S NEXT BOOK, COMING SOON IN 2024!

READING GROUP GUIDE

AUTHOR'S NOTE

When I was growing up, it was a truth universally acknowledged that Sacramento was a place to leave—at least in my experience. The theater was in New York. The beaches were in LA. The culture was two hours west in San Francisco. And what even *was* CSU Sacramento? I grew up surrounded by people who agreed that Sacramento is a great place to raise a family, but if you're going to be an artist—get out. And I did. But like most Hallmark love stories where a city girl must return home from New York and learn to love her hometown roots with the help of a rough and rugged carpenter or mechanic or boatswain, I came home to Sacramento. And that boatswain, for me, was *Forget Me Not*.

Setting this book in Sacramento didn't seem like a huge deal to me until I was a quarter into writing it. Suddenly, everything was very specific, and there was no way to get the book *out* of Sacramento. It was incredibly easy to know where Ama bought her donuts, where Elliot takes her for a date, which high school Ama went to, and what other people think of that. Some things were instinctual, like the precise location of Elliot's flower shop—it's the shop where I picked up prom corsages and boutonnieres, though now closed. About seventy-five percent of the locations mentioned in this book are real, and of that remaining quarter, about fifteen percent are locations that have either closed their doors or will be an inside joke with Sacramentans. Some names are cleverly veiled to protect my town, but if you know, you know.

I grew up driving past weddings in the McKinley Park Rose Garden, where a huge part of this book is set. I was never a little girl who dreamed of her wedding day, but when I sat down and tried to figure out what a perfect Sacramento wedding would look like, I found myself gravitating toward the Rose Garden and Midtown. Is it how I'd like to do my wedding one day? Maybe not. But I know I'd like to have Ama as my wedding planner.

It was important to me that Ama hadn't left town for college or a big career and then had come back to Sacramento, as if it was a second choice. That's something I always regret about my first several years back in my hometown—that I felt like I'd failed the quest to get out of Sacramento. For Ama in *Forget Me Not*, her dreams had always aligned with where she lived. She didn't need to go live the city girl life before coming home to fall in love. She knew she could accomplish everything she wanted from two blocks east of where she grew up. And sure, I threw in a rough and rugged boatswain who owns a flower shop, but can you blame me?

DISCUSSION QUESTIONS

1. At the end of the book, Ama's and Elliot's positions on marrying each other seem to have flipped. Ama is open to it and proposing to Elliot every day, and Elliot is the one saying no. What do you think Elliot is waiting for? Do you think he still believes Ama is opposed to getting married? What do you think she could do to convince him otherwise?

2. When we first meet Elliot, he states that he hates flowers, but by the next time we see him, he has learned to enjoy them. Have you ever reluctantly accepted a work assignment or a family responsibility that you grew to love and understand?

3. Why do you think Ama's position on getting married changed?

4. Both Ama and Elliot take on huge projects without getting a lot of assistance. Why do you think it is hard for each of them to ask for help?

5. The Greek myth of Amaryllis is mentioned briefly. Do you see any similarities in that story and in Ama and Elliot's relationship? Who is who?

6. Why do you think it is hard for Ama to see how Whitney has been two-faced to her? Do you think Ama owes Whitney any loyalty?

7. Ama's mom and Elliot's dad both affect their children's lives in some way. For Ama, her mother shaped how she views

relationships and marriage, and Elliot's dad's death pivoted Elliot's career path. How have your parents influenced and maybe even dictated your life? How hard is it for children to separate themselves from their parents' values, expectations, and plans?

8. In the first chapter Ama tells someone that weddings are not marriages, that they're just a moment in time. What do you think about this? Do you feel that people make too big a deal of weddings? Do you think the bride should not have gone through with the wedding and party when she wasn't sure about the marriage?

9. We see throughout the story how social media has both helped and harmed various characters. Do you think social media is a good thing? What are the pitfalls of social media for someone's career or reputation? How has social media affected your life—in good and bad ways?

10. Ama is constantly reminding herself to "be professional." Do you feel that Ama conducts herself in an unprofessional way? Do you think that some jobs allow for some so-called unprofessionalism like befriending your clients?

ACKNOWLEDGMENTS

OMG IT'S A BOOK! I cannot believe you paid for, checked out, or pirated my book! What fun!

I might have to thank Ali Hazelwood first. That might be in the contract I signed with her. So thank you, Alison, for convincing me to pull-to-publish a (completely different) story while we were browsing a toy store, like the adults we are. Without your encouragement, guidance, and support, these people would never have been able to pirate my book.

Gaia Banks—my agent, my mother earth—deserves all my affection for lighting up like a Christmas tree when I told her my idea for this book. I must thank her child for coming into the world at exactly the right time so that this book exists in the way it does. Thank you, Gaia, for believing in me, and thank you for staying up way past office hours during That Week due to the time difference. Thank you to everyone at Sheil Land Associates, including Maddie and Alba.

A huge thank-you to everyone at Forever and HarperCollins UK for believing in *Forget Me Not*, especially my INCREDIBLE editors Junessa Viloria and Martha Ashby, who believed in this book whole-heartedly. Thank you for pulling me back from my questionable jokes and reminding me that not everyone lives in my head, like I'd always assumed. Thank you to the marketing and publicity teams, especially Dana Cuadrado and Queen Estelle, for every little bit of creativity and passion you put into this. And thank you to Beth, Sabrina, Leah, Stacey, and Daniela, and anyone I forgot at Forever and HarperCollins UK, which is probably a lot because I have literally spoken to only three of you at the time of writing this. Thank you to Lori Paximadis! Thank you to my German, Polish, and Brazilian editors, Maria Runge, Alicja Oczko, and Frini Georgakopoulos, for taking a chance!

Thank you to all the brides I've bridesmaided for—which is a lot. While not yet at *27 Dresses* level, my future is clear.

In much of this book, I'm sure I sound like I don't know what I'm talking about, but these ladies did their best to help me on all sorts of subjects: Cat Dionisio, Michelle Adamsky, Angelica Whaley, Ashley Mortensen, and Adriana Daft née Zerio all deserve the world. (But anything I got wrong is clearly their fault, thank you very much.)

The only way to survive publishing or a pandemic or publishing during a pandemic is with supportive spaces. Thank you to my besties in Gremlins, MW, Krampus, Words Are Hard, and especially Claire, Jen, Ali, and Kate Goldbeck in The Edge Chat, who wanted good things for me and this book when I couldn't wish for the good things myself. Thank you, Lucy, for always having my back and setting me up for success. Thank you, Anna Conathan, for being the best coach ever and for introducing me to my Creator Goddess. And to Mar, Cat, and Amanda— thank you for being my cheerleaders, sidechat bitcas, existential crisis counselors, first beta readers, and all-around best friends— fandom or no fandom.

Special thanks to Fran, not only for the nugget that became this book, but also for your selfless creativity that leads so many people to create good stories (Follow her at @galacticidiots on the bird app). Thank you to Abby Jimenez for the early blurb! Thank you to NikitaJobson for THIS COVER! *heart eyes* Thank you for every piece of art you've ever been kind enough to create for my fics. I'm so honored to have you as my cover designer and glad you're getting the recognition you deserve.

To everyone who knows me as Juls or LovesBitca8, thank you. Fanfiction is not a stepping stone to traditional publishing. It's a home that will always be a part of me. Thank you to the Rights and Wrongs members and the friends at RoR. Thank you to everyone who left a comment or a kudos or reached out to tell me that my work matters.

Thank you to Sacramento, for being the place you always want to leave, but can't seem to get your heart out of. About seventy-five percent of the places in this book are real. I recommend visiting this terrible, wonderful city (just not in the summer) and going to the McKinley Park Rose Garden.

Thank you to Jennifer Borasi, Richard Weldon, and Joshua McKinney for teaching me how to write and how to enjoy words. Thank you to my family, especially Grandma Glo, whose dirty mind and wicked humor I inherited, and Grandma Marion, of whom I have one memory—giving her a flower. And finally and most importantly, thank you to my parents for believing in me when I wanted to be an actress, when I wanted to be a musical writer, and now, as I have become an author. Third time's the charm, maybe? Thank you to my mother for the title of this book, and thank you to my father for reading my *edited* version.

ABOUT THE AUTHOR

JULIE SOTO is an author, playwright, and actress originally from Sacramento, California. Her musical *Generation Me* won the 2017 New York Musical Festival's Best Musical award, as well as Best Book for her script. She is a musical theater geek, fandom nerd, and the author of many spicy fanfictions. Julie now lives in Fort Bragg, California, with her dog, Charlie. She is probably drinking coffee as you read this.

Find out more at:
    JulieSotoWrites.com
    AO3 LovesBitca8
    TikTok JulieSotoWrites
    Instagram @JulieSotoWrites
    Twitter @JulieSotoWrites
    Facebook.com/JulieSotoWrites